led the world twice over,
mous: saints and sinners,
artists, kings and queens,
and hopeful beginners,
where no-one's been before,
crets from writers and cooks
ne library ticket
nderful world of books.

JANICE JAMES.

SPECIAL M

This
THE ULVERS
a registered ch

The Foundatic
provide fund
diagnosis and tr
are a few exam
THE ULVER

A new Ch
at Moorf

Twin o
Western Op

The Frederic
Ophthalmolog

Eye Laser equ

If you would li
Foundation by
legacy, every co
received with gr

THE ULVE
The Gree
Leice
Tel

I've trave
Met the f
Poets and
Old stars
I've been
Learned s
All with
To the w

ORBS OF JADE

For as long as she could remember Janine had been envious of her pretty younger sister, Cassandra. Cassie who always seemed to get her own way despite the wishes of their autocratic father, while Janine was constantly at war with both her parents. As the sisters grew up the jealousy that had marred their childhood was to poison their adult life. Set in Durham and Alsace, the author explores the insidious and self-destructive effect of envy between two people thrown together by reason of common parentage.

Books by Barbara Masterton
in the Ulverscroft Library:

ISLAND OF GLASS
LATE HARVEST

BARBARA MASTERTON

ORBS OF JADE

Complete and Unabridged

ULVERSCROFT
Leicester

First published in Great Britain in 1989 by
Souvenir Press Limited
London

First Large Print Edition
published February 1991
by arrangement with
Souvenir Press Limited.

British Library CIP Data

Masterton, Barbara
Orbs of Jade. — Large print ed. —
Ulverscroft large print series: general fiction
I. Title
823.914 [F]

ISBN 0–7089–2372–0

Published by
F. A. Thorpe (Publishing) Ltd.
Anstey, Leicestershire
Set by Words & Graphics Ltd.
Anstey, Leicestershire
Printed and bound in Great Britain by
T. J. Press (Padstow) Ltd., Padstow, Cornwall

LONG, long ago, when I was real and the world existed only as an intrusive dream, I used to wish that Cassandra would disappear forever.

Make her go away, I would think fiercely, kneeling in my nightdress beside my narrow bed, my hands, palms together, held rigidly against my nose; while my mother knelt beside my sister's cot and prayed to God, mildly yet earnestly, to make us all good and the world a better place to live in. Make her go away and I'll be good, I promised, my eyes screwed up tightly to give my wish more power. But when I opened my eyes Cassandra was still there, curly-haired and cherubic, regarding me knowingly through the white-painted bars with large blue eyes, her chubby fists clasped beneath her round chin. My mother would finish her plea to the Almighty with a softly sighed Amen, as if acknowledging the futility of such a prayer for universal benevolence, but I always suspected that it was my salvation for which she had the least hope.

To be a petted only child until one is four, whose baby ways are treasured and applauded, then to become, quite suddenly, an older and wiser child in comparison with the new, utterly helpless arrival, is a painful transformation. To make matters worse for me, we had moved farther away from my grandparents only two months after my sister was born. Alone in the new house with a busy mother, whose lap seemed to be constantly occupied with one end of the baby or the other, I resorted to stubborn silences or noisy tantrums, whichever in the prevailing circumstances would cause the most distress and earn me the maximum attention. Desire and encouragement for me to be polite and winsome before visitors only made me stare wordlessly into their affable faces, until their ready smiles faltered and grew strained; whereas on shopping expeditions, trotting beside the pushchair firmly fastened by a hand, I was at my noisiest and nastiest, until my harassed mother was driven to smack me – something she hated to do, especially in public, and for which she despised herself as soon as she had calmed down.

She read books on child psychology, which proved, as she frequently explained to my exasperated father, that sibling jealousy, with all its distressing symptoms, is perfectly normal in a four-year-old who has been supplanted by a new baby; but it did not make it easier for her to cope with me.

Once I had started school the situation eased considerably. I was introduced to a freedom outside the home and one-year-old Cassandra became more of a nuisance than a threat. I loved school — eventually. For the first week I refused to be abandoned there and struggled and shrieked that I would not stay, while my mother tried to let go of me, holding back tears caused by distress and the pain of a bitten arm; the teacher, with the practice of years of similar scenes, won the battle over my flailing limbs and marched me into the classroom, where I became, almost at once, a model of willing docility. Soon I made friends who were far more necessary to me than a baby sister. My relationship with my mother improved as I felt more important again in her eyes. I was the big girl, who could read, after a fashion, make greeting cards, dog-eared pictures and ramshackle cardboard models to bring home for display and admiration. I could go out to play on my stabilised two-wheeler with Lois, who was my very best friend, and Jane, who would not go away no matter how much Lois and I ignored her.

Yet the latent jealousy persisted. Cassandra was so good, so placid, so sweet. Everybody said so, especially my mother. Indeed, Cassandra was all those things. She seldom cried and when she did she cried quietly, in order not to cause a fuss, with large tears flowing copiously down her pink cheeks from beautiful clear eyes. She cried reproachfully and it was an urgent pleasure to hug and kiss her into smiles again, something that I did with energy. I was the cleverest at making her laugh. I was also the cleverest at making her cry. I was applauded for the first; I took care that only Cassandra knew about the second. Nevertheless, she adored me despite my small cruelties to her, which were mainly of a tormenting nature, such as being spiteful to her favourite dolly and not letting her share in my games, or spoiling her own. I envied her her sweet temper, her soft, plump prettiness and her curls, all in contrast to my own meagre attributes. I was thin, nervously energetic, with a volatile temperament, always wanting to do something more exciting somewhere else — and I had straight hair. The only thing we had in common was our fair colouring. I was quick and clever — Cassandra would never match me in the classroom — but she was calm and wise in other ways that I could not understand but grudgingly admired. She always got her own way and, bright as I was, I did not know how she managed it. When we both wanted the same thing, effortlessly she obtained it. Cassandra sat back and received while I laboured and lost. It was to be the story of our lives — or so it seemed.

When I was fourteen and Cassandra was ten, we experienced two exciting events and I began the awkward process of growing away from childhood. In the late autumn of that year our brother Roderick was born and my mother's younger brother came home from Hong Kong. These events were like one really, because Cassandra and I were staying with our grandparents while Mum was in hospital having the baby, so that when Uncle Daniel arrived we were part of his excited reception. Grandma Harris had been beside herself for days with happy anticipation, and we had had to help her prepare his room and shop for his favourite food. Grandpa smiled a lot behind his pipe and remarked a few times that he could not think what all the fuss was about, but we could tell from the way he said it that underneath he was as excited as we were. Uncle Daniel had been away for six years, every year of which he had been expected to return, but something always happened to prevent him. Dad used to say that it was because he could not leave his 'currant woman', which intrigued me for ages, until I came across the word 'current' in the course of my reading and realised that Uncle's woman was not so much fruity as flowing. I formed a mental picture of a willowy female with long hair and diaphanous clothing streaming away from her, as if she were standing serenely in a perpetual Force Ten gale. Even when I could define the term 'current woman' more accurately, I retained the first image in my imagination, subtly transformed into a glamorous version of my own skinny form.

The day before Uncle Daniel's arrival, Grandma took us to visit our baby brother for the first time. He was just twelve hours old. I must say I rather hoped Cassandra's nose would be put out of joint just a little, at finding herself no longer the youngest in the family, but not a bit of it: she was as thrilled with Roddy as I was. Mum looked contented and happy in her neat hospital bed, surrounded by cards and flowers. She greeted us as if she had not seen us for ages and held us close, asking if we were being good girls for Grandma and expressing the hope that I was being helpful about the house. Grandma scooped the baby from the depths of the crib at the side of the bed and handed him first to me to hold. He was so tiny, wrapped up firmly in a thick blue cotton square, with the ends tucked in so that he felt like a soft, warm parcel. He was fast asleep, his red face all scrunched up and peaceful, and I could have held him forever.

"Good gracious!" Grandma exclaimed ten

minutes later, breaking off her conversation with Mum to look at me in amazement. "It's the longest time I've ever seen you sit so still, Janine. Here, let me have him, it's Cassandra's turn."

"What time does Dan arrive tomorrow?" Mum asked.

"Early evening."

"It will be wonderful to see him again. Cassie was only four when he went away. Perhaps he'll stay at home for good."

"I wish he would," Grandma sighed. "It's about time he settled down."

"I wonder what Oliver will think of his new son." Mum gazed fondly at the picture made by Cassandra with the baby cuddled on her small lap.

"He'll be delighted," Grandma asserted briskly. "He always wanted a son."

"Did he?" Mum said, taking her mother's word for it.

Grandma always knew what people wanted, because she assumed that they wanted the things she thought they ought to have. If one happened to disagree with her, as I sometimes did, and say, "But I don't want that," she would answer in her quick, no-nonsense way, "Of course you do, dear!" and one resigned oneself to receiving it, whatever it was. She had made up her mind, I had overheard her telling Grandpa, that Uncle Daniel needed a wife. It would be interesting to find out what Uncle Daniel thought about that.

Cassandra and I accompanied our grandparents to the station the next evening to meet the London train, which was en route to Edinburgh. It was November, so it was already dark, with a cutting wind that gave us sniffy noses. Cassandra kept going to all the bother of removing a woollen glove in order to get her hankie from her duffle coat pocket, but I just kept sniffing, much to Grandma's annoyance. "Have you got a cold, Jan?" she asked, pointedly, and later, with irritation, "Haven't you got a handkerchief, child?"

By the time the train drew in alongside the platform, approaching it across the slender height of the viaduct which arched gracefully above the compact city of Durham, most of the passengers must have been weary from the hours of enforced passivity in a stuffy atmosphere. The tables of the pullman coaches were littered with empty cans and crumpled packets. Those passengers who, when they felt the train slowing down for a station, were still alert enough to gaze curiously from the windows past their own reflections and those of their fellow travellers, would have been rewarded by the sight of the massive floodlit splendour of the cathedral and adjacent castle, prominent above the almost encircling arm of the River Wear. As soon as the train halted, doors opened and people burdened with luggage lurched down onto the chilly platform on stiff legs. Other people struggled aboard, eager for warmth. They began a quest for seats, intruders upon the lethargic scene, their suitcases and bags held awkwardly before them, thumping extended limbs as they went.

"There he is!" Grandpa exclaimed.

Coming towards us with a large suitcase in each hand and overtaking groups of other travellers with long, purposeful strides, was Uncle Daniel. He was tall and hefty with a square face, close-cropped hair and a chin like a spade. He shook Grandpa's hand vigorously, hugged Grandma so hard he made her squeak and said to us, "Hello, kids!" He did not remark how much we had grown. I thought all adults did that

10

if they had not seen a young person for six months or more. He just grinned at us and then proceeded to ignore us. He strode off with Grandpa towards the exit, refusing to let him carry a case. We hurried after them.

"It's so lovely to have you back," Grandma said a little breathlessly, getting into the back of the car with Cassandra and me.

"Great to be back," her son said, "but it's bloody cold. I don't know how you all stand it."

"Wait till the winter comes, my boy," Grandpa chuckled. "Hong Kong has made you soft."

"Where's Lorna?" Uncle Daniel asked.

Three voices from the back started to tell him all about the new baby. Grandma won.

"And Oliver, the tycoon?"

"In Luxembourg," Grandpa told him. "He'll be back tomorrow. Business comes before babies, you know!" There was the faintest note of disapproval in his voice. It was often there when he spoke about my father. Whenever Cassandra and I complained about Dad being away a lot, Grandpa said it was because he was

11

a success and no one ever saw much of successes, they were obliged to make sacrifices of their private lives and we should be proud of him; nevertheless, I had the impression that Grandpa considered too much sacrifice a self-indulgence.

Uncle Daniel had brought expensive presents from Hong Kong. There was a beautiful silk table cover for Grandma and an intricately carved ivory box for Grandpa's pipes. Actually, he had not remembered Cassandra and me, but he had been generous in his gifts for my mother and at Grandma's whispered suggestion he took one of them and handed it to me, saying, "Here you are, Jan. Choose the one you like and give the other to Cassie." The pretty box with its oriental design was very heavy, and I placed it carefully on the table before pulling off the sticky tape around the edges of the lid. Inside, surrounded by masses of filmy shavings, were two golden Chinese dragons, handsome and fierce, sitting proudly upright on weighty bases. They were meant to stand back-to-back as book-ends and were identical with the exception of their huge, bulbous eyes, which were coldly glittering like unpolished jewels. One pair of eyes was an opaque, deep blue and the other a frosted green. They were curious, glaring eyes, sightless yet all-seeing. We stared back at them with delight and wonder, fascinated.

"Which one are you going to choose, Jan?" Grandpa asked. "Lapis lazuli or jade?"

I glanced at Cassandra. Her shining gaze was fixed upon the dragon with the green eyes. Quickly I put my hand on it and said, "This one. I like this one best."

Cassandra accepted the other without demur. She did not look at me, but the closed expression upon her face as she reached out both hands to grasp the heavy ornament made me certain that, as always, she had got exactly what she wanted.

My father returned from Luxembourg the following day. He went to see his son on the way home from the airport and looked in on us afterwards to pronounce himself well satisfied. He said it was a pity that Mum could not have timed things a bit better, but at least she would be out of hospital before his trip to Norway the following week.

I have to explain something fundamental about my father. No one could remain unaware of him. Everybody reacted to him in one way or another, usually by vying for his notice. Even those who disliked him, and there were a few, could not bear to be ignored by him. He was an aggressively cheerful man, of medium height, with keen blue eyes in a smooth-skinned face beneath short, smooth hair. He had a compact figure and was always neatly dressed, whether in a suit or in perfectly matching casual clothes. He gave the impression of having just stepped from a tingling cold shower into clean white underwear. His hands and feet were small, his expensive shoes always well-polished. He was energetically optimistic and could not bear people to remain unresponsive towards him. If one persisted in being quiet and unappreciative of his efforts, he gave up and one became as good as dead in his company, to be ignored forever after as unworthy, invisible and voiceless, for if one spoke he would not hear. Not many people were reduced to the living dead; most competed for his approbation, laughing at his jokes even when they were aimed at themselves. Good-naturedly, he once told the wife of a colleague, who had failed to spot an insignificant grammatical error in an inscription on a wall plaque, that she was an ignorant bitch. She was supposed to take the remark in the spirit in which it was intended. She did not. He was not aware that she was a writer with a reputation for precise and beautiful prose and, when my mother pointed this out to him later, he was unrepentant. The lady never forgave him — not that he cared; after all, she was not in a position to be of use to him and her husband had laughed with the other men, albeit uneasily, at his wife's obtuseness.

Almost every man who knew Dad, however slightly, regarded him as a friend. Women, understandably, were more wary of him; they took offence too easily. He was a man's man, because men took him at his own valuation based on achievement: they admired his exuberant personality and his success in their world of business. Perhaps, too, they admired the crushing effect he had on their confident wives, who would start by rising to his lively wit and feeling encouraged to put in a few witty observations of their own, and within ten minutes were smiling politely, laughing appropriately and speaking only when called upon to say a few words in corroboration of a story being told by Dad or one of his cronies. These were usually reminiscences of pleasures they had shared in the past, often of a sporting-spectator sporting-type, or of a social occasion connected with their business affairs when 'old so-and-so' had made a fool of himself and provided them all with amusement; more often they were tales of triumph over an adversary on the glorious and fertile fields of finance.

When Dad walked into my grandparents' home that evening after his visit to the hospital, we all reacted predictably and became animated and eager for his attention; it was as if it were he and not Uncle Daniel who had been absent for six years.

"What did you think of your little son, Oliver?" Grandma wanted to know, as pleased about the baby as if she had ordered him especially.

"Third time lucky," Dad said, tweaking

Cassandra's nose as she hung upon his arm, and grinning at me. "Hong Kong too hot for you, Dan?"

Uncle Daniel smiled. "A cooling off period was called for," he admitted.

"Look what Uncle Daniel's brought us," Cassandra said, pointing to the golden dragons which were side by side on a low table. "They look like funny lions, but they're dragons really. The one with blue eyes is mine. Jan chose the green one."

"That follows," Dad said, putting his arm round my shoulders and giving me a quick hug. "Two little green-eyed monsters together."

Everybody laughed.

I blushed with shame. "I'm not a green-eyed monster," I protested, avoiding looking at Uncle Daniel for whom I was developing a devastating crush. It was not fair of Dad to suggest that I was consumed with jealousy. At fourteen I disliked most things about myself and I was struggling to be a better person within an unpromising physical form. Whenever a small flame of jealousy licked into life, I quelled it resolutely, telling myself that it was despicable to envy a sister whom, paradoxically, I loved.

"Blue is my very favourite colour," Cassandra said conversationally. "It used to be yellow, but now I like blue best."

You would! I thought, pretending not to care.

"Would you like something to eat?" Grandma asked Dad. "I expect you're hungry."

"Love something," he said. "I can't say I'm eager to return to an empty house. How long do you reckon on being here, Dan? Or are you home for good?"

I waited anxiously for the reply.

"Only a month," Uncle Daniel said.

My heart sank.

"Good," Dad said, "because there's something you can do for me out there — to your advantage, of course."

2

WE had moved house twice since Cassandra was born, each move reflecting an increase in my father's fortunes. The house we then occupied was on the banks of the River Wear, just before it swept moat-like round the promontory bearing Durham's splendid Norman cathedral. It was an elegant old house. The steps up to the cream-painted front door, which was set beneath a stone portico, led directly from the pavement of a long, curving road that descended into the city. At the back of the house was a large private garden, over-stocked and in its farthest corners given back, in desperation by my mother, to unbridled nature. There were six stone steps from the kitchen onto a sloping lawn, which was overhung at its borders by rampant herbaceous plants. At the far end of the lawn, scarcely discernible in summer amongst the flowering shrubs and leafy trees, was a tiny wooden summer-house. This had a verandah from which one could look down upon the river in its deep, semi-circular channel; the vegetation of the steep, wooded banks, smothered with daffodils in the spring, was reflected in the flowing dark water. The summer-house was mine. That is, I thought of it as mine. When the house and rest of the world became intolerable, I sought refuge there, leaning against the rough walls to weep stormily in rage, or gently in the perplexed sorrow of the youthful misunderstood; leaning across the peeling balustrade of the verandah to watch the small boats passing beneath me, while I dreamed sweet dreams of the future. The loosening timber of the ageing structure and the fragility of my adolescent emotions were as one; the dust and insects, the smell of the wooden planks, sometimes warm and redolent of cedar, sometimes damp and earthy with the smell of fungus and rotting leaves, were mingled in my senses with the intensity of my changing moods. Visiting that retreat was like trysting with an understanding lover: the world receded and I was soothed.

During the warmer months, Cassandra often played in it with her friends and, occasionally, my mother sat on the verandah to read or write a letter. Their visits were transitory and made no difference to the ambience of the place. Whatever possessions they left behind — a skipping rope, a hair ribbon, a book, magazines — were inconsequential, lying at random on the two long benches or the rickety trestle table. Against one wall was a locker, in which we kept an assortment of racquets, hockey sticks, shuttlecocks, bats and balls — none of them in good condition. Propped in a corner were two folded deckchairs, their faded striped canvas dirtied and torn.

Sometimes, I wondered about the people who had used the summer-house before us. Someone had desired it to be built and had no doubt sat in it during the long, hot summers that are always in the past. Mostly I thought about myself and those things that were making my present either pleasurable or painful.

On the day that Uncle Daniel left for Hong Kong, I sat hunched up on one of the benches, wrapped against the invasive December cold in an anorak and fur-lined boots, and wondered about the life he was returning to and the woman who was waiting to share it with him.

He had spent a lot of time at our house, talking to Mum. It was obvious that there was a strong bond of affection between them, but for some reason they were careful to minimise this on the rare occasions when my father was present. Mum was the only one who got to hear about his life in Hong Kong. Grandma often complained that Uncle Daniel told her nothing. Drifting in and out of their conversations, aware that I was an intruder, I gathered snippets of information. He was going back to a new job and, after careful consideration, the woman he had left behind — absence having done what absence is said to do, made his heart grow fonder. He was in some kind of financial difficulty, but whatever he had promised to do for Dad should see him straight and, in the meantime, Mum had helped him out. That was a secret. No one must know, in particular Dad, who had never lent anyone a penny in his life and would certainly disapprove of his wife doing so.

Mum was breastfeeding the baby and on several afternoons I returned from school to find Roddy having his tea and Uncle Daniel and Mum talking away across his greedy suckling. The first time I was embarrassed and quickly left the room, but as my presence, embarrassed or otherwise, was merely an irritant to them, I learned to take the scene for granted. Mum and her brother talked as if they were trying to make up for six years of lost verbal contact. They had exchanged letters, but not many. They needed to be near in order to relate to one another, using the language of fond siblings in which one word would recall a whole episode of shared existence and provoke laughter, while a sigh could convey an unspoken sadness, completely understood.

One afternoon, I had dumped my heavy school bag in the hall and gone into the sitting-room to find Uncle Daniel on his own, reading a newspaper.

"Where's Mum?" I enquired, sitting down, pleased to have him to myself for once.

"Upstairs, changing Roddy's nappy," he answered without looking up.

"I wish you could stay for Christmas," I said wistfully.

He looked at me and smiled, "So do I," he agreed, but I did not believe him.

As a means of holding his attention, I said, "I should like to go to Hong Kong."

"Well, you're nearly fifteen. In a few more years you'll be able to come for a visit. You can do what you like when you're twenty-one, you know. You could bring Cassie."

There was no place for Cassandra in my plans, but I let that pass. "Could I stay with you?" I asked. "I mean, would you have room?" and I blushed as if I had proposed something immoral.

"Probably," he said.

Such an enigmatic reply portended a shift in his circumstances, perhaps a change of accommodation or even, heaven forbid, marriage.

"How's school?" he asked in that bright tone normally adopted by our elders when they mention the place. I suppose he could not think of anything else to talk to me about.

"All right." I did not want to be reminded of the fact that I was still a kid in his eyes. I was trying desperately hard to think of something sophisticated to say to stop him returning to his newspaper, when Mum came in.

"Hello, Jan. Haven't you got homework to do?"

"I'll do it later," I muttered sulkily. I wished she would mind her own business.

"You know you're suppposed to do it before dinner," she reminded me.

"What difference does it make to you when I do it?" I asked rudely. "I always get it done, don't I?"

"Please yourself, darling," she answered with a shrug, then turned to her brother. "Will you take a pair of curtains when you go, Dan? Mum said she would alter them for me."

As I was leaving the room, I heard Uncle Daniel remark, "She's the image of you at that age, Lorna." To which Mum replied, "I was never so difficult." "Oh yes, you were," was the retort and they both laughed. I picked up my bulging briefcase and dragged upstairs with it. Cassandra hurtled past me on her way down, landing with a leap at the bottom.

"I've made my Christmas list," she called happily. "Want to see it?"

"No," I said ungraciously, having already

been told by Dad that I could not have what I wanted most of all for Christmas — a pair of black patent shoes with stiletto heels to wear at the discos.

Dad was in for dinner that evening. "Done your homework, Jan?" he asked cheerfully as I took my place at the table.

I answered grumpily that I had. Was that all they had to speak to me about?

"I did mine as soon as I came home," Cassandra informed him.

"Good girl!" Dad said approvingly. "Got it all right, I hope?"

"Uncle Daniel corrected it for me."

"Oh, was Dan here?" Dad said, looking at Mum.

"He looked in to get the bedroom curtains that my mother is going to alter for me," she told him, handing her plate to him for some meat and avoiding my eyes.

"I need to have another talk to him about that business he's going to do for me," Dad said. "Perhaps I'll go over this evening."

"May I come with you?" I asked eagerly.

"May I?" Cassandra chimed in.

26

"I'll be rather late getting back, Cassie, but Jan can come."

I was triumphant for once. During our meal, Dad and Cassandra did most of the talking. Mum listened and answered occasionally; I ate and thought dark thoughts, mostly about the blind boil I could feel coming on my chin and a loose filling in one of my back teeth which meant I had to concentrate on chewing on the other side. I would have to dash upstairs as soon as dinner was over and dab spot-stick on my face and pray that Uncle Daniel would not notice the glowing blemish.

"You're very quiet, Jan," Dad observed as I began tucking into a large slice of lemon meringue pie. "Not unhappy, are you?"

"No," I reassured him hastily, smiling to prove it, "of course not."

Dad took it as a personal affront if we were miserable. Like his employees, we were supposed to be contented. He was loud in their praise and proud of them — he let everyone know that — and in consequence they were supposed to be galvanised into doing their best for him for what he considered a generous return. He could not give a damn for their private lives. It was much the same with his family. It was our duty to share in the satisfaction of his success, to boost his self-image as a clever, caring human being and to put up with any amusing tale he had to tell at our expense. If we were unhappy, we had learned not to pain him by showing it, for it would never occur to him to enquire too deeply into its cause. After all, he had a constant grief of his own, one which he bore bravely because he had no choice, but one which he kept very much to himself: he was not tall. Four more inches would have made him perfect. Man may strive for perfection, but never attains it — even Dad was aware of that. Tall men who could not make him like them wondered what they had done to offend him and, try as they would, were unable to make amends.

Dad gave his family everything, even a considered amount of his precious time. We should be pleased and gratified, but most of all we should be happy. If we were not, it was a positive disgrace; he was hurt, incredulous and, when we refused to abandon our misery even after bribery, he grew angry and we were accused of biting the hand that fed us: we were letting him down and he was cut to the quick. It did not matter that the reason we were low in spirits had nothing to do with him, he could be relied upon to take it personally. We found it very trying.

Mum suffered most from this egotism, which made it necessary for him to feel the most important person in the lives of his family and close friends. Watching her behaviour over the past few weeks with Uncle Daniel, realising that she was the same with her parents and personal friends, made me aware of something I must have noticed long ago, yet failed to register: she had two personalities. Out of her husband's company she was lively, talkative and ready to express a controversial opinion, with plenty of bright ideas and schemes for enriching her life. When she was with Dad, she became a supportive listener, a backer-up, almost colourless in comparison with him. People who only knew her by her husband's side thought of her as charming, but reticent and shy. How wrong they were! Very occasionally she seemed to tire of this superficial role and would dare to call attention to herself by entering energetically into a discussion dominated as always by Dad. He would pause, as if in deference to her opinion, then at the first opportunity either disagree with her viewpoint, ridicule her lack of real knowledge on the subject or argue about the accuracy of her memory — his own being infallible! They never agreed about incidents in their shared past. In company, Mum always conceded the argument in order to save her husband's self-esteem, but privately she never did and they enjoyed some tearing rows over what seemed to Cassandra and me mere trivialities. When their tempers had cooled it was always Dad who relented — he had to, it was one small victory that Mum would not forgo. Perhaps she counted it as recompense for her diligent love, a small mark of which was that she never wore high-heeled shoes when she was with him, ensuring that, with her at least, Dad was the big man he so much desired to be.

Mum's own friends were few and firm. There were two from her schooldays, three from her university days and one from the months of her first pregnancy, whom she had met doing similar antics at the ante-natal clinic. These women hardly knew my father. On the other hand, of social necessity, Mum knew many of Dad's friends and their wives, although her association with them never progressed beyond polite and agreeable discourse. These were the people to whom she appeared likeable but shallow, completely overshadowed by her husband's dynamic personality and drive. Out of her company, the thing they remembered best about her was her looks. It was generally conceded that she was extremely attractive and that Oliver Chandler had chosen his wife for beauty and docility rather than brains.

In fact she was an astute woman. I was reaching an age to be able to appreciate that she managed her difficult husband with consummate skill, and sometimes I felt a little sorry — just a little — for the arrogant man who loved her and confidently lorded it over her. When it came to wheeling and dealing outside the boardroom, my money was on Mum.

Within a couple of weeks of Uncle Daniel's departure, the infatuation that had engrossed me for a month faded. I transferred my tender longings quite painlessly to a student at the local boys' school and was happy if I could pass him anonymously in the street once a day, accompanied by his noisy mates all wearing scruffy black blazers, scuffed shoes showing plenty of sock, and burdened with the inevitable load of ink-stained books slung in grubby haversacks over their shoulders. His name was Martin. That was all I knew about him, except that he was gorgeous to gaze shyly upon and most of my friends fancied him as well.

Uncle Daniel's significance was retained in two ways. It was through him that I began to perceive the complexity of my parents' relationship with one another and it was through the baleful green eyes of the golden dragon, which seemed always to reproach me for jealousy from its position of state amidst the clutter on the top of the chest of drawers in my bedroom, that I began to appreciate the complexity of my own feelings, especially where they concerned Cassandra.

When Uncle Daniel visited England again, five years later, I could not imagine what I had found so attractive about him; for a start, at thirty-seven he seemed so old. The woman, by then his wife, turned out to be a pretty Chinese of great delicacy of mind and form, only three years older than myself. She was only eighteen when he left her behind on that first visit and it made me realise how very immature I must have seemed to him then.

However, on that December day in the bleak beginnings of an English winter, huddled up on the summer-house bench in a mood of utter dejection, I felt very grown-up indeed and was convinced that I should never cease grieving. I was morbidly feeding my emotions with romantic literature the sort my mother dismissed disparagingly as 'Enid Blyton for adults'and tender songs of unrequited love, played interminably on the record player in my room.

"How the hell that girl can concentrate on her homework with that row going on, I'll never know!" Dad used to say. He made the mistake of supposing, in common with many parents, in particular the parents of girls, that the hours that their daughters spend in their rooms are devoted to study, when in fact 'study' is an approved excuse for getting out of doing anything unpleasant and boring about the house, such as their own ironing. Were our parents so different when they were young? I wondered. It was inconceivable that they had all been model children, like Cassandra, evenly good-tempered and always willing to be useful; unless marriage and children of their own had transformed them. In which case, I looked forward with interest to Cassandra's eventual transformation and shuddered to think what would happen to me, already so imperfect. Perhaps I should do the next generation a favour and not contribute to it.

3

LATE one Saturday morning, during Roddy's second year, he and I were at the summer-house, waiting for Mum and Cassandra to return from shopping. Roddy was fast asleep in his pushchair, cool in the lacy shade of an ash tree, and I was reading *To Kill a Mockingbird,* to please myself and oblige my English master, but I was feeling too restless to concentrate and left my seat overlooking the garden to go onto the verandah, where I could watch people enjoying themselves on the river. Milling about beneath me in the hands of amateur sailors were four rowing boats, three of them with young children aboard, and two canoes. One of the rowing boats, with a small fellow aged about eight at the oars, was describing lazy circles, jumbling the colourful reflections into winking patterns beneath the high sun. I was watching this entranced, hoping the boy would never get the hang of it, when around the curve shot a swiftly moving skiff, darting purposefully in mid-stream between the sluggish, broader craft. The rowing boat nearest to me hastily pulled across, well away from the skiff's smooth passage, and one of the youths in it looked up at me and smiled. My heart stuttered in its rhythm with pleasurable surprise. He knew me! I had not been invisible to him all these months. I smiled back and watched until he and his companions had rowed out of sight around the broadly sweeping bend, their prowess not improved with the knowledge that my eyes were fixed upon them.

The next afternoon, Sunday, I put on my best pair of jeans, with a new baggy cotton top, and strolled along the river bank, hoping that I would see him again. There was little chance. He could have been anywhere else in the wide world. When I reached the slim, Ove Arup bridge which links the university with Palace Green, there he was, leaning on the parapet, alone and idly watchful.

We said hello to one another. I hesitated and then began to walk on, not knowing how to capture this familiar stranger. He fell into step beside me and said, "You're a friend of Lois Grant's, aren't you?"

"Oh, do you know Lois?" I was amazed, because she had led me to believe that it was her dearest wish to know him. He began to explain that in fact he did not know her personally, but his brother knew her cousin. Within five minutes of stilted conversation we had forgotten Lois and were beginning the complex game of getting to know one another without being too inquisitive — or informative, for that matter. There is a unique chance at the start of an association to be the person one would like to be, before one's true nature surfaces and spoils the fantasy. Often, by then it is too late: one has fallen for the other's masquerade and has to live with the unmasked.

"When shall I tell Leila to expect us this summer?" Mum asked Dad one morning, almost a year later.

He was about to rush off to descend with brisk authority upon his unsuspecting workforce at an electronics factory on Teeside. "It doesn't look as if we'll be able to go this year," he said. "Perhaps later, in the autumn."

"It has to be during the school holidays," Mum reminded him, "and I don't want to wait until October half-term. If you can't come, we'll have to go without you. I shall tell Leila to expect me and the kids at the end of July, as usual. You may be able to get across for a few days, surely?"

We were sitting round the breakfast table in what we called the garden room, which was an airy extension to the dining-room. It was decorated with a pretty trellis-effect white and green wallpaper. It had white-painted woodwork, lots of small-paned glass and tall, glossy green pot plants strategically placed to make it appear that the vegetation in the garden had overspilled into the house. The furniture was made of light ash and the upholstery was in a satinised cotton print of full-blown roses which matched the curtain fabric.

Dad bent and kissed Roddy on his plump cheek carefully avoiding his eggy mouth, then he kissed Mum. "We'll talk about it later, Lorna," he promised. "I have to go, the car's waiting."

"Will you be in for dinner, Oliver?" she called as he was leaving the house.

"Yes, all being well," he called back.

Mum looked at me and smiled. "He'll come," she said with confidence. "If there's one thing your father can't stand, it's the thought of the rest of us enjoying ourselves without him."

"What if he really can't come?" I asked, pouring myself more orange juice.

She smiled again. "Give Cassie a shout, will you? If she doesn't get up soon, she'll be late for school."

I walked through the cool, shaded dining-room into the bright warmth of the hall and yelled for Cassandra. If my sister had a fault, then in my opinion it was her great capacity for sleep. Morpheus had only to beckon and she crept trustingly into his arms with a sigh of pure pleasure. He had never found me so willing to be seduced. No doubt that was the reason why Cassandra had been the more attractive child. There is nothing more frustrating for tired parents who are craving sleep themselves than a baby who fights it with every breath in its healthy lungs. I still begrudged the beguiling god every hour he stole from me, but now of course I kept no one awake but myself.

Cassandra appeared at the top of the stairs in her nightdress. In the morning sunlight which was streaming through the landing window, her rounded young body was clearly visible beneath the fine cotton. She was thirteen years old and already physically maturing. With a shock, I realised that her developing breasts were almost as full as mine. God, how I hated being so skinny!

"Get dressed," I told her. "You'll be late for school." Then I went back to the garden room. "I don't want to come to Alsace this summer," I said.

Mum put down her coffee cup. "Don't be difficult, Jan. Where else would you go?"

"I could stay with Grandma and Grandpa."

"I want you to come," Mum said. "That's naughty, Roddy. Use your spoon." Then to me again, "Next year you'll be going off to university. This could be our last family holiday. Please come, darling."

"I'm fed up with Alsace," I said ungraciously. "Other people go to more exciting places. Lois is going to Austria with her cousins. I wouldn't mind going off somewhere with a friend."

"You can do that next year. Your father will be so disappointed if you don't come. You know how much he likes us all to be together."

"But he might not be going either," I reminded her.

She looked vexed, but did not answer. She turned her attention back to Roddy, who was bashing the daylight out of the remains of his bread and butter soldiers with his empty mug.

I glanced at my watch. It was almost eight-fifteen, time for me to go.

"Bye, bye, Roddy." My little brother put up his face to be kissed. I took a tissue from the box on the window ledge and thoroughly wiped away the breakfast from his mouth and the end of his snub nose, then I lifted him into my arms and hugged and kissed him until he squealed to be set free and punched me with his tiny fists.

"Don't be excessive, Jan," Mum sighed. "You are either all over him or ignoring him. I can't think why he is so fond of you."

I dumped him back on the cushion on his chair. He let out a yelp of pain as his chubby knees came in contact with the edge of the table.

"Sorry, Roddy," I said contritely, giving him another quick kiss on the top of his head. I ran upstairs and stood at the landing window. Cassandra passed me on her way down to breakfast, looking demure in her school uniform, her curls well-brushed, the nascent woman no longer apparent. As she turned the corner of the staircase, she glanced back and said, "He's gone. I saw him from the bathroom window." She continued unhurriedly down the stairs.

I raced after her, grabbed my blazer and school bag and slammed out of the house. I need not have worried. He was there on the corner, waiting for me, patient, shy and utterly dependable. From our first meeting, when had he ever let me down?

"You're late," he said equably.

"My watch must be slow," I explained and we set off side by side towards my bus stop. He was fortunate, he was within walking distance of his school. "Mum is trying to persuade me to go to Alsace with them again this year." The first words I spoke to him were usually of my problems.

"You might as well," he said.

He was my faithful friend and ally, tolerating my varying moods with calm perplexity; calming my anger with cool reason and curbing my exuberance with quiet amusement. I tormented and sometimes hurt him, goading him to retaliate, but it was not in his nature to be provoked. He was sober and sensitive and I needed him during those last years at school.

"When you phone Leila," Dad said to Mum that evening, "don't say I won't be coming with you. There's a chance that I might manage it after all, but it'll probably mean I shall have to fly back for a few days in August."

Mum's expression did not change as she said how pleased she was. She waited until after dinner to tell him that I did not want to go.

"Whyever not?" he asked me, astounded.

"Sooner or later I shall stop going on holiday with you, why not this year? I'm seventeen."

"Age has nothing to do with it," he said. "It's not as if we keep you tied to us while we're there." That was a lie for a start. "You know the place well enough now to be able to get about on your own if you want. You'll be able to please yourself what you do."

"That's the trouble," I complained, "I know the place too well. I'd like to go somewhere different or even just stay at home. Gérard and Jean-Michel haven't come across with Leila and Lucien for years now. They are allowed to do their own thing."

"They are both older," Dad said, and when I opened my mouth to protest that Jean-Michel was only one year older than I was, he started on about all the things he had planned for us to do that year, such as spend a few days in Metz on the way there and a long weekend in Geneva during the course of our stay.

"I thought you might not be coming," I remarked coldly.

"That's supposing I do," he replied. Then a thought struck him. "You weren't planning to do anything with that young man of yours, I hope!"

"Such as?" I enquired rudely.

He glowered at me.

I only want his company rather than yours, I thought, but I said, "He's got a summer job behind the bar in the County Hotel. His family can't afford to go abroad."

"Anyone can afford to go abroad these days," Dad scoffed. "They go on package holidays." He despised package holidays. I could not imagine Martin's parents anywhere but in their well-cared-for modern semi-detached house on the outskirts of Durham, tending their neat, geometrically laid out garden, nursing their elderly car which they seldom used, and being proud of their two clever sons who were going to have the chance of a good education, which was something they themselves had missed.

"Poor, are they?" Dad asked, as if poverty was a disease.

"It depends what you call poor," I answered stiffly, ashamed that we had so much and in a mood to condemn him, as if he were a criminal, for providing it.

"It usually means having very little money," he replied witheringly. "What does his father do?"

"He's retired," I said shortly. I was not

going to discuss Martin's parents with him. His standards were not theirs.

"I want you to change your mind about Alsace, Jan," Dad said in the tone of voice that defied defiance. "Last year you were a great help to Lucien with the *dégustation.*"

There were not many British visitors in Alsace. South of Strasbourg, GB plates were few and far between. I had helped out whenever there was a party of British tourists handicapped by rudimentary French and eager to sample Lucien's excellent wine and visit his *caves,* the chilly rooms where the precious grape harvest was fermented, bottled and stored. Although Lucien's English was good, he had a typical French perversity about using it to help out lazy foreigners.

Lucien and Leila Amberlé were the only friends that my parents had in common. They cultivated the vine in a small village called Grutenheim at the feet of the Vosges mountains. Dad and Lucien had spent alternate summers at one another's homes when they were young and Lucien eventually met and married a girl from Newcastle. They had two sons, Gérard who was three years older than I was, and Jean-Michel. We had seen a lot of this family when I was a child, but once the elderly Amberlés had retired from the family business, Lucien was kept far too busy most of the year to be able to visit us very often and Grutenheim became our second home. It was beautiful and I loved it, but it was an integral part of the family life I was becoming so impatient to shrug off.

Over the next couple of weeks I put up a good fight, pulling out all the emotional stops from tears to sulks, but I was no match for my father when it came to getting my own way.

"Give in graciously, Jan," Mum pleaded, when I told her, wearily, that I had decided to go after all. "The thought of a month spent in an atmosphere of tension between you and your father is more than I can bear. Take a leaf out of my book for once: let him organise and boss to his heart's content. Conserve your own energy for his absences. If I fought with him all the time, I'd have to take to my bed when he was away in order to get up the strength to start all over again when he came back."

"It's a wonder you aren't on tranquillisers," I

said morosely. "Does he never get tired?"

Mum laughed. "Do you? Frenetic vitality is one of the things you and your father have in common."

"And the other things?" I asked in dismay, not feeling in a mood to relish having anything whatsoever in common with him.

"You're both 'having' people," she said regretfully.

"What on earth does that mean?"

"It means, Jan, that you must have everything you want and you can't bear to lose anything you have. What is it going to do for you, I wonder?"

"Cassie always gets what she wants," I pointed out.

"You think she does, because she keeps quiet about her defeats. Cassie never lets anyone know what it is she desires until she has it. She schemes while you storm. You couldn't be more different."

"It's worked all right for Dad."

"Has it?" Mum asked. She paused for a moment, considering, then she said, sarcastically, "Oh yes, your father's a big man in the big world, if that's what you mean."

Implying what? That he was not so big in the small, intimate world they shared? I could not say that I had noticed it. We certainly felt the full weight of his presence. "He's a pain," I said.

"Yes, isn't he? The kind of pain you miss dreadfully when it stops, because it means you've lost something vital — like a limb."

4

SO I went with them on that familiar journey to north-eastern France, taking the ferry from Hull to Zeebrugge, then travelling on the motorway that skirts Brussels to the south and on through Luxembourg to Lorraine, where we were to spend a few days. My father had suggested, time and time again, that we should travel by air and hire a car while we were in France, but Mum would never hear of it. She always had so much to take. Some of the things were commissioned by Leila, such as a couple of legs of lamb and packets of Twining's tea, and there was even more to bring back, including our full allowance of Lucien's wine.

The drive from Durham to Hull was not so bad, about a hundred miles, but from Zeebrugge to Metz was a longer haul. So far that year, the northern English summer had been unsettled and we were hoping for an improvement in Alsace, where the weather had been kind to us on previous holidays. When we left Zeebrugge after an overnight crossing, a cool, early morning mist was hiding the flat Belgian countryside, but by the time we reached the rows of filling stations near the French border with Luxembourg and stopped to take advantage of the cheaper petrol before we crossed, the sky was virtually cloudless — a deep, endless blue. Gazing from the window into the bright sunlight, I felt myself slipping back into all the past summers spent there, sliding into the slower pace of stretched-out time-tables, where if one is going somewhere, one will go — eventually and come back at any time; if one is eating, one eats long and leisurely, with wine, water and *salade* always on the table, except at breakfast which is crusty bread with coffee and hot chocolate for the children.

Cassandra and Roddy slept most of the time in the car and only woke when we stopped to eat and relieve ourselves. I was sitting on one side of Roddy's safety seat, directly behind my mother, helping her to keep a look-out for the vehicles overtaking us in the fast lane with no intention of ever leaving it. When we were approaching a motorway it was necessary for both of us to crane our necks backwards, because it was extremely difficult for Dad to see whether or not it was safe to leave the slip road. The hazards of driving on the wrong side of the road — as we always thought of it — were as much part of the holiday excitement as the well-remembered scenery through which we were driving.

Instead of passing Metz on the motorway, glad to put the ugly great pipes of Thionville behind us, and stopping only long enough to use the toilets at the La Maxe service complex, we spent two nights in the city, staying at its ancient, commercial heart, near the Place Saint-Louis, where the tall, austere façades of the buildings have arched arcades which house rows of small, exclusive shops and flower stalls.

Dad had decided what we should do and see in Metz. No stone of its history should be left unturned, starting with the Romans. I rebelled. They could traipse from museum to monument if they liked, but I had no intention of going with them.

"I suppose you want to mooch about on your own," Dad said over breakfast in the hotel. "It's not my idea of a holiday."

"We are well aware of that, Oliver," Mum said with a hint of resignation in her voice. "Jan can do what she likes and meet us for lunch."

"I wasn't going to bother with lunch," I said untruthfully. I intended buying some bread and cheese and a delicious fruit-filled pastry to eat on the banks of the Moselle. "I'll take Roddy with me if you like."

"What a good idea," Mum said.

"No," said Dad at the same time.

I was ruining his day by not wanting to share his planned pleasures.

"We may as well all go round the town window shopping and wasting our time," he said.

"I wasn't going to window shop," I told him — well, only a little bit, perhaps.

"What were you going to do then?"

I was becoming thoroughly exasperated. I knew I should not have come. It was only the second day of the holiday and Dad and I were at loggerheads. I wished I was back in Durham in the rain with Martin and that Dad was away as usual on one of his business trips, leaving us all in peace. I was ready to answer him in

53

an extremely sarcastic manner, describing walking from the hotel towards the river in minute detail, explaining that I might blow my nose when I got to the corner, but then I caught the expression on Mum's face. A day mooching around on her own would have delighted her as well, but there was never any question of that. Roddy was grizzling, because he did not like his cereal. Cassandra was trying to coax him to eat it. He flung his sturdy arm at the spoon and accidentally knocked his plate to the floor. Mum picked it up and soothed him. Dad, a map in one hand and his coffee cup in the other, ignored the antics of his little son, as he ignored all domestic trivia that did not concern him. He was still waiting for me to answer him.

"I'll go wherever you go," I gave in sulkily, "seeing as it's positively the last time I shall be coming on holiday with you all."

That was a battle he would fight another year. He was satisfied with his present victory. "Good girl!" He looked pleased but Mum tightened her lips and frowned at me. She was worried that I would pay him back by being awkward. I decided to be docile all day for her sake and gave her a smile of reassurance.

"Have we all finished?" she asked on a note of hope.

"I'll have another cup of coffee," Dad said.

Mum lifted the heavy silver pot and felt it. "It's not very hot."

"Then I'll ask for some more." He beckoned imperiously to the waiter who moved smartly to his side. We were used to his demands for extra attention, however small, in hotels and restaurants. Unless he had people running round after him he did not consider that he was being properly served. This attitude went down better in France than in England and I did not feel obliged to look away so often, pretending I had nothing to do with him.

Roddy said he needed the bathroom. Both Cassandra and I quickly offered to take him.

"You take him, Jan," Mum said, and I had him out of the chair and clear of the dining-room in a matter of seconds, while Cassandra equably resigned herself to at least another ten minutes at the breakfast table.

With Roddy in his pushchair, we set off to explore Metz. Luckily, although my father wanted to see everything there was to see, he was not one to hang about while doing it and in that way was a person after my own heart. Mum and Cassandra would have lingered longer in the museum, gazing at the paintings and enquiring into the natural history of the region and the Roman artefacts, but Dad breezed through with me and Roddy not far behind. We spent longer over monuments and places of interest in the open air, such as the old Porte des Allemands, which is a mighty gateway astride the River Seille, guarding the city from Germany. On one side of the river, the towers have pointed slate tops, resembling conical hats, and on the other they are squat and massive with stone battlements.

I loved the soaring, Gothic cathedral of Saint-Etienne which, unlike Durham Cathedral which overlooks the river, is hemmed in by the narrow streets surrounding its own small square, busy with people and buses. Inside the cathedral, the stone-slabbed floor and tall pillars were awash with the colours of its glorious stained glass windows, some richly hued and as old as the building itself, others bright and clearly modern.

After lunch in a restaurant, recommended to Dad by Lucien — which looked seedy outside and not much better inside, but where the simple food was good and most of the clientele was local — we persuaded Dad to leave visiting the oldest basilica in France until the next day and instead walk along the esplanade on the banks of the Moselle. We sat for a while on the terrace overlooking the river and Mont St Quentin and I wrote a postcard to Martin. I was feeling guilty because, despite my reluctance to be there, the special magic of France was stealing over me, even as I wrote, permeating my senses. Behind us there was a fragrant shrub, covered in deep red flowers, such as I had never seen at home; not far away was a pungent public lavatory and we had eaten mussels in garlic for lunch. Martin, so very English, was becoming unreal against the lively sound of French voices.

A middle-aged woman, wearing a dark blue, heavy cotton dress which hung about her spare frame, and expensive leather sandals on her stringy, sunburnt feet, was walking past with her dog, the ubiquitous German Shepherd. She stopped and spoke a few words to Roddy. He screwed up his eyes and looked up at her as if she was insane. Mum answered for him and explained that Roddy did not understand because he was English.

"What about the rest of us?" I asked her, amused.

"Oh yes," she told the woman, "we're all English, of course." She spoke as if she was surprised to remember this.

Roddy said loudly, "Go away, bad dog!" just to prove his origin, although his blue shorts, just as short as shorts could be, were a dead giveaway. Had he been French, they would probably have been knee-length with turn-ups.

Cassandra remarked as she was watching the woman walk away from us, "Tomorrow, I'm going to buy a straw hat, with flowers on it. I don't want to get freckles."

"You've got them already," I said.

"No, I haven't. You have! I want to stay pale, it's more interesting. Everyone here is so brown.

"Why do you want to look interesting?"

I asked her at thirteen, surely it was enough to look healthy.

She lowered her long, fair eyelashes and smiled demurely, saying in her maddening, illogical way, "Why not?"

I wrote Martin's address on the card and wondered if the time would ever come when Cassandra and I would have a proper conversation. The four years between us presented a gulf we were unable to reach across that and our temperaments, which were so different that the motives and aspirations of one were incomprehensible to the other. At any rate, if Cassandra had made up her mind to buy a hat in the morning, the chances were that my desire to go shopping would be fulfilled. Dad would have to drag Mum and Roddy around that old basilica.

"I'll go into the town with Cassandra in the morning," I offered, as if I was doing everyone a favour.

"So shall I," Mum said firmly. "I need to buy a couple of things myself." She used the word 'need' judiciously, spurning the word 'want' as ineffectual.

Dad snapped shut the guide book he had been reading and sighed. "God, you women! I don't know how you would exist without shops. I'll give you an hour. Roddy and I will go on the river in the morning, won't we, son?"

I would make sure that I stretched that hour to its limits — that is, to the limits of my father's patience.

We arrived in Grutenheim just after three o'clock on a swelteringly hot day. The busy main road from Strasbourg had been a thundering nightmare of assorted vehicles and it was a relief to turn off it, south of Colmar, into the quiet country roads which linked village to village between endless sloping squares of densely cultivated vines. The red-roofed villages appeared deserted; the houses were closely packed, higgledy-piggledy, around the church, and everywhere colourful window-boxes of bright geraniums. The narrow roads and alleyways had not been built for motor traffic; nevertheless, every household owned at least one car. How else did one bring back the litre bottles of water from the hypermarket? The quiet of the somnolent countryside was broken only by the strident chirping of crickets — a vibrant non-stop hymn to the ecstasy of summer, accompanying us through the open car windows.

We had to pass through two villages before reaching our destination, then we saw the square tower of the church at Grutenheim, topped with its steeply angled red roof. Modern chalets, built above garages and utility rooms, straggled along the outskirts of the village near the empty tennis courts and playing field, and then we were passing cautiously between the older buildings, through the cramped church square with the *boulangerie* and modern telephone kiosk, and round two sharp corners into a leafy lane which led upwards through green vineyards set in close, neat rows, to the tree-clad hills beyond. Fifty metres along the lane, we turned through open wrought-iron gates into a sun-drenched courtyard surrounded by buildings and irregular patches of dense, black shadow. We had arrived.

There were two other cars parked there. One we recognised as Lucien's large, white Renault, the other probably belonged to a customer. On the left of the gates was the original old house, where Lucien and Leila now lived. His elderly parents had moved into a new one on the other side of the courtyard, which had been built for them on their retirement. Directly opposite the gates was another modern building, partly hidden by the pendulous blue blossom of a venerable wistaria, where the wine was made and stored; a controlled and chilly environment, the Amberlé *caves*. The apartment with the geranium-edged balcony was ours. We never wanted to hear of the family's other visitors who were granted the same privilege.

It was too hot and the journey had been too long for us to spring animatedly out of the car. We sighed heavily with relief, opened the doors and uncurled from the seats, almost as if we were sorry to have to make the effort, yet one more kilometre in the car would have seemed intolerable. Roddy, unharnessed from his safety seat and woken up in the process, stood in the baking yard holding his comforter, a woolly rabbit, by its ears, and whimpered as if he had been deposited on an alien planet. At the fourth car door slam, someone appeared in the deep shadow of the family house and an English voice called out cheerfully.

"Hello, you lot. You've arrived at last!" Leila walked towards us, smiling broadly, wiping her hands on her apron. "Hello, pet," she greeted Roddy, picking him up and giving him a big kiss.

Suddenly, Roddy remembered the planet. He had been here before and liked it. "Where's Tonto?" he asked, looking round.

"We haven't got him any more," Leila said sadly, putting him back on his feet.

"Why not?" Cassandra asked with disappointment, because the large dog had been a great favourite with us all.

"Dead!" Leila said. "Run over by a *camion.*" The brutal statement of the plain fact was typical of her.

I glanced round the courtyard, not wanting to believe it. No large shape detached itself languidly from the shadows to wag itself towards us.

"How are you all?" Leila asked, regarding us critically, one after the other. "Apart from being tired and hot, I mean. That car," indicating the one in the shady corner, "should be going soon, then you can put yours there. Come in and have some lemonade." She paused until my mother reached her side. They exchanged slow smiles which expressed the satisfaction they felt at being together again, and we followed them from the glare of the courtyard into the low-ceilinged dimness of the family house, shuttered against the unrelenting sun.

My parents and Leila began talking nineteen to the dozen, exchanging news. Leila took a large brown jug of lemonade from the refrigerator and placed it on the kitchen table, its stained wood bashed and scored with years of use and abuse. We knew the stone jug and the table well, as we knew everything about the place. I perched in my favourite spot, on the cupboard beside the coffee machine, and held out my hand for one of the glasses which Cassandra was taking from the shelf over the draining board. These glasses had once held mustard. We usually took some back with us to replace the ones we had smashed since our last visit.

Leila was fussing over Roddy again, slipping back into the endearments of her childhood. Roddy was by turn a pet and a canny bairn. She'll be calling one of us hinny next, I thought. It was a strange thing about Leila. She had spent more than twenty years in France and remained stubbornly English. "I gave up a lot when I came here," I once heard her telling Mum. "I'm damned if I'm going to become French into the bargain." Yet she loved her adopted home and wanted to be nowhere else. Leila was of average height with a slim back, narrow, sloping shoulders, full hips and shapely legs, and she had a disproportionately large bust. I use the word bust, because it seems more appropriate than any other term, although perhaps chest would serve as well. Her bust, then, was large, firm and astonishing. It was the first thing one noticed about her and one had difficulty in politely ignoring it. Whenever she came to visit us, Grandma Harris used to say, "I'd do something about that bosom if I were her. It's not nice!" However, it did not embarrass Leila as much as it embarrassed others on her behalf. Needless to say, she had to have most of her clothes made for her. This bust was the subject of some ribald amusement, but only in her absence. Jokes were made by the men and regretted by the women, who thought it was a shame for her to be so encumbered.

The customer's car passed the kitchen window and turned left through the gates.

Dad went out to move our car into the patch of shade and begin removing the luggage. We heard him greet Lucien and they stood talking just outside the door beneath the sheltering overhang of the first floor. They spoke in English. I am ashamed to say that we made little effort within the family to speak French unless Lucien's parents were present, when it became a necessity. The fault was Leila's, not ours. Her French was good, as one would expect after so many years, but she was too perverse to make the effort required to perfect it. One advantage was that her boys were bilingual. Lucien's English was about as good as her French, and although Leila used her own language to him and their children most of the time, they answered her in whichever language they fancied — always their own when they were annoyed with her.

Dad came in carrying the large ice-box.

"Good! My legs of lamb!" Leila exclaimed, and while she was emptying the contents of this plastic container into the refrigerator, Lucien walked in with his parents, old Mathias and Marie-Louise, and his younger son.

"Jean-Michel is helping Lucien this summer," Leila explained.

At last we were engulfed in a proper French welcome — kiss, kiss, kiss, time and time again, *"Ça va?"* *"Ça va bien, merci,"* and, becoming animated and excited, we all began talking at once.

5

"**W**HAT about Martin?" Cassandra asked softly, her unsmiling blue eyes regarding me from beneath the wide brim of her new straw hat, which had a deep band of cream lace around the crown and a cluster of pink rosebuds. She was sitting on the grass with her legs curled under the skirt of her pink cotton sun-dress, an open book in one hand.

I was watching the small boats on the lake, searching until I found the one containing Mum, Roddy and Leila. "What *about* Martin?" I asked coldly, because Martin was none of her business. She did not answer. I swivelled round on the wooden bench to stare at her, raising my eyebrows. She returned my look without expression, then dropped her eyes to her book.

Cassandra was a watchful child. She was quiet and complying. People easily forgot that she was there. She listened, observed and said nothing. What she learned, she kept to herself, but occasionally she made a remark that showed her perception and left one feeling strangely uncomfortable and in a mood to reflect upon one's words and actions, sometimes regretting them. She watched with calm detachment while the rest of us interacted impulsively around her.

What about Martin? I asked myself, thinking of Jean-Michel as she had no doubt intended. I left the bench and the picnic boxes and wandered along the side of the lake until I reached the busy boating area. I bought a can of fizzy orange and sat at a white metal table near the landing stages to drink it.

Lake Gérardmer stretched before me, surrounded by low, tree-covered hills. Here, set amongst the Vosges, the heat of the plain was tempered by a refreshing breeze which licked across the water, ruffling its surface texture. The small craft bobbed about with sudden splashings against the tiny waves, moving haphazardly between the smoother, swifter passages of the light wind-surfers and the slower, purposeful passenger boats, which were making stately circuits. Next to the wooden jetties was a tiny shingle beach, where small children played and swam in the shallow water. Behind the café where I was sitting was a crowded car park and long, impatient queues for the public lavatories — sit-down or stand-up varieties, the choice being between convenience and hygiene. I drank my orangeade and opted for hygiene.

I walked back to our picnic spot holding Roddy's hot little hand and listening to his chatter about the delights of getting wet in a rowing boat. Mum and Leila were sauntering on ahead, deep in conversation to the exclusion of all else. That is how they always were, learning from one another how to cope with the complexities of marriage and bringing up a family, stage by stage — putting their problems into perspective, was what Mum called it. Neither of them was aware of the admiring glances being bestowed on Leila's bust by a group of lounging youths with nothing better to do than comment upon features of interest.

Dad was back in England. He had left only three days after our arrival, hoping to return in time to spend the last week with us. In his absence, our holiday was taking on a lazy casualness that he would not have tolerated, our family unit fragmenting according to the whim of each individual, which was how things always were when Dad was away organising other people.

The fact that Jean-Michel was there that summer made a great difference to me. He had just passed his driving test and was using Leila's beloved *deux chevaux* with the obligatory round 90 kilometres sign on the back, as a sweetener for helping his father with the vines. Unlike his elder brother, Gérard, he had little interest in the family business and would be going to Paris in the autumn to begin studying civil engineering.

Cassandra and I went swimming with him and his friends in Colmar and in the evenings I played tennis with them. I talked Mum into promising that I could have driving lessons when we returned home; in the meantime Jean-Michel let me have goes in his mother's car on land belonging to his grandparents. Leila and Mum were using our car since Dad had gone, which left the little green Citroën 2CV free. We were having a great time gadding about in it. Once a week I sent a picture postcard in an envelope to Martin, using up every blank space with cramped handwriting and trying not to think of his dull working holiday or give him reason to suspect that, despite all my protestations to the contrary before I left, I was enjoying myself. I was no trouble at all to my mother, indeed she scarcely saw me, except at dinner. She and Leila did the marketing together in the mornings, mostly at Colmar or Rouffach, and afterwards, frequently, they took Roddy and Cassandra to one of the lakes, Gérardmer or Longemer, for swimming and boating. I could please myself whether or not I accompanied them and most of the time I did not.

Sometimes in the early evenings, before the leisurely meal that we all took together any time after eight-thirty, Lucien would drive us up into the hills beyond the vineyards and we would leave the car to walk up steep paths through fragrant pine woods until we reached a chateau, a church, a monastery — some ancient pile of stones built strategically on the heights to overlook the wide valley of the Rhine, far below. We would gaze into the slanting evening sunlight across the tranquil green plain to the Black Forest in the distance, and the long history of trouble and brutal conquest seemed like a dream, related by the old ones when only half-waking.

Occasionally, I helped Lucien show visitors around his *caves*. I poured the excellent wine for them to sample at a narrow table in the special room set aside for the tastings. I did a little surreptitious sampling myself, of wines with which I was already familiar: the delicious white wines of Alsace — Riesling, Gewürztraminer, Muscat, Sylvaner, Pinot Blanc — or the Pinot Noir, the local red wine, served in green-stemmed glasses, cool in the shaded length of the traditionally furnished room, which offered refreshment and relief from the hot sun. The Crémant d'Alsace was never sampled. It is a sparkling white wine, similar to Champagne, although not so expensive. It was kept for special occasions.

When the ornate iron gates, with the sign saying 'Lucien Amberlé, *Proprietaire-Viticulteur'* were open, there was a constant coming and going of cars containing customers for the wine. The gates were opened first thing in the morning and shut well before the *vigneron* and his family sat down to dinner.

That afternoon, when we returned from Lake Gérardmer I walked across the courtyard into the room where the wine was bottled. Lucien and Jean-Michel were there beside the large, sloping, three-dimensional rectangular rack which held the bottles of Crémant and automatically turned them one eighth of a revolution every day, obviating the necessity for the numerous lightning flicks of the wrists that the two-handed job used to entail and which Lucien would often demonstrate for the amusement of his visitors.

The men turned at my entrance, their discussion ceasing.

Both Lucien's sons resembled him physically. They were above average height, lean and athletic. Lucien in his younger days had been a keen tennis player and skier. All three had mid-brown hair, very blue eyes and dark complexions. Mathias and Marie-Louise Amberlé, although now grey-haired, had similar startlingly blue eyes which had not dimmed with age. They looked more like brother and sister than husband and wife, but whereas he was plump and good-tempered, she was tiny and sharp-tongued, with a face lined and puckered like scrumpled, coarse brown linen. Leila, with her fair hair, grey eyes and matt white skin, was a foreign cuckoo in that French nest. I suspected her of playing up her difference, so that the rest of them were not sure what they should expect of her. She was never asked to participate in the wine business and would not have known a Pinot Gris grape from a Riesling. I thought that this ignorance, assumed or real, was deplorable and wondered how long it had taken Mathias and Marie-Louise to adjust sufficiently to this English daughter-in-law to grow to love her; for love their *belle-fille* they obviously did.

When he saw that it was only me, Lucien smiled and excused himself, saying he was needed elsewhere. As he was leaving, a car drew into the courtyard and we heard him greet a friend from a neighbouring village.

"I don't want to play tennis this evening," I said to Jean-Michel.

OOJ6

"Pierre will be disappointed," he mocked. Pierre was a friend of his.

"He'll have to find someone else to partner," I answered.

"He's not interested in your tennis," Jean-Michel laughed. "Haven't you noticed?"

Well yes, I had, but I was not interested in Pierre. The last thing I wanted was to form an attachment in France; after all, I had made up my mind not to return to Grutenheim. I was going to put the place behind me, as one does treasured possessions one has outgrown. I was there that year on sufferance and would have had a much less enjoyable time if my father had not been called away. After three years of not seeing one another, Jean-Michel and I had met as young adults and discovered that we got on very well. We were allies in pursuing our own selfish interests, not yet knowing what it was like to be tied by responsibilities. All we knew of duty was the obligation we owed our parents and, seeing it as a restriction, we evaded it whenever possible. Jean-Michel did what his father required of him as quickly and efficiently as possible, then disappeared with haste, just in case Lucien thought of something else for him to do. I employed similar tactics with Mum.

"Janine!" That was her voice now, calling me to hang up the washing. She could not stand the heat trapped between our apartment and the steeply sloping roof, and Cassandra could not stand the spiders, so I always had the job.

"Coming!" I yelled back. "I've got to go," I said to Jean-Michel. "Sorry about the tennis."

"That's all right. I'll probably go to Colmar instead."

I went outside and up the stairs to the balcony of the apartment, directly above. Mum was in the kitchen, giving Roddy his tea. The washing was waiting for me in a plastic bowl next to the sink.

"The machine's broken," Mum said. "It won't spin. Ask Leila if you can spin it in hers."

"It's not necessary," I answered. "You know what it's like in there — an oven." I picked up the heavy bowl and went along the hall and up a staircase to the door into the loft. As I went in the oppressive heat engulfed me. The vast, low-raftered area was well lit by tiny square openings

77

beneath the eaves, through which birds and bats made their nocturnal flights and insects flitted in and out constantly. I glanced around as I always did when I first entered, just to make sure that I had the place to myself. Near the door were stored old brushes, dustpans, mops, an ancient vacuum cleaner, an ironing board and a metal bucket. Three long, plastic-covered lines were strung between the heavy wooden beams and fastened on them was an odd assortment of pegs and clothes hangers.

I began to hang up the sopping washing, mainly Roddy's little garments which dripped copiously onto the baking concrete floor. I knew from experience that the deluge would dry out in a matter of minutes.

I quite liked the loft. It was a world apart, rather like the summer-house at home, into which sounds of the other world drifted spasmodically with a faraway quality: a cry, a call, a car engine, church bells and here, the clang of wine crates. Only outdoor sounds were heard. The apartment beneath, the two houses and other buildings round the courtyard, hugged their sounds within their walls, as if they too were in need of protection from the sun. There was a heaviness in the air that meant a thunder-storm in the offing. I bent down for the last garment which was soaking in a pool of lightly scented rinse water. It was the blue blouse that Martin liked, the one he said was the same colour as my eyes. As I pegged it up by its hem, I thought again, What about Martin? Well, he was still there, wasn't he? Dear, dependable Martin, his Anglo-Saxon reticence in contrast to the lively, Gallic charm of Jean-Michel. Perhaps it would be prudent to remind Martin that I still regarded him as indispensable.

After dinner, late in the quiet, bat-filled dark, I went along to the telephone kiosk in the village. As I was making my way past the silent, huddled-together old houses with their closed, shuttered façades, guard dogs hurled themselves against garage doors and hedged fences, barking noisily at my soft, sandalled steps and leaving me in no doubt of their displeasure at my fleeting presence. Even though I knew where to expect each noisy onslaught, I still jumped and side-stepped hastily at every sudden outbreak of barking. By the time I reached the telephone which was in the heart of the village, opposite the tall, looming shape of the church, black against the thundery sky, the air was vibrating with canine unease and I sensed that while people were holding themselves still, listening, the dogs were restlessly prowling about, muttering deep in their furry throats, waiting for my nervous return journey.

"Mrs Proudfoot?"

"Yes," a voice answered cautiously, not wanting to give too much away.

"This is Janine. Is Martin there?"

"Oh, Janine. I thought you were still in France, dear."

"I am."

"Good gracious!" There was a pause, no doubt caused by shock at the extravagance of the call, then she gabbled, "He's still at the County Hotel. He won't be back for another hour. I'll tell him you called."

I was going to ask her when he would be at home the next day, so that I could telephone again, but she replaced the receiver as soon as she had finished speaking and there was nothing left for me to do but retrieve my unused pile of francs from the glass tube.

I went to bed that night thinking of Martin, busy behind the bar. I pictured him pulling pints and smiling his shy smile at the good-natured remarks of the customers, and I felt a little homesick — just a little.

The following evening, Dad came back and spoilt it all. He insisted on carting us off to spend three days with some friends of his in Geneva, even though I begged to be left behind. Cassandra, who usually did as she was told with every appearance of enjoying it, fixed me with a limpid gaze and said quietly, "If Jan can stay here, then so can I." That did it! Dad, wavering a little about letting one daughter off the hook, especially after I had reminded him bitterly that he had promised I would not be tied to them that year, had no intention of releasing two, and that was that. Cassandra had cleverly made sure that I accompanied them.

We spent two days back in Grutenheim before returning home. On the day we arrived there so, unexpectedly, did Gérard. His family were delighted to see him and it meant they could do what they loved best — open some bottles of Crémant as an aperitif and enjoy a celebratory meal. The dish of the evening was Gérard's favourite, *choucroute garnie*, which is smoked sausage and pork with fermented, shredded white cabbage, cooked in white wine and washed down with local beer or Lucien's lovely Riesling.

The excited conversation around the table, because Mathias and Marie-Louise were present, was in the Alsatian dialect neither French nor German, but related to both. I was in my element. Like my mother, I have an ear for language and could easily differentiate between the dialect and pure French. Dad and Cassandra stuck to elementary French, the former holding forth in his normal, uninhibited manner, mainly addressing the men, the latter saying very little and saying it softly. This was an affectation of Cassandra's. She had read somewhere that if one spoke almost inaudibly, people paid more attention to what one said — well, they had to if they wanted to hear what it was — and gave it more consequence than it probably deserved. I found this habit very annoying, but I had to admit that, like all her ploys, it was proving effective. Even impatient, sour-faced Marie-Louise leaned attentively towards her when she said something in her prettily accented French and actually smiled at her encouragingly, whether or not she had understood. The only person to whom Cassandra spoke in a normal tone of voice was Dad, otherwise he just ignored her.

All of us, even naturally white-skinned Leila, were tanned in varying shades according to our complexions; all, that is, with the exception of Cassandra. Beneath the wide brim of her straw hat she had managed to stay relatively pink and cream. She was sitting opposite Gerard. As the welcome newcomer in our midst, he was receiving most of the attention, especially from his adoring grandparents. I was amused to see that Cassandra, despite her efforts to disguise it, was suffering a crush for Gerard similar to the one I had experienced at her age for Uncle Daniel. She was hanging on his every word and blushed when he turned towards her, even if it was only to ask for the salad bowl. It was comforting to realise that undereath that undemonstrative exterior her emotions were as ungovernable as everyone else's.

At the other end of the table, Jean-Michel and I were enjoying ourselves. He was teasing me about his friend Pierre and I was laughingly denying any interest. I turned away from him to pass the bread to Mathias whose plate was already surrounded by a mess of crumbs. Jean-Michel put his arm around my shoulders and said to Gérard.

"This girl has every intention of beating you at tennis tomorrow."

"Really?" Gérard smiled.

I caught Mum and Leila regarding Jean-Michel and me speculatively, with expressions of expectant satisfaction. I shrugged out of his light embrace and, looking Gerard in the eyes, said boldly, fortified by my strictly controlled allowance of Lucien's wine and a second glass taken when no one but Jean-Michel was looking, "Of course!"

Cassandra looked at me as if she disliked me. Oh well, she would probably like me well enough again when Gérard had thoroughly beaten me, for I had no doubt he would. I remembered his expertise of old. What I lacked in skill on the tennis court, I tried to make up with energy. He had plenty of both.

The telephone in the hall rang. Jean-Michel went to answer it and came back grinning to say it was for me.

It was Martin. He just wanted to know if I would be back on Tuesday as planned and when I answered that I would, he said he was glad because he was missing me. His weekly letters, short, stilted affairs, had said much the same thing. He said the weather wasn't very good in Durham. His letters had contained that information as well.

"Have you got through all your 'A' level reading?" he asked.

Trust Martin to remind me of that. "More or less," I told him untruthfully.

"The results are through. I've got the grades I needed."

"Congratulations!" I said warmly.

"What's all the racket about? Sounds like a party."

"No, it's just dinner."

"What, at this time of night? I've got

to go, Jan, the money's running out. See you soon."

"See you," I echoed, replacing the receiver. I returned slowly to the conviviality of the table, having already left it in spirit. I should have asked Martin what his grades were.

"Has he told you that he's found someone else while you've been away?" Jean-Michel teased, noticing my thoughtful expression.

"No!" I laughed at the very idea. If either of us was to find someone else it would be me, not Martin. That was not conceit but a measure of my utter confidence in his loyalty. One day I was going to hurt him — it seemed inevitable.

6

SEPTEMBER in Durham was beautiful. The sun, so fickle there all summer, made up for it by its constancy. Autumn was already in the air. It was arriving benignly, with cold breaths in the mornings and evenings which gave way to warm sighs and only occasional light tears during the course of the month. As the weeks progressed, the leaves started to change colour and were waiting for the first strong winds of October to cascade earthwards. A few could not wait and, floating downwards on the fresh breezes, lay lightly scattered in the long grasses and beneath the untidy hedgerows like scraps of damp paper.

Martin and I sauntered along the overgrown river banks catching up on the weeks spent apart. His summer job had ended and he was preparing to go to Cambridge. I envied him. He knew it and did not speak about the excitement of his own coming year but dwelt upon how quickly my last year at school would pass, urging me to work hard and have patience.

"I find it difficult to have patience," I said. "You have enough for us both."

"Implying what? That I have too much?"

"It wasn't meant as criticism," I said, but perhaps it was. We walked on in silence for a while, separated by our thoughts, then I asked, "Do you think our friendship will survive four years of separation?"

"Friendship?" he asked, giving me a long, serious look. "Who knows?"

"You sound as if you don't care," I accused him.

"I sound despondent," he corrected me.

"Then you don't think it will?"

Martin shrugged noncommittally and, taking my hand, drew me closer to his side, slipping his arm round my waist. "Jan, you might find this difficult to believe, but at this moment in time, as the current saying goes, there is something just as important as you in my life."

I giggled. Not because I did not believe him, but because I was immediately confronted by a mental picture of Uncle Daniel's 'currant woman'.

Martin compressed his lips, hurt and annoyed.

I tried to explain but it was a silly concept, so much out of step with what he was trying to tell me, that I gave up and began apologising.

"I'm sorry, Martin. What is this very important thing?"

"My degree, Jan. I owe it to my parents to do well."

"I have a degree to get as well, remember."

He smiled slightly. "You'll succeed, you always do."

"So will you."

"I don't want just to scrape through. I've got to make you all proud of me, to make my parents' struggle worth the effort, worth the faith they have in me, if you like."

"I have faith in you, Martin."

His arm tightened around my waist as he asked, "What about love, Jan?"

"It's too soon to talk of love," I protested.

His clasp loosened and I stepped away from him. "Four years is a long time. Don't let's complicate things. I'll be free for the first time in my life."

"Free from what, Jan? You've always

been able to think and say what you like. What other freedom is there?"

"The freedom to *do* what I like, of course."

"An illusion," he said morosely. He stopped to look across the river at the splendid cathedral, a monument to faith and endurance. I stopped a few yards farther on, waiting. He turned towards me with a huge sigh and as he caught me up, said, "I wish we were going to university together. I age a hundred years when we're apart."

He looked so young and boyish in his T-shirt and washed-out jeans, with his hair a little too long, curling round his ears and on the nape of his thin neck, that I was overcome with a maternal, protective feeling such as I often felt for Roddy. I wanted to hug and kiss Martin into a happier frame of mind. Instead, I grabbed his hand and said lightly, "Oh dear, I'm not very interested in ancient monuments. How about going to the disco tonight before your rheumatics set in?"

I had been at university a year when Martin and I had our first serious quarrel. I came home for the long summer vacation with every intention of taking off again on a Euro-rail card within a week or so, with a group of student friends. Dad said I could not go. How ridiculous! I said, of course I could, it was no longer any of his business where I went or what I did and he said, all right then, miss, your overdraft is none of my business either. He had just discovered the overdraft. I appealed to Mum, who gave me petrol money for my mini which had been my parents' eighteenth birthday present to me, and advised me to change my tactics with Dad.

"Take a leaf out of Cassie's book," she said.

Unbelievably, they were having trouble with my sister. She was so devious about getting her own way, they were unable to do much about preventing her.

"What's Cassandra doing?"

"If I knew that, I wouldn't worry so much," Mum said. "She's not doing any work at school, that much I do know."

"Are you going to Grutenheim for August?" I asked.

"Yes, but Cassie won't come."

"Won't come!" I was amazed. She was

91

only fifteen. Dad had made sure that I went with them until I reached the magic number eighteen.

"She's going to stay with Grandma Chandler."

"In Alnwick? What's she going to do there for a month?"

"She says she'll keep the old lady company. Your father is grateful." Mum smiled ruefully.

Dad always felt guilty about his mother living on her own and had tried many times to persuade her to come and live with us. We were thankful that her reply had always been a firm no. She was a vain, fussy, finicky person, not very fond of young people. She lived in a stone cottage surrounded by fields and patches of woodland on the outskirts of Alnwick. She read, watched lots of television, talked to her numerous cats, fed the birds and telephoned her only son every time a tap dripped, a tile loosened, a cat died, a shrub needed pruning — anything at all that she could not or would not do herself. Dad was usually away from home or too busy to be much help, so Mum drove to and fro, doing the necessary fixing and the hours of listening — for of course it was the listening that was the real necessity. Grandma Chandler existed entirely in two states, either hurt silences or endless monologues. I don't know which was the more trying.

"I had no idea Cassandra was so fond of Grandma Chandler," I remarked.

"Neither had I. I hope she is good at burying cats and washing in cold water." Grandma did not like wasting money on things like electricity and gas. For ages Dad had been trying to talk her into allowing him to modernise the cottage, but she said he could do it when she was dead.

"Cassie will hate it there. After a week, she'll be joining you in Alsace."

"I hope you're right," Mum said.

I set about getting my own way with Dad. I had to wait for three days until he returned home and by then I had devised a new strategy.

That evening I knocked on Cassandra's bedroom door. She was supposed to be doing her homework. She had two weeks left of the school term.

There was a rustling noise, then she

called languidly, "Come in."

She was lying on her bed with her text books scattered around her. The room was an absolute mess. At least mine was only untidy. On the floor next to the bed was a waste paper basket. Cassandra had been scoffing chocolate, the evidence was clearly visible. It was not a crime to eat chocolates on one's own, but there was a certain decadence about the act, a self-gratification which we had been encouraged not to indulge. Families must share the good things in life: Dad said so. Ignoring everything but my reason for being there, I said, "I want your advice," and sat down on the edge of the bed.

Cassandra rolled onto her stomach, put her chin in her hands, her heels in the air and raised her eyebrows at me in enquiry. If she was surprised at the unusual request she did not show it.

"Dad won't let me go to Europe with my friends."

"How can he stop you?"

"Money."

"Oh, I see." She thought for a few moments, then she said, "If Martin went with you I expect Dad would let you go."

"Martin has to work during the summer. I've already asked him."

"Ask him again." Cassandra would never take no for an answer.

"It's no use." I had learnt from experience that 'no' was sometimes the only answer I would get.

"Then tell Dad that Martin is going. It will amount to the same thing."

I looked into her large, guileless blue eyes, at the whole plump prettiness of her, and shuddered with foreboding. "Tell lies, you mean."

"It depends how much you want to go, doesn't it?" She rolled onto her back and picked up her maths book, bored by my obtuseness.

I took the hint and stood up. When I reached the door, I asked, "How did you manage to talk Dad into allowing you to go to Alnwick for August?"

Without taking her eyes from the book, she said, "I persuaded Grannie Chandler that she would enjoy my company."

"You'll be bored to death there. What will you do?"

"I'll think of something."

"This room is a pig-sty," I remarked.

"Yes, isn't it?"

"I pity Mrs Basset." This was the woman who helped Mum with the housework three times a week.

"You needn't. Mum won't allow her to come in here."

"I'm not surprised. She'd never get out again." I left her to her homework. Perhaps she was turning over a timely new leaf in preparation for her '0' levels next spring.

"Would you object to me going to Europe if Martin came as well?"

"No," said Dad. "That young man strikes me as having a sensible head on his shoulders. I would certainly consider it."

"The trouble is," I told him, "Martin has to work, but perhaps he could have a few weeks off. I'll ask him."

"I don't mind helping out financially."

"He won't let you do that."

"Then I'll give you enough money for both of you and you can be as discreet as you like about sharing it." Martin was working for a friend of his father as a petrol pump attendant. I took my mini to be filled up as it was approaching the time for him to leave that evening, and drove him home.

"Could you take a few weeks off?" I asked him when we reached his house.

"Not until September. I told you, Mr Bliss needs me while the rest of the staff are taking their holidays. I'm doing four weeks here, having a week free and then doing two more at his other filling station. If you wait until September, we could have a holiday together somewhere, provided it wasn't too expensive. We could go camping. My uncle has a tent he would lend us."

"I hate camping."

"Have you ever tried it?"

"No, and I don't want to."

"Everybody should rough it at least once in their lives."

"Travelling around on a rail ticket doesn't include four star bed and breakfast," I pointed out.

"Very well, wait until September and we'll do it together."

I did not want to wait. I wanted to go with my extrovert friends from university. It would be fun as part of a group. Martin was too much a cautious planner to take advantage of the opportunities of such a holiday. He would be forever consulting timetables and worrying about where we would eat and sleep.

"Forget it!" I told him ungraciously.

"I'm sorry, Jan," he said in the tone of voice people use when they are more sorry for you than for themselves. "It's difficult for you to appreciate what it's like not to have any money."

"That's what you think! As a matter of fact, I have a huge overdraft and Dad is being sticky about bailing me out."

Martin laughed without humour. "I'm talking about not having anyone to bale me out. Your father will come round."

"Actually, he said he would give me enough money to cover both our holidays," I said very foolishly.

Martin got out of the car and before slamming the door said coldly, "I only do what I can afford to do. You wouldn't understand that."

After dinner that night I said to Dad, "Martin will go to Europe with me," and Dad said, "Good! Let me have your cheque book and I'll put your account straight before you go."

But I never went. Just when I was

98

successfully beating down all feelings of guilty deception in a frenzy of telephone calls, arranging times of meetings and ship and train departures with my friends in various parts of the country, Mum told me that she had bumped into Mrs Proudfoot in the market and learned that Martin was not going with me.

"You're entitled to do as you please, Jan, but only with your own resources. I'll not say anything to your father. I'm too well aware of the deceptions I have found it necessary to play on him, but I've never done it to get money out of him, only for self-preservation. I'm surprised at you. Usually, you go headlong into trouble through honesty, not deceit."

I was ashamed. I had every intention of telling Dad the truth and giving up the holiday; then Martin telephoned and I almost changed my mind. He was furious with me for involving him in my lies to my parents. He said that he, also, was surprised at me. I had changed since leaving home for university and he did not like to see it.

"Then don't see it!" I blazed. "Get lost, Martin Proudfoot!" I slammed down the receiver and rushed upstairs. I grabbed my well-stuffed haversack and flung the contents about the room, then I sat amidst the chaos of socks, underwear, sweaters and a change of jeans, and wondered what I could do to fill in the long vacation and get my own back on the righteous. The huge green eyes of my cherished golden dragon were watching me with baleful intensity. I stared back at it tearfully then reached out and placed the heavy object on my lap, my fingers exploring its smooth contours and cool, bulbous jade. I'll find a job, I decided. I'll show them!

"I'm going to get a job," I told Mum when she and I were alone at breakfast the following morning.

"Good for you, Jan. I'm sure your father will be able to find you something."

"I'll find something myself. I don't want to ask Dad for anything else."

"Even better," Mum said approvingly. "I know what it's like to be a kept woman and, believe me, its destructive. I shall be starting a job myself when Roddy goes to school in September."

"Does Dad know?"

"There's a lot of things your father

doesn't know yet. If he ever shows any interest in how I spend my time, I'll tell him."

This sounded ominous. I took a good look at her. How often do we take a good look at our parents when we are young? Usually, I saw what I wanted to see: just Mum, busy keeping us fed, cleanly clothed and housed. That morning I saw an attractive woman of — let me see, I was nineteen, she must be forty-two. She had short, fair hair with the ends tipped in a gold colour, blue eyes like Cassandra's and mine, only with a few fine lines around them, a lovely clear skin and a wide, full mouth which was always on the verge of smiling. She was wearing a cream silk housecoat, tied around her trim waist with a matching sash, and on her feet were blue leather mules. Her finger and toe nails were immaculately painted a deep pink to match the lipstick she habitually wore, but she had not yet made up her face for the day. She never wore a lot of make-up apart from lipstick — just mascara to darken her fair lashes and a dusting of powder for special occasions.

"Are you happy, Mum?"

"What a strange question from one of my children! I should be asking you that."

"Aren't you going to tell me?" I pleaded.

"Jan, who is ever really happy? To be happy, one needs to be vacuous, completely without thought. When someone says that they are happy, they are being utterly selfish."

"Then you are unhappy," I concluded miserably.

She shook her head and smiled. "Only sometimes, as we all are. What about you, my darling?"

"I have to apologise to Martin. I'll wait until I can tell him I have a job, then perhaps he won't despise me so much."

"Women must be independent, Jan, otherwise we come to despise ourselves."

I did manage to find a job, eventually, but I was forced to let Dad help me in the end, because no one else had anything to offer me. I spent six weeks in Cumbria, staying with friends of his from Brazil, teaching their young son English and French.

However, I ended up deceiving Dad after all, but with my own money which made it more excusable. I went on holiday with

Martin at the beginning of September to the West Coast of Scotland, ostensibly to tour in my mini and take bed and breakfast at guest houses. Actually, we borrowed the tent from his uncle and Martin taught me all the delights of camping — I quite enjoyed it.

7

"ONE supreme experience," my father said, leaning back in his chair. "Everybody has at least one in their lives. Something to remember with unalloyed joy. I expect we could all bring such an event to mind." He smiled expansively round the room as if he were encouraging each of us to remember.

I thought, I knew this evening wasn't going to be a success. Who is going to be foolish enough to respond to this spurious invitation? Not one of the women, I hope? Oh yes, I might have guessed, the earth mother, Gina Distom, Mum's friend from their ante-natal days, sitting there comfortably and inelegantly in her Laura Ashley cotton with her straight fringe, bare legs and low-heeled sandals.

"My supreme moments have been the births of my babies," Gina said smugly and predictably, in an 'aren't I clever' tone of voice. "I remember when Lottie was born . . . "

I glanced at my mother. She was smiling at her friend, hiding her nervousness on her behalf. Dad's face was also wearing a smile but it had become fixed, glacial, his eyebrows raised in simulated interest. The other guests were listening politely and attentively, making appropriate noises of agreement or commiseration as the story progressed. No doubt they were all eager for Gina to finish with the obstetrics, reach her climax — the birth of little Lottie, now a hulking great girl the same age as I was — and give them all the chance to relate their own ultimate experiences. Mum and I waited uneasily.

Gina finished her tale on a note of triumph. One of the other women said chattily that she agreed with her, having a baby was a most fulfilling experience. She would have said more, given the chance, but Dad beat her to it.

"Women always have the advantage over us men," he said agreeably to the other males in the room. "How can we poor sods compete with the excitement of giving birth? No, our enterprises are far more mundane, but nonetheless satisfying. I venture to suggest. I can recall a wonderful day at Lord's, when the sun shone on a perfect wicket and . . . "

Mum and I relaxed. He would tell his story as he had intended to do from the start, and to hell with the ecstatic recollections of anyone else. The men would not begrudge him these minutes of glory. Like most of Dad's stories, this one was told to give him consequence and included the names of eminent people in the world of sport and business who were either known personally to his listeners or, more often, through hearsay — subjects of apocryphal anecdotes, fodder for other people's after-dinner stories.

"Do you really know him well?" Gina's sport-loving husband asked, most impressed, referring to the famous cricketer Dad had just mentioned.

Dad laughed. "I first met him in Worcester . . . " and off he went again.

What a shame, I thought. Mum's evening, the one she had intended to be so different, was ending up like all the rest, with Mum in her usual role of listener and smoother of ruffled female feathers. While Dad was talking, she was stirring her coffee, looking intently into her cup, on her lips the half-smile of interest she reserved for these displays of genial egotism. She had something else on her mind, something that had been absorbing her thoughts for weeks, making her irritable and aloof even with Roddy.

"Wasn't that right, Lorna?" Dad appealed to her, while everyone waited eagerly for confirmation of the fantastic incident he had just related about a leading financier whose name was often in the news for the most estimable of reasons.

"Yes, quite right," she agreed as if she found the story as incredible as the rest of them.

I looked around the room. All eyes, with the exception of mine and my mothers — she was gazing into her well-stirred coffee again — were fixed upon my father who, until that evening, had been a comparative stranger to them all. The eyes of the men held admiration, they liked him; those of the women held guarded resentment: they had come to recognise him as the enemy. One did not take one's eyes off the enemy who was far more fascinating than one's friends; they could be ignored with impunity.

Gina, Brenda, Carol and Joan, four sensitive, intelligent women, had taken their cue from my mother — after Gina had been snubbed — and were leaving the forum to the men. Dad was too clever to do all the talking. He encouraged their husbands to put in a pertinent word or two.

"Would anyone like more coffee?" I asked, when the laughter had died down after Carol's husband had been allowed to tell a joke. I left my seat to fetch the coffee pot from the sideboard, wishing they would all leave soon. Despite the laughter, there was a strained atmosphere about the evening. It was not entirely my father's fault, the presence of the other men contributed to it as well. The women had a lot of catching up to do and needed to be alone together to accomplish it. Brenda Glendinning was visiting the area from Wales and Mum, who had not seen her for years, had invited her and three of their mutual friends who lived locally, to spend an evening together at our house. Brenda had expressed the intention of bringing her husband and so the other friends were asked to bring theirs. Dad was supposed to be away somewhere, Holland I think, but his trip was cancelled at the last moment and he was here as well. I think the other men might have been content to talk among themselves and indulge their wives urge to reminisce and bring each other up to date on events in their respective lives, but there was no way my father could have been persuaded to take a back seat, especially in his own home.

"How about a shopping spree in Newcastle, ladies?" Joan suggested while I was pouring her coffee. "I've got the car tomorrow, haven't I, Ben?" She was merely checking on his greater claim to it. "I could pick you all up and we could have lunch in Fenwick's. How about it?"

It was arranged. Not much shopping would be done, but I had no doubt they would enjoy themselves and learn some astonishing facts.

Two weeks later Mum and Dad left for a holiday in Hong Kong. I had promised to look after Roddy while they were visiting Uncle Daniel and his wife, Meng. Cassandra was working. She had left school at sixteen, having done abysmally in her examinations. There had been a tremendous fuss at home, with Dad insisting that she re-sat her '0' levels, but she had obstinately refused and, without saying anything about her intentions, found herself a job in a travel agency. She was still living with my parents, but more in the manner of a lodger than a member of the family. She was out more often than she was in, kept erratic hours, some nights not coming in at all, and had numerous telephone calls from a variety of male voices which she was rarely available to answer for herself. Mum was distracted by her behaviour; Dad was only partly aware of it. Cassandra had always been such a quiet, tractable, good girl. She was still quiet and, as far as Mum knew, good, but that was not very far at all and left a lot of room for doubt.

I had two months to wait until I started work. Despite the pleasures of sharing a tent with Martin, he and I had gradually drifted apart during the years that I had been away from home. I had made many friends at university, most of them of the type my parents would have considered undesirable, and had avidly explored every avenue of experience that became open to me. However, my restless craving for amusement and change had been seriously quelled at the end of my second year by a tragic incident involving a close acquaintance, whose similar questing for novelty had led her to drugs and death. Sobered, I had dropped out of the wild group and put my considerable energy back into my studies, just in time to catch up on the months of neglect and assure a respectable degree.

When my parents departed for Hong Kong, Roddy, who was seven, still had three days left at school before he broke up for his six-week summer holiday. He was no trouble and we got on well together. I took him on day trips to Beamish Open Air Museum, to the beach at Tynemouth, the skating rink and the swimming baths. When the weather was fine we had our tea picnic style in the summer-house, and afterwards he played with his toys on the lawn or rode round on his bicycle, while I wrote long letters to Martin in the United States where he had been sent for two years by the pharmaceutical company for which he was working. I was trying to atone for the in-between years, when our correspondence had almost petered out through my carelessness and his misunderstanding. On the few occasions when I went out with friends or visited the hairdresser, I left Roddy with my grandparents. Grandpa was not well, otherwise they would have been happy to care for him all the time.

One morning I received a telephone call from Grandma Chandler at Alnwick. She sounded distressed.

"Tell Oliver to come at once, the fox has eaten my ducks," she wailed.

"He's not here, Grannie. He and Mum have gone to Hong Kong." How could she have forgotten? It was only a week ago that Mum had told her all about the holiday.

"Hong Kong!" She sounded incredulous, as if they were visiting the moon. "Oh yes, I remember. Daniel. Well, you'll have to come and clear up then, Jan."

"Clear up?" What was there to clear up?

"Bits of duck," she said. "The fox left heads and feet and feathers all over the place."

"Oh lord! All right, I'll come." I did not fancy the job at all.

Roddy and I went to her rescue with rubber gloves and a big black plastic sack. Grannie met us at her cottage door, all frail and twittery, going on indignantly about the fact that the wicked fox must have killed her precious ducks just for fun, because it had not eaten all the bodies.

"I don't know how he managed to open the door of the hut," she said. "He must be very clever."

"Perhaps you forgot to shut it last night," I suggested, and immediately regretted it. She could not bear the thought that the massacre had been her own fault and started to wring her hands in distress, saying, "I'm sure I didn't. I'm sure I did," over and over again, trotting behind me down the garden towards the duck pond. Roddy saw a dismembered webbed foot and decided to go back and visit the goat instead. I did not blame him.

I had no sooner finished the grisly job, depositing the sack next to the dustbin into which I threw the soiled rubber gloves, than Grannie Chandler said, "There's a screw loose on my kitchen cupboard door." I followed her into the poky, dismal kitchen and began opening drawers looking for the screwdriver, which she was convinced she had put in one of them. Heavens, what a load of junk she hoarded! I found it at last amongst the cutlery, and while I tackled the loose screw Grannie put the kettle on for a nice cup of tea and started to tell me about the incident with the fox all over again, until Roddy came in to say that the goat had eaten his balsawood helicopter. She broke off her monologue to tell him, unsympathetically, that it was his own fault. "I've warned you about the goat, Roderick."

They scowled at one another with mutual antipathy. "Give my love to Cassandra," were Grannie's parting words.

"I will when I see her," I promised, driving off with Roddy kneeling on the back seat, waving vigorously, relieved to be going.

We did not see much of Cassandra. She never sat down to a proper meal with us. Sometimes, Roddy and I encountered her in the kitchen, stuffing down anything she could find that did not require cooking. Roddy adored her and would hover round her waiting for a smile and a little attention. She was as pretty as ever; she could even be described as beautiful if one were being objective, but that was something I could never be about Cassandra. Behind her beauty was a hidden flaw, marring it for me; a negative attitude towards those closest to her, a disguised luxuriousness. Cassandra pursued her pleasures relentlessly, using whatever and whoever came to hand without remorse, yet no one criticised her for this. She smiled, and one felt the urge to protect her from the big, bad world, although she had proved already that she could take care of herself. I suspected that self-preservation was her main concern. My jealousy persisted. I could never rid myself of the suspicion that she was cheating me, if only out of the coveted place of favourite in the family.

While Mum was away I was doing all the washing and ironing. I tidied the house with the exception of Cassandra's room which remained a no-go area, and kept the refrigerator stocked. Cassandra slept and ate, changed her fashionable clothes every time she entered or left the house, took frequent baths, eating and drinking while soaking, made a mess of the bathroom and went out, either to work or to play; but where she played, with whom and at what, I had no idea. I did throw occasional questions at her in the kitchen and through the bathroom door, such as, "Are you going out again?" and "Where are you going tonight?" To the first she would invariably reply, "Yes" and to the second, "Out", and when I asked, "Do I know him?" referring to one of her boy friends who had actually been privileged to talk to her on the telephone for an hour, she had answered, "I shouldn't think so." I gave up.

Grandma Harris and I had some cosy heart-to-hearts, in which she expressed her concern, not for Cassandra who could do no wrong in her eyes, despite my constant moaning about her laziness and lack of consideration, but for my mother.

"I'm so glad Lorna and Oliver have managed to go away together. They need some time alone. Lorna is left too much to her own devices."

"What devices, Gran?"

She gave me an old-fashioned look and said obliquely, "At least she cannot accuse your father of keeping her short of money. I can't think why she had to go back to work. It was unnecessary."

"She enjoys it," I said. Mum was helping her friend Carol run a small, smart dress shop. "She needs to be independent."

"Independent, fiddlesticks!" Gran retorted. "Look where independence can get you."

"Where?"

"To the point of no return," she snapped with grim satisfaction.

What on earth was she talking about? "Has Mum reached a point of no return?"

"I sincerely hope not!"

"Return from what, Gran?" I persisted, searching for comprehension. We often had these baffling conversations, but this time I was determined to find her fine thread of reasoning and follow it to its end.

However, she proved too crafty for me. Her eyes slid away from my face. She tilted her head, listening. "Is that your grandfather calling me? Yes, I do believe it is. Time for his medicine. I'll take it to him."

A week later my question appeared to be answered: Dad returned from Hong Kong, Mum did not.

"When will she be back?" I asked him, puzzled and alarmed.

"I have no idea," he answered irritably. "She says she's staying there forever."

Back I rushed to Grandma.

"She'll come back," she consoled me, resolutely setting aside any alarms about the point of no return. "She's teaching him a lesson. Though if you ask me, she's the one who should be told a thing or two. Poor Oliver! I expect he's upset."

"So is Roddy," I pointed out coldly. Not to mention me, I thought. I was not too old at twenty-one to feel abandoned.

What had been going on in the three years while I had been immersed in my own rackety affairs? If I had spent more of my vacation time at home instead of abroad, I might have found out. As it was, I could only conjecture. It seemed likely that my mother had grown tired of role-playing. I could not blame her. I made it cruelly obvious to my father that my sympathies were not with him. When Mum came back, as I confidently expected she would after deliberation, he would be constrained to take her back on her own terms, whatever they might be.

Then I received an apologetic letter from Mum. She had every intention of staying away for ages. She wanted Roddy to be sent out to her in a month's time. I could not believe it. Suddenly I knew the meaning of the word 'flabbergasted'. Back I went to Grandma with the dreadful news. Grandma was absolutely livid. Even her grey curls seemed to stiffen with outrage.

"How could she!" she exclaimed at least twice. "What a wicked thing to do. How could she leave her husband and children? What on earth's come over her? Your poor father!"

"She wants Roddy sent out to her. But Dad says he won't let him go." "I should think not indeed! Sent out to her!" She was scandalised. "Sent out to her like a parcel! He most certainly will not be sent out to her. She'll have to come back if she wants him, the poor little lamb. How is Oliver taking it? He should never have let her take a job. I knew no good would come of it."

"How could he prevent her?" I enquired crossly. "She has a mind and a will of her own. He's not her master. That was the trouble — he liked to think that he was."

"Nonsense!" Grandma said. "He thought no such thing. Women nowadays are not content to be good wives and mothers, they want more."

"Of course they do," I agreed, but I knew it was useless to start arguing with her about the rights of women. She had not had the same choices when she was young. Who knows what she might have done if she had? Perhaps she felt cheated of those choices, or perhaps she genuinely had not desired them.

I left Grandma fuming about her inconsiderate, ungrateful daughter and fretting about her rejected, hard-done-by son-in-law and went home to telephone Leila. I was badly in need of comfort and advice.

Leila knew all about everything. I could tell.

"Bring Roddy to us for a while, Jan," she suggested soothingly. "We'd love to have you. Don't worry about Cassandra, she'll manage on her own. I'll write to Lorna and set her mind at rest. It'll all work out, you'll see. Most couples reach a crisis at some time in their married lives. It's best to keep out of the way until your parents have resolved theirs."

"I had no idea there was a crisis," I complained miserably. "I don't think Dad knew, either."

Leila laughed a short, bitter laugh. "No pet, I'm sure he didn't. Poor Oliver."

Everybody kept saying 'poor Oliver'. Even Cassandra had murmured, "Poor Daddy," after reading Mum's letter.

That evening, when I told him that Roddy and I had been invited to Alsace for a month, I understood why. I had prepared myself for a fight. I was sure he would not want us to go. What I received was chastened acquiescence.

"Do what you think is best for Roddy, Jan," he said quietly.

All the bouncing conceit had gone out of him. He was tired and haggard, a man who had been ambitiously and confidently reaching for the stars, whose wife had suddenly stopped supporting the ladder and kicked it from beneath his climbing feet. Dismayed, he found that he was left dangling in mid-air with a heavy rope of responsibility around his neck.

Who would listen to his boastful stories

now, in the knowledge of the defection of his chief acolyte?

"Poor Daddy," I said, kissing him lightly on the cheek.

He was astonished, as well he might be, hearing those words from me. The next instant he looked utterly defeated. The last thing he wanted to hear was pity in the voice of one of his children. My words, meant to draw us closer in our shared sense of desertion, had driven us farther apart. I wished I had only thought them.

I caught Cassandra in her dressing-gown between bedroom and bathroom at eleven-thirty on Sunday morning, the day before Roddy and I were due to fly to Strasbourg. Her fair, clear skin was glowing with health. Despite all the make-up she lashed upon it and her junk food diet, she never suffered from spots. Other girls of her age, with similar rounded contours, would have been worrying about their weight; Cassandra always gave the impression of being perfectly satisfied with her body the way it was, verging on the voluptuous. I must admit, I would have swopped figures with her, given the chance. Kind people called me slim, but it was a euphemism for skinny.

"Do you mind if Roddy and I go to Alsace?" I asked her, out of breath from dashing up the stairs to reach her before she disappeared into the bathroom for ages.

"Of course not. Why should I?"

"Will you manage on your own?" I was not so confident about this as Leila had been.

"Yes, perfectly."

"What about the laundry? There's Dad's to do as well, a clean shirt and underwear every day. Mrs Basset can't come in more then three times a week and she hates ironing." She complained that my father changed too often just to make work for Mum. Until recently, I had not realised how much Dad's crisp, smooth image depended on Mum's diligence.

"Grandma Harris is going to do the laundry and the shopping. No bother, well get on fine." And she went into the bathroom, humming a tune to herself as if she was completely happy, although how she could be with Mum defaulting, I could not think.

"Lunch will be ready in an hour," I

shouted over the sound of running water. Then I ran down to the kitchen to see how Roddy was coping with podding the broad beans that Grandpa had sent over from his garden.

8

DAD drove Roddy and me to the airport. Roddy was not sure he wanted to go. He was torn between the excitement of travelling in an aeroplane for the first time and his desire to remain at home and wait for Mum's return. He could not understand her lengthening absence, but he was taking it philosophically and had not yet considered desertion as a possibility.

Dad and I talked to one another with false cheerfulness for his sake. For the first time I knew what it was like to feel responsible for a child's happiness and have the wish to protect him from the cruelties of grown-up perversity. Nothing Dad said that morning could have provoked me into quarrelling with him, it would have been too upsetting for Roddy. Without being aware of it, I was understudying for one of Mum's roles. As it happened, Dad was as determined as I was to remain friends. While I had him beside me for such a length of time, it was a good opportunity to probe the rift between him and Mum. I had so many questions to ask. I kept quiet. Some of those questions I felt sure Leila would be able to answer. The most important question of all was, when would Mum return? Even Dad could not answer that one. I had written to her, enclosing an earnest scribble from Roddy. My letter had spoken longingly of seeing her again and expressed the hope that whatever reason she had for delaying her journey would soon be explained. I was trying to be understanding and sympathetic, but it was difficult because I understood so little and was beginning to sympathise, against my early inclination, with Dad, as my maternal grandmother had all along. I was sure that he had always been the same overbearing, conceited, thrusting personality. Why had Mum married him if she disliked this so much? There had to be more to it and I wondered dismally if she had fallen in love with someone else while she was in Hong Kong. How could she, in a mere fortnight? Or rather, how could she fall far enough to forsake her husband and children?

Roddy's note, painstakingly printed in

pencil and smothered in heavily scored kisses, had said simply, "Come home soon, Mummy. Love from Roddy." Thinking about it prompted me to turn to look at him. He was sitting in one corner of the back seat of the BMW, small and solemn, thin like me but with Dad's brown hair and hazel eyes, his stick arms and legs protruding from his short-sleeved T-shirt and cream shorts. On his feet were stripy socks and navy and red trainers.

"Excited?" I asked him.

He nodded and smiled, then went back to his protective daydreams.

How vulnerable he was! Come home soon, Mum, or I may never forgive you.

"It's a long time since you've been to Grutenheim, Jan," Dad observed.

"Yes, four years."

"Nothing has changed there," he said enviously.

"Dad, you'll have to go to Alnwick to see Grannie. She'll be lonely if no one visits her and she always has lots of things that need doing."

"I will if I have time. I have a hectic couple of weeks ahead of me. If I weren't so busy, I would have stayed in Hong

Kong until Lorna decided she had had enough."

"Enough of what?" I could not help asking.

He gave me a swift glance, trying to read my expression, then said irritably, "Of Hong Kong and that feckless brother of hers. God knows what he and his wife exist on, it certainly isn't earned income."

"What does Uncle Daniel do?"

"On the surface, not a lot, but plenty of shady deals, I suspect. Nothing I should care to be mixed up in, yet give him something decent to do and he makes a mess of it. I had to send someone out there to sort things out." He was referring to the business he had asked Uncle Daniel to do for him when Roddy was born. "Dan has been putting wild ideas in your mother's head. Look, we'll stop at the next services for some coffee. You have plenty of time."

Leila was at Strasbourg airport to meet us. "I've had a letter from Lorna," were her first words to me as she made a grab for a shyly reluctant Roddy, embracing him against her substantial bust and smiling at me over his trapped head. "Everything is going to be fine. You're not to worry. She'll probably be back by the time you are."

"Another month!" I said with dismay.

"How else is Oliver to be shocked into submission?" she laughed.

I was not sure that I wanted my dynamic father shocked into submission. Was that really what my mother was hoping to achieve?

"Don't look so serious, pet." Here I received my kiss and hug. "Sometimes drastic measures are called for."

"What if I hadn't been at home to look after Roddy?" I remarked, taking hold of his hand protectively.

"Then Lorna would have had to think of something different, something much less effective, I'm sure."

Following her out to the car with the heavy suitcase, I asked her quietly, so that Roddy would not hear, "Do you think she has found someone else?"

For an Englishwoman, Leila gave a very Gallic shrug. I heaved the case and the flight bag into the back of her car, no longer the dear old 2CV but a smart Peugeot 205, and wished crossly that my parents would sort things out between them. Dad might be insufferable, but I did not think he deserved to be usurped. Either their life together so far had been reasonably successful or Mum had been duping us all, including Dad.

"She always seemed happy enough," I said grumpily, getting in beside Leila. But I was deceiving myself. I remembered how often I had wondered how she put up with Dad and marvelled how, given enough time, she would cleverly and patiently achieve her own way without him realising it. I knew she resented the duplicity she was forced to practise to keep Dad's image of himself as the king-pin firmly in place, and the rest of the household ticking over quite smoothly with the king-pin carefully removed and set on one side.

"You've been away a lot these last years, Jan. Things change between couples as they grow older. Why do you assume that it's your mother at fault? As I recall, you have never got along particularly well with your father."

"I didn't choose him but Mum did. Anyway, Mum's the one who stayed in Hong Kong." I winced as Leila swung out from the parking bay, the Peugeot narrowly missing the car next to it.

"It was business that brought Oliver back," she said, which I knew to be true, and before I could reply, she added, "Don't judge until you understand, Jan." There was a short silence, then she said in a brighter tone, "Gérard is looking forward to playing tennis with you. He's working with us now, of course. It's made a great difference to Lucien."

"What about Jean-Michel?" I knew him much better than Gérard.

"Working in Marseilles. We rarely see him, but he telephones once a week. He's got a girl friend there. We haven't met her yet."

I was disappointed.

Once more I was on the busy trunk road between Strasbourg and Colmar. I had intended never to visit Grutenheim again, it was to have been put behind me with the restrictions of an indulged, protected childhood. In a way it would remain in the past. Visiting it as a woman with the responsibility for my little brother, fast asleep in the back of the car, and preoccupied with concern for my parents' marriage, I was to see it in a different light, stripped of the illusion of childish subjectivity. The village had once existed as part of my holiday pleasure, in isolated summer, with the Amberle family there solely to provide us with a warm welcome and four weeks of leisure and friendship.

Today, sitting beside Leila, listening to her as she brought me up to date with her family affairs, hearing her speak to me for the first time, woman to woman, about her concerns and anxieties, the way she would have confided in Mum if she had been sitting beside her, I began to perceive the realities of life in Grutenheim. Apparently Marie-Louise was becoming more sour and difficult as she aged. She and her husband were in their eighties. She was physically frail yet her mind remained sharp and calculating. Lucien, technically the boss for many years now, had to account to his mother for every move he made, every innovation, every franc he spent, just as his father had done in his day. It did not bother Lucien too much, he was used to it, but Gérard objected. It was bad enough having to consult with one's father when one was ambitious and trained to make the most of modern technology in viticulture, but it was intolerable to have to explain everything to one's suspicious, carping old grandmother who was a relic of the days when there had been no alternative but to do things the hard way, up and down the vines beside one's mate, weeding and pruning. Lucien could pander to the old girl if he liked, Gérard would have none of her interference, even though he loved and respected her. Mathias was easy-going. He listened to his wife's constant complaints about the way the business was being run, just as he had listened years ago to her complaints about her English daughter-in-law. Marie Louise could not see the sense in buying new machinery, no matter how advanced and clever it was, while the old was adequate and still working. Diplomatically, he agreed with her; he also agreed with his son that she was impossible and with Gérard that Lucien was too slow in making changes.

"I'm glad I've kept out of it all these years," Leila said. "I plead ignorance and they leave me in peace. The old man is canny. He comes to my kitchen for coffee and cake and a bit of quiet when the atmosphere across the courtyard is at its most rancorous, but he's not there long before Marie-Louise is shrieking for him, complaining of his laziness and listing all the jobs he hasn't done that day. They've known hard times, and perhaps she begrudges the younger generation the comparative ease of their more mechanised work. They should be taking life easy now, enjoying their old age together, but she refuses to fade from the scene and won't allow Mathias to fade either. She's always nagging at him, it's very sad. She's unbelievably penny-pinching or, I should say, franc-pinching, but it doesn't sound right, somehow." She smiled at me. "She makes me feel like a kept woman, frittering away the family substance. See this blouse? I had it a month before I could bring myself to wear it. Marie-Louise never buys new clothes. Five years ago I remember her buying a coat to replace one that had literally worn out. As she always wears sombre colours, all her clothes look the same anyway. She probably thinks it's about time I stopped wearing what she calls 'frivolous colours'. How is Cassie?

Growing into a beautiful young woman, by all accounts."

"Yes, quite beautiful," I agreed.

Leila smiled at the unspoken reservation in my reply. "So are you, Jan." She was being kind.

"I'm not in the same league as Cassandra," I admitted without reservation.

"You were always very different," she conceded, adding quickly, "but not in looks."

"It's obvious we're sisters," I acknowledged.

An hour and a half later we were wending our way between the shuttered houses of Grutenheim, clustered together peacefully in the late afternoon heat. By the time we reached the church square I felt I had never been away, and it was with elation that I saw again the familiar iron gates, wide open for trade, and the sunny courtyard, an enclosed world of precious memories which encapsulated my tender, growing-up years. It was strange to be there with only Roddy.

There was Lucien, coming out of the bottling plant to welcome us. As he stepped from the shadow cast by the apartment balcony into the brightness of the afternoon, I realised that it was not Lucien but Gérard. While Leila and I were getting out of the front of the car, he scooped Roddy from the back, holding him in his arms while his sleepy brain cleared.

"You've grown," he told him. "You'll soon be as tall as I am."

"Taller!" Roddy stated. "I'm going to be six foot two like Uncle Daniel, Mum says so, 'cause I've got big feet. Where's Lucien?" he asked, looking round eagerly. "He promised I could have a go on the little tractor." He meant the tractor that went up and down the tracks between the rows of vines.

Gérard smiled at me, looking into my eyes with a long, keen appraisal. I could not take my eyes from his.

"Welcome, Jan," he said.

Roddy squirmed to be set free. Gérard bent to put him on his feet and I was released from a spell which had lasted mere moments and from which I emerged utterly enchanted. I was in love.

Gérard took the suitcase and the flight bag from the boot of his mother's car and Leila, oblivious of my shattering

136

self-revelation, said, "You'll have to share the flat with Gérard this year, Jan. It's his now, but don't worry, he only uses it for a retreat. He still eats with us and expects me to do his laundry."

I caught Gérard's eye and hastily looked away in case he could see how happy I was to share anything with him. Then I was resurrecting my long disused patois, for coming towards us slowly with a dragging, sideways motion, leaning her frail form heavily upon a stout stick, was Marie-Louise, wearing a long black dress which I must have seen many times before, her grey hair scraped back from her wrinkled, sharp-featured face, her eyes as bright and shrewd as ever.

"The child has grown," she said of Roddy. "The girl is a woman," she said of me.

I embraced her gently, conscious of the brittle bones beneath the thick material of her dress.

"You are tall, Jan," she said reprovingly as if it was my fault. "Tall and too thin. Leila must fatten you up."

"She has a very elegant figure," Leila said defensively.

"I agree," Gérard said, and I blushed like a teenager, quickly reaching into the car for my shoulder bag to hide my happiness.

While Gérard took the luggage up to the flat, the rest of us went across the courtyard into the family house. Lucien was working in the small room next to the entrance, which was set aside as an office. He came out to say hello and embrace us.

"Where's Mathias?" I asked, for Cassandra and I had long been aware that he enjoyed kissing and embracing young ladies and was usually among the first to do so, much to our amusement.

"Huh!" Marie-Louise ejaculated scornfully.

Lucien explained. "He's with one of his cronies in the village. He'll be back soon."

"Discussing the wine. Always discussing, never doing," his wife grumbled, hobbling away to her own home.

Mathias loved to talk, it was probably his favourite occupation after kissing young ladies. He took pleasure in endless, gentle discussion with a group of friends who shared the same closed memories: similar small shames and satisfying minor triumphs during the long years of two wars. They discussed the present, never the past, but their opinions of the present were coloured indelibly by their bitter experience. They had worked doggedly throughout every difficulty, but had not counted on reaping the rewards. There was only one enemy now, picking them off with patient precision, biding his time for those who had temporarily drifted out of his sights. Food and wine were good, discussion with one's intimates was comforting and the headstrong young were a race apart, knowing nothing except what they had been taught, yet thinking they knew it all. *Mon Dieu!*

Roddy had a prejudice against milk in France. He insisted that it did not taste the same as the milk at home. I think he had once been given the long-life sort by mistake, so he would not drink his usual mixture of weak tea there either. I left him eating bread, garlic sausage and tomatoes, washed down with white grape juice, and went to unpack.

It was strange on entering the flat to find no evidence of my family's occupation. Everything was still and tidy, cool behind partly closed shutters. I let a flood of early

OOJ10

evening sunlight into the kitchen and jumped when the old refrigerator motor thrummed noisily into action, then I went along the passage to find the luggage. I opened the door of the first bedroom, the one which was always used by my parents and Roddy, to discover that the double bed now belonged to Gérard. The little truckle bed was folded against a wall. I shut the door quickly, retreating from what seemed like a breach of privacy. I went next door to the room Cassandra and I had always shared, and there, beside the twin beds which were encased in heavy green tapestry covers, were the suitcase and holdall. I crossed to the window and opened the shutters, looking out nostalgically across the sloping vineyards, an immobile sea of serried green waves stretching up to the round-topped, forested hills.

When the clothes were neatly stowed away in the old fashioned *armoire* and the ugly chest of drawers which smelled of the apples that had once been stored in its deep bottom drawers, I took the toilet things along to the bathroom. Here there was more evidence of Gérard, but I could not back away this time: this was one room we were going to have to share. I placed my hairbrush and comb next to his on the windowledge, caught sight of my reflection in the mirror over the handbasin, blushed at the serious blue-eyed gaze that confronted me, snatched up my brush and comb, thought, What am I doing? and replaced them with a shrug. Love was having a peculiar effect on me.

From the bathroom I went into the silent living-room. The round, highly polished table was covered by a brown chenille cloth with a straggly fringe. That cloth, I was convinced, had been there always. We had removed it countless times for meals, carefully folding it and putting it on the horrid, shiny sideboard with its veneer chipping off the corners of the cupboard doors and cutlery drawer. Today, the table, which usually had a glass jar containing field flowers in its centre, was covered with papers and books and there were more books and magazines on the other surfaces in the room — the card table, the two easy chairs and the six dining chairs, of which two were pushed against the table and four were standing along the walls.

The flat itself was roomy and modern, but

the furniture, extraneous to the requirements of Marie-Louise, was old, cheap and hideous, yet familiar. I was fond of its nastiness.

When Roddy was having his bath that evening, he saw me glance at my watch and, realising that I was anxious to get him into bed so that I could join the Amberles for dinner, he decided to be difficult. First he did not want to leave the bath, then he dropped his knitted rabbit into the bidet. I callously wrung the thing out and wrapped it in a towel to pat it as dry as possible, while he cried noisily that he could not sleep without it. He had grown out of his dependence on it when he started school, but it had been surreptitiously resurrected from the bottom of his toy trunk just before we left for Alsace. It was the only sign that Mum's long absence was making him feel insecure. He would not put his pyjamas on and when I had succeeded in roughly pushing and pulling him into them, my temper barely under control, he stubbornly refused to remain in the flat by himself.

"I don't like it here," he stated mutinously, flinging the damp rabbit and a picture book I had thrust into his hands to the bottom of his bed. "I want to go home."

"Of course you like it here," I told him briskly, sounding just like Grandma Harris. "Don't be silly, Roddy. I'll only be gone about an hour, and if you want me you can go out onto the balcony and shout across the courtyard."

He jumped out of bed and stood in front of me, rigid with resolve. "I won't stay here on my own."

"You've done it before," I reminded him.

"No more!" he shouted, then his voice changed tone, taking on a pleading quality designed to melt my heart. "You come to bed too, Jan."

Wordlessly, I handed him his dressing-gown and slippers. As soon as he had scrambled into them, I took him over to the house.

"Put him in the big chair in front of the television," Leila said. "He'll either fall asleep or learn some French and I bet I know which it'll be. Put that disgusting rabbit in the airing cupboard until he goes to bed. Will you make the salad dressing for me? You'll find another bottle of oil in the cupboard, that one's nearly empty."

After dinner, Dad telephoned to make sure that we had arrived safely. I asked if Cassandra was there and Dad said, "Of course," as if it was the natural place for her to be at that time of the evening; it was eight-thirty at home, an hour behind us in Grutenheim.

"Is she all right?" I asked.

"Yes, perfectly. She helped me eat the excellent meal she cooked."

"I'm glad she's looking after you," I said, jealousy struggling to overcome my better nature. "May I speak to her a minute?"

"She's in the bath. I'll ask her to call you back."

That was normal behaviour, at least. "Don't bother. I'll speak to her another time."

Gérard carried a sleeping Roddy back across the warm dusk of the courtyard.

As I was tucking the blanket around him and his tightly clutched rabbit, Gérard, who was standing next to me, asked, "Are you going back to the house, Jan?"

"I'd like to, but if Roddy wakes up and finds himself alone here he'll be frightened, so I'd better stay. Hopefully, he'll soon get used to it."

"Then I'll stay with you, if you don't mind. I usually come over here after dinner when I'm not going out. It gives me a break from work, otherwise Dad goes on talking shop, especially if the old couple are there."

"I don't want to intrude on your solitude," I said. "I'll stay in here and read."

"Don't do that. Come and talk."

I went gladly.

9

MY mother had said that, in her opinion, to be happy one must be either thoughtless or selfish. I am ashamed to say that for the next four weeks I counted myself happy, except for those rare moments when I thought about anyone other than myself and Gérard.

During the day I was Leila's companion, helping her about the house and going with her to do the marketing, taking Roddy with us. We wandered with large metal trolleys around vast, cool hypermarkets, buying such things as biscuits, apricot-filled madeleines for Roddy, washing powder in giant packets, milk, two kinds of bottled water — one for drinking neat and the other for making coffee — or we jostled our way around the stalls in the centres of small, busy towns, snapping green beans, tasting local cheeses, poking, sniffing and prodding the ranks of colourful produce, on the eternal lookout for the freshest, the tastiest and the keenest priced. Leila bought first and decided what we should eat for dinner afterwards. She had become more French than she knew.

While we were shopping or drinking coffee at tables set out on the pavement, we talked, woman to woman. Each day I knew my mother a little better as I filled her place as confidante and friend. When Leila remarked with some surprise how like Lorna I was, I realised with similar surprise that she was right. Superficially I resembled my father in character — impulsive and quick tempered. However, whereas I charged through life with a care not to knock anyone over, Dad kept his eyes on the challenging horizon, unaware of the difficulties experienced by those who were desperately trying to keep up with him. Somewhere along the line, Mum had faltered and fallen and she was having to draw his attention to the fact.

"What do you suppose is wrong between my parents?" I asked Leila while she was waiting to buy a plateau of peaches and Roddy was engrossed in watching a miniature woman dexterously mending the cane seat of a chair, while squatting in the back of a scruffy van which was partly filled with broken bits of cane furniture.

Leila completed her purchase. As we were walking back to the car park, she said, "It's impossible for anyone except the couple involved to know what really goes on inside a marriage. Intimacy breeds nuance. There's always the right thing to say and the right way to say it at the right moment. In some marriages, this matters more than in others, but one must never become careless about hurting the other's feelings, because then all the harmony disappears and who can be happy living in constant discord? Marriage works best on mutual self-sacrifice. Unfortunately, it's too often left to one partner to do all the sacrificing. When Lorna returns and offers you an explanation, you still won't understand completely, but Oliver will, if he takes the trouble to think back and remember."

"You're putting me off marriage," I protested with a smile, waiting for Roddy to catch us up before we crossed the road.

Leila laughed. "I don't believe it."

"I'm afraid that's one of the ways I'm like Dad. I am not very self-sacrificing."

"I don't believe that either. I'd say you are being very generous, giving up your holiday to look after your little brother."

"But I love Roddy," I said, reaching for his hand.

"Exactly!"

In the afternoons we walked with Roddy through the forested slopes of the Vosges, along shady tracks padded with pine needles. We took him to the lakes to swim, to play long, long games of crazy golf, and to mix with other children. Occasionally, Leila took us to visit some of her relations-in-law. It seemed strange to me that after living in France for so long she should have no close personal friends there.

We called on Lucien's two sisters and their respective families, and on the families of his elderly aunts and uncles. Leila had never taken any of us to meet them before, not even Mum, and at first I assumed we were going just to fill in the lazy afternoons, but gradually it dawned on me that Leila was presenting me to them for their approval. The expression on her face whenever I entered into the lively conversation was one of smug gratification. See, she seemed to be thinking, she can speak French already. This one is not like me, you would be able to absorb her without abrasions.

One afternoon we went to call on Lucien's younger sister, Thérèse, who lived in Cernay with her husband and two little girls. While Roddy was playing with her daughters in the garden and getting by extremely well, much to our amusement, with his own version of despotic 'Franglais', Leila, Thérèse and I chattered over coffee and cake at an ornamental white metal table on the lawn.

"It's easy to forget that you are English, Jan," Leila remarked on our way home. "I've made things awkward for Lucien with my stubborn foreignness. You would fit in here like a native. You seem to belong, somehow."

Perhaps because I've fallen in love with a Frenchman, I thought. I glanced at her, sitting beside me in the driving seat of the car. She returned my look as if she was reading my mind. She smiled.

"It would be a coincidence if both father and son married English girls, wouldn't it? Once I thought Jean-Michel would be your choice."

Was it all wishful thinking on her part, because she found the idea of having her best friend's daughter as her *belle-fille* an attractive one, or had she reason to believe that Gérard was as crazy about me as I was about him? If she was planning ahead then I could not blame her, for I was doing the same thing myself.

Gérard was devoting to me the evenings after dinner and any time he could wangle off from his work in the vineyards. He began by making the excuse that he ought to entertain me, it was his duty to a guest, but soon he admitted that he was entertaining himself with my company and we were seeking every opportunity, with the connivance of his mother and the indulgence of the boss, his father, to be on our own.

We travelled around the area to places of interest. Most of them I had visited already, but I was seeing them now through Gérard's eyes and hearing about them from his lips, which made them all the more fascinating. I sat beside him in his car for mile after contented mile of twisting, almost empty road as it wound endlessly through the dense forests and past the clearings which held the ubiquitous war cemeteries. From a distance these tranquil memorials resembled smoothed green quilts of white *petit-point* crosses, which I fancied were spread over hosts of numb sleepers who lay insensible to the sun's fierce summoning. Above the tree-line, the blunted noses of the hills extended in flower-filled meadows which were alive with insects and shrilling with crickets. As the road snaked round and downwards once more, there were breathtaking views into the wooded valleys.

One afternoon, Gérard took Roddy and me to the *Fête du Vin* in Ribeauvillé. The steeply ascending road through the centre of the little town, prohibited to motor traffic for the day, was dominated by the Castle of St Ulrich, high on a hilltop. The road was crowded with people and stalls of goods which had been set out before the shop fronts. We edged in to the side to watch a brass band make its noisily tuneful way through the town, the young men wearing red monkey jackets and black trousers and shoes. They were followed by horses with garlands of flowers round their sturdy necks and straw hats jammed over their ears, drawing carts decorated with vines, in which sat young people dressed in the regional costume of scarlet and black. We sat at a café table on the road leading up to the castle, eating ice-cream and watching the festive world pass by, pestered by flying insects which, much to Roddy's dismay, kept settling on our arms and necks and on his bare legs, ready to administer sharp bites if not smartly brushed away.

Adjacent to the car park at the entrance to the town was a small fair. Before leaving, Roddy had a go on the carousel. Standing in the centre near the mechanism, starting and stopping the rides, was a hard-faced, dark, gypsy-type woman who was holding a mangy, ginger toy monkey on the end of a pole. As the ride speeded up, she dangled and dipped the monkey over the heads of the revolving children, who were reaching up excitedly to grasp the long tail. The one who managed to snatch it off would win a free ride.

"Careful, Roddy!" I shouted as he made a lunge for the tail, almost falling off his painted horse which went on disdainfully sliding smoothly up and down its vertical post.

"He's enjoying himself," Gérard said. "If it comes to that, so am I, thanks to you, Jan. I shall always remember this summer as one of the happiest of my life. The last time you were here, you were great friends with Jean-Michel. I used to watch you both laughing and talking together and envy you the fun you were having." He put his arm round my waist and said, "Now I have you all to myself and need envy no one."

The ride was slowing. We moved closer to it, walking round with it until we were opposite Roddy. When it stopped, he promptly scrambled off the horse and raced to the other side to climb onto a cockerel. The vile-looking woman, a veritable 'Madame Defarge', was holding out a soiled hand for his money.

"Only one more go," I told him as Gérard stepped forward with four francs.

On the way home we were thrilled to see an inhabited stork's nest. It was a huge affair, set on the top of a cone-shaped chimney and overlapping the edges, rather like an upside-down cossack's hat made in twigs and straw. Perched inside it, over-large and absurd at such a height on such an edifice, was a long-legged, long-necked, long-beaked white bird, feeding an offspring almost as big as itself, of which only the top half could be seen against the sky as it squatted with its beak wide open. We had seen many life-like models of storks placed strategically on roofs and chimneys throughout the region and many empty nests, but these were our first real-life specimens and Roddy was thrilled to bits. He took a photograph of them with Gérard's camera and was reluctant to leave the scene.

The evenings were my happiest time, when Roddy was fast asleep in bed and I was alone with Gérard in the dimly lit living-room of the flat, drinking coffee and talking.

"I shall always be here in Grutenheim, Jan," he said, after I had told him about the job I would be starting in Newcastle in September. "Fortunately, I want what my father and grandparents want for me, to remain a part of the family business. Jean-Michel doesn't want to know. One day I shall move into the old house and

Mum and Dad will migrate to the one the old couple live in."

I wanted nothing more than to move into that old house with him.

The following Sunday we left Roddy with Leila and went to Riquewihr, a tiny medieval town surrounded by ancient ramparts with no access for cars. The narrow streets of leaning, black and white timbered houses, many of them with projecting upper stories, were packed with tourists, most of them German. We were strolling up the steep incline of the main street when Gérard spotted an artist's studio. We went in to browse around and admire the prolific collection of oil paintings and prints. The artist was working on a canvas in a side room and keeping an eye on potential customers through the open door with the aid of a spotty youth, who lurked about the premises distrustfully as we wandered round with other people between the stacked canvases. The minute Gérard and I showed sufficient interest in the work to suggest that we might buy something, the youth discreetly reported this to his master, who left his painting and, wiping his brush on a piece of stained rag smelling strongly of turpentine, sauntered out with assumed nonchalance to make our acquaintance. He was a very large German in vigorous middle-age, with light blue eyes, smooth tanned skin and a superb beard. He greeted us affably and, quickly detecting from my accent that I was English, complimented me on my French and deplored the fact that he knew hardly any English at all. Meanwhile his discerning eyes were taking in the other people around us — mainly Americans — and I did not believe him. From the loudly decisive way he had spoken, I had the impression that there was an advantage for him in disclaiming any aptitude for my native tongue — perhaps it would encourage some of those people to say what they really thought about his work.

While Gérard and I were turning over a pile of prints, with the amiable giant commenting upon each one over our shoulders, there was a commotion at the entrance, a bright rectangle of dazzling sunlight against the dimness of the interior, and a harrassed woman made her appearance, carrying a box of groceries.

"There's another one outside," she said sharply in French to the spotty youth, and then she said something equally sharp in German to the artist, before struggling up the rickety wooden stairs in the far corner of the room.

"My wife," the artist said disparagingly, and deftly turned his attention and ours back to the unframed print which Gérard had been admiring. It depicted a young woman with a rapt, animated expression on her face, wearing a simple white shift and clutching a bunch of wild flowers to her breast. A bit like Ophelia, I thought.

"She reminds me of you, Jan," Gérard said and, of course, the artist agreed effusively. Gérard paid him 250 francs and presented the print to me. I was thrilled to have it. It was not until much later that I revised the significance of the gift.

Two days before Roddy and I left for home, I spent the entire morning in the apartment, cleaning it and doing the washing so that everything would be clean and fresh to pack. I took the damp clothes into the loft to hang them up to dry, overcome with nostalgia for past holidays when the apartment had been home for all my family and this had been my special job. As I was pegging up the clothes between the low wooden beams, I could hear Roddy in the courtyard below talking to Lucien in his shrill, bossy little boy's voice, demanding, as all protected and spoilt children do, the attention and concern that is their right.

I was anxious to return home in order to sort things out: to deliver Roddy to my father or my grandmother, and to start my new job. Then I could begin to think about coming back. All my plans were directed towards my eventual return to Gérard. Next time I came, I hoped he would ask me to stay. In the meantime, perhaps I could coax him to visit Durham. I intended finding myself a flat as soon as possible after starting work and then, perhaps . . .

"Oh!" I jumped as the door opened behind me. I turned round in consternation. As far as I knew I had the place to myself. My heart tripped in its rhythm. It was Gérard.

"I thought you were working," I said to him.

"I came to find you." He smiled. "I was amongst the vines when suddenly I thought, Jan will soon be gone and life will be dull again. So I came to find you." He approached me, took Roddy's shorts from my hands and dropped them into the basket at my feet, then he put his arms round me and kissed me, long and lingeringly. He laughed down into my bemused eyes and said, "It's about time we progressed beyond holding hands, don't you agree?"

I wished he had not waited so long. I had been burning to touch and be touched. I raised my face to be kissed once more, and afterwards, when he released me, I told him, how rashly, that I loved him.

"Do you, Jan?" He looked pleased and assured me that he loved me too, but I wished I had not been the first to say it. As always, I had been too impulsive.

During those four weeks in Grutenheim I had developed a warm sense of belonging there, and now I regarded my imminent departure as a necessary yet frustrating break in the continuity of my happiness.

Marie-Louise had looked on approvingly

whenever she came across me helping Leila in the house or helping Lucien in the room set aside for the wine tasting. Mathias liked to find me on my own and talk at length about the wine business, or about his grandsons whom he described, proudly and lovingly, as the cool-headed, hard-working Gérard, and that clever scamp, Jean-Michel, who was fonder of drinking the wine than producing it and fonder still of the opposite sex. Occasionally, the old couple had dinner with the rest of us; then Mathias, mellowed and incautiously merry after liberally imbibing the product of his own land and past labours, would, if I was not careful to avoid him, pull me playfully onto his knee as if I was still a little girl and, much to my embarrassment, fondle me around the waist and hips, declaring to the company that I was too thin and in need of an extra helping of *choucroute* to fatten me up.

"Leila could spare you some of her fine figure," he once suggested, with his moist, approving eyes on the buxom breasts of his *belle-fille.*

Leila did not take offence, but his wife did. "Enough of that kind of talk, old man!

Leave Janine alone. Can't you see that you making a big fool of yourself?"

I left his knee thankfully, yet slowly and with a smile, to show that I did not really mind. He was kind and harmless, with fond thoughts which outran his desires. I could not help wondering what solace he had ever gained from the sharp scrawniness of the woman he had always slept beside. I could imagine myself becoming like Marie-Louise as I grew older, and wished that second helpings of *choucroute* were really the answer to obtaining a few extra pounds of soft, strategically placed, desirable flesh.

"When will you come back again, Jan?" Gérard asked, very late on the night before we left, as we sat together in the living-room of the apartment.

"I don't know. It depends what happens at home. I'll have my job, don't forget, and then there's Roddy. If Mum doesn't return from Hong Kong, I don't know what we'll do. He'll have to stay with Grandma Harris during the week, but it would be difficult for her to take him backwards and forwards to school now that Grandpa's health is poor."

"What a pity you live so far away. I'll miss you, Jan."

"And I'll miss you," I told him miserably, moving closer, enticing his arms to receive me, his lips to seek mine.

Gérard took us to Strasbourg to catch the plane.

"Don't look so sad," he said, just before we parted.

"I hate leaving the sunshine," I answered, smiling ruefully.

"You mustn't only come in summer, Jan. Things are very different here in winter. The sun doesn't always shine, you know."

We embraced and, grasping Roddy's hand very tightly, I followed the other passengers to the departure lounge, willing myself not to look back with longing.

10

"WILL Mummy be there to meet us?" Roddy asked when we boarded the plane.

"Daddy, I expect," I said, preparing him for disappointment.

I was wrong. Mum was there. She swooped upon us before we had recovered from our surprise. We returned her hugs and kisses spontaneously, yet I was interested to notice that Roddy's delight, like my own, was tempered with reproach.

"You've been gone a long time," he told her accusingly, withdrawing from a fervent embrace to stare coldly into her face as she bent over him. "Me and Jan have been with Leila for yonks!"

"Ages," Mum corrected him gently.

"Yonks!" he stated stubbornly.

Mum took his hand, firmly, because he showed signs of pulling it away to mark his protest. I picked up the baggage and we went to find the car.

"Thank you, darling," Mum said to me

warmly. "I knew I could rely on you."

"Have you got everything sorted out now?" I asked. She certainly looked radiant, as if she had not a trouble in the world.

"Yes," she said confidently. "I've made my point."

"With a vengeance," I remarked acidly.

"Don't be cross, Jan," she pleaded. "Roddy is cross with me as well, I can tell."

He glanced up at her gravely and did not contradict her.

"I've brought you a lovely present from Hong Kong," she coaxed him with smiles.

His face brightened, than he remembered his displeasure and scowled.

Mum laughed and kissed him on the top of the head. "Don't pretend you've missed me," she teased.

We were halfway home before I ventured to ask her why she had been away so long.

She glanced quickly behind, to remind me that Roddy was listening, then said, speaking softly, "It's between me and your father, Jan. He understands now, I hope. He says he does. He was at his most appalling in Hong Kong. We spent most of the time visiting his business associates and friends — I'd no idea he had so many friends there — and I found myself playing the same old yes and no game, isn't Oliver wonderful! We were supposed to be there on holiday, after all. The only time I really enjoyed myself was when we were with Dan and Meng in their delightful home, but that didn't suit Oliver. He has never liked Daniel very much. They have absolutely nothing in common. When I started to complain to your father about seeing too much of his friends, he blamed my unreasonableness, as he called it, on Daniel. I looked at the life Dan and Meng have and I saw quite clearly what was wrong with ours. I started to explain to him, he went off the deep end and I decided, right we'll sort this out once and for all. He had to return, I didn't, so I stayed." She placed her hand over both mine, which were clasped together in my lap, and gave them a squeeze. "I couldn't have made that decision without knowing my Jan was at home, looking after my little boy."

I was only partly mollified. "So Dad realises how appalling he is now, does he?" I enquired sarcastically.

She raised her eyebrows. "Do I detect a subtle shift of allegiance?"

"I didn't realise I was meant to take sides. Dad has never said one word against you while you've been absent." I emphasised the 'you'.

"This is the girl whose favourite occupation was quarrelling with her father," Mum remarked incredulously.

"I'm not a girl any longer," I reminded her.

"No, of course not. How silly of me! You are a woman and you will reserve your quarrels for the man you love."

"That's Gérard," Roddy piped up from the back. "She kept kissing him."

I blushed.

Mum laughed. "I know all about Gérard," she confessed. "Leila and I have kept in touch. By the way, Jan, I had no intention of having Roddy sent out to me. It was just a ruse to make your father take me seriously."

I was so incensed, I decided to change the subject. "How has Cassie coped?" I had not given her a second thought for weeks.

"Marvellously. Your father is full of praise for her, especially for her cooking. I wasn't aware that she could boil an egg. It just goes to show what people can do if they have to. I was beginning to think that my sweet, willing Cassie had disappeared forever. I should go away more often. It gives you all a chance to redeem yourselves. Cassie has a new job, by the way. In London. She'll be starting next week, the same day as you start work."

"What kind of job?"

Mum shrugged. "I don't know. She's a bit cagey about it. She says it's much the same as she's doing now at the travel agency, whatever that may be."

"Where will she live?"

"She has that all fixed up. She's moving in with a friend down there." She turned to me with a smile. "I haven't told you my news yet. I'm taking over the dress shop. Carol wants to get out. And I shall be acquiring another one, if all goes well. I tried to persuade Cassie to join me in the venture, but she's not interested. I can count on your advice about the merchandise occasionally, I hope, Jan?"

"Of course."

"I love that outfit," she said, referring to the pink cotton blouse and skirt I was wearing.

"I love that suit," I said. "I'll have it when you've finished with it." We smiled happily at one another, friends again, but not so close as we once had been; the mined area of no-man's-land had imperceptibly widened.

Dad was pleased to see us back. He arrived home early, soon after five o'clock. He opened the front door and the whole house sprang to life. It was as if even the furniture stood to attention, quivering to be noticed. Roddy ran the length of the hall into his arms, crying, "Daddy, did you miss me?" and I came halfway down the stairs and hung over the banister to receive my share of the enthusiastic homecoming. Once again, I was struck by the fact that we were making as much fuss of Dad as if it were he and not the rest of us who had been away. Over Roddy's head, my parents' eyes met in mutual expressions of secret satisfaction, and when Roddy ran off to fetch the present he had brought for Dad from Alsace, Mum slipped into her husband's arms. Quickly, I went back upstairs, experiencing that warm feeling of security which comes to an individual of any age from witnessing forgiveness and accord between its frequently sparring parents.

Cassandra put in an appearance at dinner, much to Roddy's delight. He sat between her and Mum and beamed around the table at us all, with evident satisfaction at having his family together again.

I watched Dad discreetly for signs of improvement. He appeared to be more puzzled than reformed. He was determined not to put a foot wrong, if only he could be sure where to put a foot right. He started to tell us about how ingeniously he had sorted out a tricky industrial problem while we had been away. Mum listened patiently for a while, expressing admiration when appropriate. Eventually, she put down her knife and fork, looked him straight in the eye down the length of the table until he faltered, actually faltered to a stop, then declared that she had something to tell him. Dad's apparent keenness to hear was quite diverting. She began describing the size and location of her proposed new shop. When Dad opened his mouth to interrupt, she said firmly, "I haven't quite finished yet, Oliver," and he shut it again, looking as if he did not mind in the least.

That won't last, I thought. She'd better make the most of it.

"Tell us about your holiday, Jan," Dad ordered magnaminously, when Mum had had her say.

I obliged, but he had no qualms about interrupting me, and when Roddy started to describe the wonderful stork's nest, Dad had seen umpteen in Scandinavia, much to Roddy's amazement and envy.

"What have you been doing with yourself?" I asked Cassandra. "Apart from looking after Dad, of course."

"Working. What else? Has Mum told you I've got a job in London?"

"Who will you be living with?"

She mentioned a girl from school, someone the rest of us did not know very well, but the familiar name allayed our misgiving.

"Did you know that Martin has a girl in Philadelphia? Mrs Proudfoot told Mum." Cassandra had a way of telling you something significant as if it was the merest trifle.

I looked at Mum.

"I met her in Marks and Spencers," Mum explained, as if that mattered.

"That's nice for him," I said trying to sound pleased. I was surprised to discover that I minded, just a little bit, yet I knew in the circumstances I should not have minded at all. I had scarcely thought about Martin for the past month and had not written to him for twice that long. I owed him a letter. He had been faithful for so long, how could I help experiencing a sense of loss?

"You don't need Martin now, do you, Jan?" Cassandra said sarcastically.

There had been times when I had needed Martin very much indeed. Now I had Gérard. I told myself sternly that I was glad Martin had found someone else to love. It was a funny thing, but I could bring his face to mind instantly and clearly, whereas I needed a photograph of Gérard to recall his features in detail. Of the two of them, I had known Gérard the longer time. How could one account for the vagaries of the mind?

Later that evening, while I was finishing my unpacking, Cassandra came into my bedroom. The door was half open and she entered uninvited. I looked up from the task of sorting the clothes onto the bed, one pile for Roddy's room, and watched her walk across to my chest of drawers. She placed her oriental dragon next to mine amongst the clutter.

"Now you can use them as book-ends," she said, turning to look at me. "It was silly to split them. If Uncle Daniel had brought it over especially for me, I might feel differently about it." She took a pile of books from the top of the trunk I had used at university and plonked them between the dragons. Then her eyes fell on the print which I had stuck on the wall temporarily with Blu-Tack.

"Gérard gave it to me," I told her.

"Mum said that you and Gérard are sweet on one another. How serious is it?"

I had a wary reluctance to discuss my love with Cassandra. "Time will tell."

"When do you hope to see him again?"

"He might come over after Christmas."

"Poor Jan, that's a long time to wait."

Despite her words, there was no sympathy in her voice.

"I shall have plenty to occupy me. I'm looking forward to starting work on Monday. What about your new job?"

"I haven't actually got it yet, but don't say anything. I'm going to London anyway. I'm determined to get away."

"Any particular reason?"

"Not really."

She pushed the dragons closer together so that the leaning books stood to attention, but she was not concerned to tidy them. Many of the spines were facing the wall. "We both knew you preferred him," she said, making a horrid face at her dragon. "His blue eyes have always reproached me."

I laughed. "That's funny because I have always felt the same way about mine."

"How can inanimate objects hold so much hostility? As a human, they make me feel inferior." Cassandra patted her dragon on its proudly held head. "I'm leaving him to keep his stony eyes on you. A talisman, if you like. They look even more handsome together, don't they? They're utterly disdainful of those two human vices, greed and jealousy. Perhaps we had the right ones after all. Take care of mine, won't you, Jan?" She moved towards the door and, when she reached it, paused just long enough to say in her quiet, expressionless manner, "That girl in the print has green eyes." Then she left.

"She has not!" I told the closing door indignantly. "Her eyes are blue-grey." Quickly, I crossed over to the print, carefully detached it from the wall and carried it to the window. The girl with the rapt expression gazed past me with pale green eyes. How could Gérard have supposed that she looked like me? I had even imagined a resemblance myself, now I could see none. I had a sudden urge to rip her in half, to rip and rip until the strange girl had vanished forever. Instead, I rolled her up and put her in a drawer behind my nightdresses, thinking that she could stay there until I had her framed. Then I was gripped by a sudden, awful suspicion. I snatched the hand mirror from the dressing-table and once more hurried over to the window. I turned my head this way and that, scrutinising my face, watching intently to see if in different lights my eyes subtly, evilly changed colour. I even held an emerald green scarf against my skin, wondering if by some mystic alchemy my suppressed nature would react and avidly reflect; but no, my eyes remained unmistakably blue. I laughed at myself for being so stupid, yet the mirthless laughter held relief.

I replaced the mirror and tidied the books between the handsome book-ends. What a devious girl Cassandra was! I could not account for her whim to leave the blue-eyed dragon with me. Did she think I needed doubly watching over, or was she determined not to be watched over at all?

11

CASSANDRA has married the man I love.

I shall always think of Gérard as the man I love and I shall always think of my sister as Cassandra. I call her Cassie when I speak to her as I have always done, as everybody does, but in my mind she is Cassandra, the woman who stole from me and even now glories in her success. I am bitter. I shall never forgive her.

I am sitting in this northern winter wasteland, waiting apathetically for spring. One has to wait for something. I am cold, physically and emotionally, my thoughts as bleak as the scene from the unglazed window of the summerhouse — twigs black against the white of snow and berries blood-red between the sharpness of hungry beaks. Two blackbirds are pecking greedily on an evergreen shrub, their bright eyes alert as they wait motionless, between each swallow, for signs of next-door's well-fed cat, who is left unappeased by the tameness of tinned protein.

I have been unwell. Tomorrow I shall go back to my flat, ready to return to work as a trainee manager in a large department store in the city at the beginning of next week. In the meantime, my mother fusses over me, trying to make amends for the hurt I am suffering, as if it is her fault that one perfidious daughter has mortally wounded the other. I am alienated from everyone, even Roddy's company no longer has the power to divert me. I think I shall stay in the summer-house forever, shrivelling inwardly and outwardly, until I am as thin and brittle as the dead twigs which scrape and tap against the cedar logs in the biting wind.

"Jan? What on earth are you doing there? Come into the house at once!"

My mother is advancing over the snow-covered lawn. She has returned from the shop and not yet taken off her outdoor clothes.

"I wondered where you were. Then I spotted your footprints. Oh, Jan, you're shivering. This is very foolish. Do you want to be ill again?"

I don't care, but I do not say so. Why

burden Mum with my despair?

"How long have you been here?"

"Not long," I say, but really I have no idea. "I'm well wrapped-up. Don't make a fuss." I follow her back up the garden to the house. My feet are frozen and my head feels light as if it will float away if I turn it too quickly.

In the kitchen, Mum puts the kettle on, takes off her cream cashmere coat and flings it carelessly on a chair, then turns to me and says, "This has got to stop, Jan. For goodness sake pull yourself together."

"I've been ill," I complain, putting a hand on the table to steady myself.

"Yes, and you'll be ill again unless you reconcile yourself to the fact that Gérard couldn't have loved you. Where's your spirit? I don't recognise you now. Where's your pride?"

Tears fill my eyes. I moan inwardly with weak self-pity. How can Mum be so unsympathetic? She is wrong. Gérard did return my love.

"Sit down!" she orders. "You look fit to drop."

I obey her, watching impassively while

she makes a pot of tea. When we both have a cup before us, she sits down opposite me.

"If you get any thinner, you'll be non-existent. Jan, I'm sorry, I shouldn't have said that Gérard didn't love you. What I meant was that he couldn't have loved you as much as you love him. If he had, how could he have married Cassie?"

"She beguiled him. She wanted him as soon as she knew he wanted me. She always gets what she wants, you know she does."

Mum sighs. "I have never known what it is she wants. Can you imagine her being happy in Grutenheim, leading the kind of life that Leila leads? On the other hand, what kind of life would suit her? She can be very docile and willing when she chooses. Leila will be either charmed by her or exasperated. Don't let Cassie ruin your life, darling."

I sip the hot tea with my chilled hands round the comforting cup. "I've always been jealous of Cassie," I admit. "I've been ashamed of that jealousy because it has often seemed totally unreasonable. Now she has given me a reason. Like a malignant fairy, she has visited jealousy upon me for the rest of my life. I resent it. I resent it enough to resist it. One day I shall fling that unwanted gift back in her face."

"My goodness, what a difference a cup of tea makes," Mum says, smiling at me with approval. "The old Jan is reviving before my very eyes."

Almost, but not quite. As soon as I am on my own again the old Jan fades alarmingly.

The next day I walk into my cold, unwelcoming flat and am engulfed immediately with deep depression. Listlessly, I drift around in my heavy coat and knee-high boots, switching on the central heating and filling the refrigerator with the food I have bought on my way over. Each time I pass the mirror on the wall beside the kitchen door, I avoid my reflection. I know what I should see — a pale, thin face haunted by memories. People get over anything in time, I assure myself. Moderate happiness could yet be mine — inordinate happiness, never! I have tasted it, bitter-sweet it was, too heady perhaps for daily consumption. I make a mug of hot chocolate which is a poor substitute and, still in my coat, huddle by the gas fire, a dejected heap. The sooner I get back to work, the better.

The one-bedroomed flat is sparsely furnished, mainly with items given to me by my parents and grandparents. Nothing matches. When I was considering the flat in the short-term, I was perfectly satisfied; thinking of it now in the long term, perhaps the remainder of my life, I realise that something will have to be done about it. I must make it into a home, not leave it as a convenient pied-à-terre, allowing me the freedom to come and go at will in the knowledge that my parents' luxurious home is still my own when needed. As soon as I can afford it I shall get some new curtains for the living-room, instead of these rather garish floral ones from Grandma Chandler, which she bought years ago in a jumble sale in Alnwick. The carpet is all right. It is an innocuous beige colour that neither matches anything nor clashes with anything, altogether too dreary to make a statement, yet very practical, with rubber backing so that it needs no underlay. It was a present from my maternal grandparents. The bookcase and the easy chair in which I am sitting come from my home, as do the single bed, the trunk and the chest of drawers in the bedroom. All my books and ornaments are around me, as comforting as a bag of dolly mixtures, with the exception of the oriental dragons on the shelf at my side, who are performing their function as book-ends with aloof pride. I turn my head towards them slowly and reluctantly. They are staring at me — huge eyes of jade and lapis lazuli. They never take their eyes from me. They have the same uncanny gaze as the Mona Lisa; they appear to be looking straight at you, only their enigmatic regard holds no hint of humour. I could not part with them. They are as much part of my life as Cassandra is; to be simultaneously admired, disliked and unwillingly, grudgingly, loved. On the far wall, against the winter light, is the picture of the intense, enraptured young woman in the white dress, now mounted and framed. In that dim position, the colour of her eyes is ambiguous. She does not look fixedly out at you, but gazes longingly at her own dreams which, poor deluded girl, she has not yet realised are unattainable. I look across at her and see the gift for what it is. Gérard said she reminded him of me. He should have kept her. What am I doing with her, who need no reminding of him?

12

I AM emerging from the bad dream-time. Grandma Harris has said I am too young to be miserable forever, and she is right. She has guessed at the depths of my misery, for I have never revealed it to her; or Mum has discussed it with her, which is far more likely.

I have been back at work for three weeks and my spirits are returning with my good health and the pleasure I derive from my job. The company has shops on the Continent and it is expected that eventually my degree in French will be of use to them there, when in fact it is my intention never to set foot in France again.

The last time I was there was at my sister's wedding. Yes, I was there, putting a brave face on it. What else was there to do, show the world that I was to be pitied for a rejected love? Never! Not that I can remember very much about it. I arrived in Grutenheim at the very last moment and left at the very earliest, with a face aching from smiling and a throat aching with unshed tears. I held on to my shaky composure only through a belief that I should waken to embrace the merciful deliverance of reality.

Gérard had been as good as his word and had visited me in Durham soon after Christmas. We had five perfect days together and parted with promises to meet again at Easter.

While he was with me, I showed him off to my family and friends. They saw that I was in love with him; it never occurred to me to disguise the fact. First we went to Alnwick to visit Grandma Chandler.

"I haven't seen you for fifteen years," she said to him, pushing him away to avoid the second and third kisses on her sunken cheeks. She looked him up and down appreciatively then said to me, "He's a man now, just like his father."

Lucien and Leila called on her every time they came to Durham. She loved to recall the old days when Lucien and her son, Oliver, were lads together, spending alternate summers in each other's homes.

"This is the wrong time of year to be visiting people, young man," she said to

Gérard. "Especially people who live in the country. I like my visitors to see the garden and the surroundings in their leafy beauty. Make a cup of tea, Jan."

From the gloomy kitchen, I could hear her rattling on about local people and local events which would have been of no interest to Gérard. When I carried in the tea, she was saying, "I spend a lot of time on my own with my animals. Oliver leads such a busy life that he can never come to see his old mother and now Lorna has taken on those dress shops, she hasn't the time, either. Cassie had to go to London to work. I miss seeing her. Jan comes when she can, which isn't often."

Gérard commiserated with her. I did not. Nothing had changed, she only thought it had. Mum still responded to her every call for help, but not so promptly as she used to do. As for Cassandra, well, she had seldom bothered to visit her when she was living at home. What had given her the idea that Cassandra had gone to London of necessity rather than choice?

"How do you like your job, Jan?" Grandma asked when I set down the tray. "If you have to work in a shop, I don't know why you didn't choose one of your mother's. I suppose they pay you more. They certainly charge enough, but then so does Lorna. Of course, she won't sell very much. She'll be lucky to get a couple of customers a day, I should think. Mrs Belmont took me to Newcastle last week. She needed something from the Bigg Market. We went into your shop and I looked round for you. Where do they keep you? I didn't buy anything in there. I came back with some flea powder for the cats. All that way for some flea powder! Mrs Belmont said, never mind, it was a day out for me, but I would rather have stayed at home. I can buy everything I need in Alnwick. Everyone wanted to be fed when I got back and I was so tired with traipsing round all those busy streets."

Grandma Chandler rarely waited for answers to her numerous questions, which meant that she committed herself to remaining in ignorance; then she had the nerve to complain that nobody told her anything. She did not give Gérard a chance to talk about Grutenheim, which he loved to do at the least opportunity.

He seemed strangely out of place in my everyday environment, as if he were sparing me a few days from what mattered most to him. If I wanted the rest of his life, then I would have to share it with him in his own habitat amongst the endless rows of demanding vines. I appreciated that. Leila has a sister in Wallsend, but Gérard had no intention of visiting her, even though I offered to drive him over there. He said that his visit was too short and he meant to devote every minute of it to me, but I sensed a resistance in him to re-establish a connection with the English side of his family. Whereas in Alsace his English sounded flawless — not flawless if one counted the echo of his mother's North-Eastern speech — I was surprised to hear a definite French accent, even an occasional hesitancy, as if he was searching for the correct word or phrase, deliberately making his foreignness more obvious. It was a trick he had learnt from his mother, but to what end? Was it a way of holding on, or holding out? It was difficult to tell.

Grandma Chandler had treated Gérard merely as an acquaintance making a polite call. My maternal grandmother, more worldly-wise, regarded our visit to her with more significance.

She did not seem to like Gérard very much and I was hurt. When I tackled her on the subject after he had returned to France, she said that she had nothing against him except his intention to marry me and carry me off to foreign parts. Her son had disappeared into 'foreign parts' and many years went by between their brief meetings.

I tried to console her. "France isn't very foreign, Gran. People can swim there, you know. Anyway, Gérard and I haven't discussed marriage yet."

"Have you not! Together in that flat and you haven't discussed marriage! What did he come over here for, then? He hasn't been since he was a little lad. I presumed he came to pop the question, that was certainly Lorna's impression."

I had presumed the same thing, so I was intensely irritated with her for suggesting it. "It's too soon," I said. "Why must people rush you into these things?"

"Here, here!" murmured Grandpa, removing his pipe from his mouth to agree with me and receiving a freezing look from his wife in response.

"I haven't noticed any tendency in the young to be rushed into marriage these days," Grandma retorted tartly. "Marriage is the last thing they think about. Houses and babies seem to come first and not necessarily in that order."

"What difference does it make?" I asked peevishly. "Women have careers to think about as well." I was hoping that my employers would move me to France before I had to make plans to live there permanently, then I would be able to carry on with my job for a few years before settling down as the wife of a *vigneron*.

I have made two new friends since starting work. There is Mary, a dark-eyed girl with a wide smile, an uncomplicated nature and a great sense of fun, and Kay, who is tall and haughty with an upper-class accent which is perfectly genuine — her parents speak the same way yet sounds too good to be true on first hearing it, and makes one wonder if she is taking the rise out of one. Mary has many young men hanging around her, but is too good-natured to favour one over the others. Kay is engaged to be married, but is in no hurry to fulfil her languidly given promise and treats her fiancé, Francis, with a cool charm which keeps him dithering in admiring suspense.

Gérard and I met Mary, an admirer of Mary's called Tom, Kay and Francis in a pub one evening for a meal. The place was crowded and the atmosphere was lively, as was our conversation. In the company of the man I love and my favourite friends, I could not have been merrier. It was obvious that both Mary and Kay found Gérard attractive and that served to increase my pride and joy. Kay congratulated him on his English.

"I have an English mother," he told her, adding with a quick smile at me, "a very English mother."

"You don't need to use your beautiful French at all, Jan," Kay drawled. "What a waste!"

"Indeed she does!" Gérard replied emphatically. "It is impolite to live in a country and ignore its language. By ignoring the language, you distance yourself from the people. How can you understand what makes a nation tick if you cannot tune in to it through speech?" He spoke with more vehemence than Kay's original remark deserved. The others, whose French was poor verging on the non-existent, looked uncomfortable and suitably chastised. I guessed that he was obliquely criticising his mother and letting it be known that, unlike Lucien, he was not prepared to tolerate such obduracy in his own wife. Looking back, I find that singularly ironic.

I had expected Gérard to sleep in my newly acquired flat with me — after all, we had shared the flat in Grutenheim — but the arrangements had been made by Mum and Leila over the telephone and he was given my old room at home. However, he spent most of his time at the flat, returning to my chaste, little girl's bed in the small hours. Recalling the five days as dispassionately as I am able, I realise that not only was marriage never mentioned, but also I did not experience a heady sense of power over him, that delicious power bestowed by love that I once exercised over Martin; all the influence seemed to be on Gérard's side. I was the one watching for every change of mood, for signs of happiness or discontent. I suppose that was the surest evidence that I loved and he was loved. Gérard spoke words of devotion when I was in his arms, feeding them to me as one puts chocolate drops into a trusting child's mouth; little tokens of affection to sweeten the moment, given in gratitude for unqualified adoration and, in the manner of a child, I was satisfied. Ruefully, I recognise now what Martin had endured in thrall to my changeful moods and I wonder if he is experiencing a similar unbalanced state of affairs with his new love in Philadelphia, or is he now the pampered object of desire? It gives me no pleasure to suppose he may be. Whenever I think about Martin, I miss him. What woman does not miss a faithful and gentle lover, carelessly discarded?

There were no thoughts of Martin in my mind when I was saying *au revoir* to Gérard.

"You'll see Alsace in spring, Jan. I want you to experience all the seasons there. Until you do, you can't possibly know the place properly. Tell your father I'm sorry I missed him." (Dad was returning from Amsterdam that evening.) Gérard held me close, saying softly, "Until Easter, *chérie.*" He rubbed his cheek against my ear, whispered, "Thanks for everything, Jan," kissed me on the lips and departed. I smiled back happily as we waved goodbye. Five weeks were but a short pause in the continuity of our love affair. As I was driving homewards, I was already anticipating our reunion.

One evening, ten days before Easter, I was at my parents' home, sitting on the sofa in the living-room reading a story to Roddy, who was leaning against me, hot and grumpy with a high temperature caused by tonsilitis. The telephone started ringing and Mum, who was doing her accounts in the next room, went to answer it.

"Oh, it's you, Leila," I heard her say, then, after a listening pause and in amazement, "Cassie's there!"

"Go on with the story, Jan," Roddy insisted.

"How long does she intend staying with you?" Mum asked.

I read on mechanically, trying to keep most of my attention on the one-sided conversation in the hall.

I had almost come to the end of the

story by the time Mum replaced the receiver. I gabbled the last paragraph and snapped the book shut, catching the end of Roddy's finger which had been pointing to the giant's ugly feet.

"Ouch!" he cried.

Abstractedly, I kissed it better. He snatched his book and ran off, dashing past Mum who was on her way into the room. Roddy always reacted as if people damaged him on purpose.

Mum raised her eyebrows in enquiry.

"I squashed his finger," I explained impatiently. "What's this about Cassie?"

"She's turned up in Grutenheim out of the blue. Leila has no idea how long she'll be staying. She doesn't like to ask in case it sounds as if they don't want her. She says they're delighted to have her there."

"Why couldn't you speak to Cassie?" I had overheard her make that request.

"She's visiting a friend in Paris. She'll be back tomorrow. I'll ring again at the weekend and find out what's going on."

"I didn't know she had a friend in Paris."

"Neither did I."

"I bet she's lost her job," I said morosely.

I had a sick feeling in the pit of my stomach. I hoped she would be gone by the time I arrived. From experience I had learnt that whenever my plans were spoilt on a whim of my sister's, they never turned out as I had anticipated. "I wonder what she's doing there?" "Having a holiday, I suppose," Mum said.

"It seems strange that she didn't let you know."

"Do you realise, Jan, that since she went to London at the beginning of last September, we have only seen her for three days, at Christmas?"

Twice Mum had suggested going down to see Cassandra and been fobbed off with talk of her coming up to Durham any day. Dad had been allowed to take Cassandra out to lunch a couple of times when he was in London on business, but she had arranged to meet him at the restaurant and had a reason for leaving on her own as soon as the meal was over. Naturally, he took the opportunity to ask her what she was doing with herself and each time had been told that she was between jobs. "She looked well," he would tell us, and we had to be satisfied with that. Mum kept threatening to go down and surprise her, but the shops were keeping her so busy that she could not spare the time. We continued to send letters to Cassandra at the flat she was sharing with her friend, so thought it safe to assume that she was still living there. She never wrote, but telephoned at erratic intervals, usually late at night, and invariably her first words were that she only possessed a ten pence coin, so could we ring her back? She complained of destitution and money was hastily despatched. Dad assumed, naïvely, that because Cassandra was still dependent on him for money, she was still dependent. Mum knew better. Dad had been directed to visit the flat on the outskirts of London the next time he was in the city, but now she had spirited herself to Alsace and we would have to rely on Leila for any information she could glean.

"Even when Cassie does talk to you, she doesn't say much," I complained.

"I'm not going to concern myself about her," Mum said hopefully. "For years I was under the impression that she needed extra protection. Your father still believes that. In fact, he's more in need of protection from her. She was born with a gift for exploitation — I'm convinced of it."

"I wish I had that gift," I said.

Mum laughed. "One day you'll give up envying Cassie, Jan. You'll suddenly discover that you have everything you need to make you content, then you'll start worrying about losing it."

"What's the difference between envy and jealousy?" I asked.

"Not a lot," Mum reckoned. "I'm going back to my dreary accounts. Tell Roddy it's his bed-time, will you?"

I had only the Easter weekend to spend with Gérard. It had been difficult enough acquiring that, Easter Saturday being one of the busiest shopping days.

I arrived to find him waiting for me at the airport, with Cassandra by his side. He was looking lean and handsome in anorak and jeans and sporting a neat moustache which gave him an air of raffishness. She was beautiful in thick, brightly patterned woollens which were slightly too large for her and made her appear absurdly young, nearer fourteen then eighteen. On her head of fair curls, which were more frenetic than was natural to her, perched a knitted beret.

Instantly, I felt too smart in my new, wide-shouldered jacket and longer-length skirt, flaring from my narrow hips. As I walked towards them, I grew taller and skinnier by the step.

Cassandra's presence tempered the spontaneity and warmth of Gérard's welcome — at least, I put it down to that. It certainly dampened my ardour. He kissed me, but that was not exceptional; being French he would have done the same for Cassandra on her arrival, three times! I had offered my mouth, but my cheeks were favoured in the more conventional manner. Cassandra and I exchanged quick pecks with our faces barely making contact and considered we had done enough to demonstrate our sisterly affection.

On the way to Grutenheim, sitting beside Gérard in the front of the car, conscious of my sister's quiet yet all-pervading presence in the back, I gave them both an up-date on events at home, telling them about the state of Grandpa's bronchitis, Dad's irritation with the amount of time Mum was devoting to her shops,

Roddy's septic knee which had followed closely upon his septic throat, and Grandma Chandler's irritation with Mum for the amount of time she was devoting to her shops. When I paused for breath and inspiration, Cassandra said, "I'm sorry you can only stay for the weekend, Jan."

"I shall be back after Whitsun, all being well," I said, glancing at Gérard's profile.

"Good!" he remarked heartily, not taking his eyes from the road.

"How long will you be here?" I asked, turning round to look at Cassandra.

In her maddening way she did not answer immediately. After regarding me calmly for a few moments, as if considering the enormous complexity of the question, she said, "It all depends. I'm looking for another job, actually."

"In France?" I asked in astonishment, knowing the difficulty she had with the language.

"I have a friend in Paris."

"Who will be offering you a job?" I persisted.

"Not necessarily."

I cast an exasperated look at Gérard. He smiled back at me, amused by the exchange. "Don't worry, Jan," he advised. "I'm sure Cassie knows what she's doing."

"She usually does," I muttered, thinking that it was everyone else who remained in the dark.

Since my arrival, we had been speaking in English for Cassandra's benefit. Contumaciously, I switched to French for the remainder of the journey, laughingly explaining that I must practise it at every opportunity in case I was sent over there to work, but in reality doing it to give my lazy sister something to think about and to please Gérard whose views on the subject of his native language had been made plain to me.

The family in Grutenheim were delighted to see me again and made every effort to make me feel at home, especially Leila. When we were children, Cassandra had been her favourite. Now she was making it obvious that I had superseded her. She kept referring to the lovely month we had enjoyed together the previous summer, and said how much she had missed me when Roddy and I returned home. She did her best to make sure that Gérard and I had some time on our own.

"Why don't you and Jan go into Colmar together?" she suggested to Gérard when plans for the next afternoon were under discussion.

Gérard asked me if I would like to go and I said that I would, very much. So we went. The outing was not a great success. We were both trying hard, perhaps too hard, to recapture the intimacy of the last evening in my flat. Walking along the narrow path beside the river which wound between the tall houses in the oldest part of Colmar, known as Petite Venise, we discussed everything but ourselves. The future, about which I had been so confident, had become something I was fearful to mention. We even came near to quarrelling when Gérard began to talk about my sister and what he supposed were her reasons for bolting to France.

"I think she's been let down by her lover," he said. "Poor little Cassie."

"Has she told you that?" I asked, unaware that she had a lover.

"No," he admitted, "but what other reason could she have for running away?"

"Whatever her reasons, she'll keep them to herself."

OOJ14

"She's so young, so easily hurt. Why are you laughing, Jan? Sometimes I think you're not very sympathetic towards your little sister."

"One needs to be able to understand to sympathise," I observed caustically.

"She seems easy enough to understand to me."

"Oh, really? But you've just said you don't know why she's here."

"I haven't asked her," he said.

"Do try!" I urged sarcastically. "We should all love to know Cassie's motives for doing anything."

"Let's change the subject, shall we?" He led me towards a cafe with tables set out along the river bank in the spring sunshine. We ate ice-cream while swans sailed up and down in regal aloofness.

Late that evening, when Gérard and I were walking along a path between the rows of newly-leafed vines, something of the old magic began creeping back into our relationship. In the scented darkness we talked less and touched more, murmuring our satisfaction with one another each time we paused to embrace. By the time we returned to the black well of the courtyard, we were reluctant to release our hold and drifted up the outside stairs to the apartment, breathing and anticipating as one being. We stole along the balcony and let ourselves into the dark hall. The kitchen was a shadowy shell, humming to itself, containing rectangular objects of faintly gleaming white; the living-room door was shut. We turned into the passage leading to the bedrooms only to find it dissected by a segment of orange light emanating from Cassandra's room. Why had she not shut the door?

"Goodnight," she called softly as we passed.

"Goodnight," we answered with discomposure, feeling the spell quivering about us and almost dispersing.

For someone who spent most of her time shut off from those closest to her, leaving her door ajar was an act of provocation. Gérard had moved a step away from me. I pulled him close again, drawing him into my room, my intense desire exerting an influence of its own to which he responded. I loved him so much that I could not dissemble. And he returned that love, I was sure of it then. That night he was mine, completely mine, once more.

When I awoke, he had returned to the bedroom of his boyhood in the family house. Cassandra had been using Jean-Michel's room before my arrival; then Leila, in her mistaken wisdom, had decreed the change around and Gérard had given up the apartment in order that two sisters could be together.

Cassandra joined me in the kitchen late that morning, enticed there, she said, by the aroma of fresh coffee. Lazy and contented with the lassitude that follows a replete night of love, I urged her indulgently to tell me about her life in London and what had brought her to Grutenheim.

Across that tiny kitchen table with our elbows either side of large bowls of coffee, we came as close as we had ever done to confiding in one another. I thought that what she told me was important. Later I knew it was what she had not told me that mattered most.

She had been living in London with a friend, sure enough, but a man, not a woman. The old school friend had been used merely as a poste restante. She left

Colin, the young man, when he had not objected to the idea of sharing her with his friend.

"Cassie, how dreadful! How could you live with someone like that?"

"He was all right at first."

"What about your job?"

"I never had one, not a proper one."

"No wonder you were always in debt. Which reminds me, I have a cheque for you from Dad in my handbag. What about this friend in Paris?"

"Don't worry, she exists. She needs someone to look after her baby while she works."

"You wouldn't enjoy doing that, would you?"

"I might. I won't know until I try. I've always wanted to live in Paris. Perhaps you'll be transferred there and we could live together. That would be fun."

"You mean it would be convenient." I smiled ruefully, imagining myself with all the chores.

"Yes, it would," she admitted quite seriously. "I'm the kind of person who needs to be looked after and sheltered from the sordid things in life." She really meant it. The expression in her eyes was one of mute misery.

"Was he very unkind to you?" I asked sympathetically.

"Of course not. If he had been, I'd have left sooner. I can't bear to be treated roughly, can you? I'll submit to anything as long as it's done with tenderness. If you touch a flower with a heavy hand, its petals drop off, but if you stroke it lightly you do no damage and can enjoy its velvety softness."

I waited for her to continue with this strange revelation, my coffee bowl held before my face, its contents cooling. She was doing her best to explain herself to me and I was doing my best to understand, fascinated and repelled, convinced that she was about to reveal something hideous.

"Have you still got my dragon?" she asked unexpectedly. I relaxed. "Yes, in my flat. Do you want it back?"

"I never want it back. I gave it to you." She drank her coffee. I drank mine. She put the empty bowl on the table, got to her feet and said gravely, "Mathias is a disgusting old man."

"In what way?" I was shocked.

She shuddered with distaste. "You know in what way."

"He's harmless," I defended him. "You never used to mind him."

"That's the worst of growing up, you know how vile people can really be."

"Mathias isn't vile," I protested angrily. "How can you say that, Cassie? He's a dear old man."

"I didn't mean that he was vile. He's just disgusting."

"For heaven's sake, that's a terrible thing to say about him. What has he done?"

"He hasn't done anything, well, no more than usual, only his awful patting and stroking if he's given half a chance. It's all in his mind."

"Or yours! Something has happened to make you like this."

She jumped to her feet. "You're wrong. I wouldn't let it happen. I'm never going to let it happen."

"What are we talking about? Let what happen?" but it was no use, she had grown tired of the conversation. She turned and left the kitchen. I should have known better than to expect enlightenment. Already she was bringing ugliness where I had found only enchantment.

The weekend was over far too quickly. I did my utmost to persuade Cassandra to return with me. She seemed so lost and waif-like, harbouring goodness knows what memories of disagreeable experiences. I was worried about her. I pleaded with her to accompany me. She refused, making the excuse that she had promised her friend to give child-minding a go.

She left for Paris three days after I left for home. She was there for only two weeks before Leila received a telephone call from her, asking if she could return because things were not working out well between her, her friend and her friend's baby who, at ten months, was not as independent as Cassandra would have liked and, as she informed Leila with pained surprise, needed an awful lot of looking after. The friend, apparently, was having a great time going out and about while Cassandra was left at home with the baby. She told Leila tearfully that she could not travel to Grutenheim, being absolutely broke and utterly miserable, until she had received some money from Dad. Leila despatched

Gérard, a knight in shining armour, to rescue the hard-done-by damsel.

"She should have come home," Mum complained to me, after relating the details of her conversation with Leila. "What made her decide to go to Alsace instead? She won't get a job there, her French is too appalling."

Gérard's letter was lying on the mat behind the door when I went to fetch the bottle of milk one Monday morning in July, one ordinary Monday morning as I thought, about ten days before I was due to take my summer holiday in Alsace. As I bent to pick it up, I wondered why he had bothered to write — after all, we had spoken on the telephone as usual on Saturday evening. I tore at the envelope, impatient to get at the contents and, if I am honest with myself, I was apprehensive. I had not seen Gérard since Easter. I had not been able to take time off at Whitsun, and our frequent telephone conversations were unsatisfactory, to say the least. I had often complained to him that he never answered when I wrote, and now he had. The letter was in French, but whatever language he had used would neither have softened the cruelty nor made it completely comprehensible to me at the first reading. Standing on the mat in my dressing-gown, I read it a second time — slowly.

Dear Jan,

This is a very difficult letter to write, but after what my mother said yesterday, I feel I must. Apparently, she has made up her mind that we are going to be married. She is old-fashioned and imagines that every love affair must end the same way. We know better, of course. I am sure that, like me, you have loved before. Cassie tells me that there was once a man called Martin in your life. We shall both love again, Jan. You have your career to consider and carrying on a long-term relationship with so many miles between us is not fair to you. I think you will agree that it makes things difficult and unsatisfactory for both of us. I could not expect you to give up everything and come here, and there is no way I shall ever live anywhere else, the wine business is part of my life. You will always be special to me, Jan. Take care of yourself, *chérie*.

Long-lasting affection from,
Gérard.

I stumbled back to the kitchen, fell on a chair, put my head on the table and cried until I was exhausted; the letter scrumpled up in my hand, held rigidly away from me in futile repudiation.

By the time I heard the news from an apologetic and indignant Leila that Gérard intended to marry Cassandra, I was expecting it.

"Of course, she must be married in Durham," Dad declared. "No daughter of mine is going to rely on someone else for her wedding."

"But in the circumstances, Oliver," Mum reminded him.

"What circumstances? Oh, you mean that Jan was going to marry him. He never actually asked her, did he? She probably read too much into the affair. You know how impetuous she is."

"She loved him, Oliver. She still does. We have to consider her feelings. He must have returned her love a little. He came over here to be with her in February and, after all, Leila was expecting them to make a match of it. Leila and I have talked it over. She thinks it would be better to have the wedding over there and I agree with her."

"What about all our friends? They won't want to travel so far."

"Then we won't bother to ask them," Mum said.

"It's not what I planned for a daughter's wedding," Dad complained sullenly.

"No, I can imagine. No doubt the cathedral featured large in those plans, but that wouldn't have been possible in the circumstances — don't forget Gérard is a Catholic. I don't expect the question of his religion has ever entered Cassie's head."

I was listening-in to the conversation, unashamedly hanging about in the hall, waiting for them to finish. My father, I thought, is an insensitive pig! No wonder Mum had wanted to remain in Hong Kong. He was delighted that one of his daughters was to marry the son of his greatest friend and he did not give a damn which daughter it was. As to the subject of religion, I thought how lucky it was that Cassandra had only lived with the man in London, for had she been divorced from him the Church would have raised difficulties about her union with one of its sons.

When Mum told me later that Dad had eventually agreed to having the wedding in Alsace, I told her categorically that I would not go.

"You must please yourself, dear," she said mildly, putting her arm around my shoulders. "Only consider what they will all say if you stay away. In your place I would rather face them as if I didn't care."

"How could I?" I cried.

"Think about it," Mum advised.

It took me a long week of misery to make up my mind.

"I'll go," I told Mum dispiritedly.

"Good girl," she said approvingly.

"Go where?" Roddy asked.

"To Cassie's wedding. She's marrying Gérard."

"I thought Jan was going to marry him."

"Well, I'm not!" I shouted at him. "And don't you ever say that I was! I never said it, did I?"

"No, but . . . "

"Go to bed, Roddy," Mum advised him. "You look tired."

"I'm not tired."

"Go to bed anyway. It's late."

The marriage was in the autumn, a week after Cassandra's nineteenth birthday. Gérard was twenty-six. I put a brave face on it behind make-up designed to put colour in my cheeks, and wearing clothes designed to make the most of my bean-pole figure. I was not going to have anyone look at me and think that it was no wonder he chose the other one. What I lacked in beauty I was determined to compensate with style. Hardest to bear was my father's ebullient enthusiasm and his obvious pride in his younger daughter, the beautiful, self-possessed bride. I detested her. While Dad was behaving as if the father-of-the-bride was the most important person there, Mum was being torn between manifest happiness for one daughter and concealed sympathy for the other.

"We'll face it out together in our glad rags, darling," she had said, before we left for Alsace. "Much as Leila loves Cassie, she wouldn't have chosen her for a daughter-in-law. She has confessed to me that they have no rapport."

Who does have rapport with Cassandra? I wondered. Presumably Gérard does.

Leila made all the arrangements for the wedding. Cassandra had talked about coming home beforehand to choose her gown, but Mum, after many lengthy telephone discussions, persuaded her, without letting my father know, to stay where she was and she went over there for a few days instead. Dad forked out handsomely, urging Leila to spare no expense on his behalf.

Grandma and Grandpa Harris were puzzled by the whole thing. Grandma kept repeating the same questions over and over until I could have screamed. "Why is she getting married in France? I didn't know she was fond of him, did you? Did you quarrel with him, then, Jan?" She came to the conclusion that it was most inconsiderate of Cassandra to be married so far away. "I won't be able to go. Henry isn't well enough to travel and I wouldn't dream of going without him. I would have to get a passport and what do I want with one of those at my time of life? It's all most unsatisfactory. That's the second wedding I've had to miss. First Daniel's and now Cassie's. I hope you'll manage things better when your time comes, Jan. Oh. I know what you're thinking, that you will never marry now. You should have kept him at arm's length, my girl, like we used to do in the old days. That's the way to make sure of your man. I bet your sister was cleverer, the little madam. There's no need to become uppity. You're only twenty-three. Plenty of time to meet someone else. Gérard is very nice, I'm not saying otherwise, and I'm sure he'll suit Cassandra, but he has too much conceit about him for my taste. What you need is someone quiet and dependable, a bit shy. I like shyness in a man, it means you don't have to keep an eye on him all the time. Your grandfather was shy when he was young — with the ladies, anyway. Whatever happened to that boy you used to know? Martin something or other."

"Proudfoot," I muttered. "He's probably getting married as well."

"Lots more fish in the sea," Grandpa said consolingly. "Don't be in too much of a hurry, lass." And when his wife had left the room to make some cocoa, he said quietly, with a sardonic smile, "As I remember, some of the young ladies had very short arms."

Grandma Chandler had treated the news more casually. "I'll send sheets," she said. "White ones, they go with anything."

"You must come to the wedding, Mother," Dad said, making a special visit to Alnwick on purpose to persuade her and taking the opportunity to have a poke about, assessing the state of the house with his eyes and doing sums in his head.

"I told her I would have the place done up for her while she's away," he told Mum and me. "Well only be there for three days, but there would be no need for her to return until the work was completed and then I could go over and bring her back. The stubborn old woman said she couldn't possibly leave those blasted animals. I said I would get Bert Carr to look after them." Bert was the local handyman who stepped in when Mum was faced with something beyond her capabilities, such as digging

OOJ15

the vegetable patch. "She said the goat doesn't like him and the mangy old cat she calls Mimsy needs special care. I tried talking her round, but it was useless. She accused me of bullying her and shook her fist at me."

"It's going to be a one-sided occasion," Mum sighed. "Apart from us, all the other people there will be relations and friends of Leila and Lucien."

"I told you we should have it in Durham," Dad fumed. "Bloody hole-in-the-corner affair! People will think we have something to hide."

God, how I dreaded that wedding! I dreaded it so much that afterwards I could remember very little about it and the pain of witnessing was expunged by a great tide of relief. I spent most of the time avoiding looking at people, especially the principal performers, and on the occasions when I did look, quickly and covertly, while they were engrossed in the ceremony or absorbed with one another, I was left with vivid pictures, coloured snaps which haunted me for months afterwards, in the manner of a photograph album which opens of its own accord at captured moments best forgotten. There was Gérard kissing his bride; Gérard helping his wife into the car; Gérard's expression as once, fleetingly, his eyes met mine in the split-second before I could avert them. I smiled stiffly, hoping to convince him and anyone else who might be interested that I did not mind at all and he — well, he was the one who turned away, as if he minded for me. That made me try harder to appear insouciant. I was one of the first to wish the pair every happiness in their life together and then, for the first time that day, for the first time since I had arrived in Grutenheim, I really looked at Cassandra, into her lovely, serenely smiling face. She reminded me of the cat that has triumphantly swallowed the plump pet bird but must keep the secret to itself.

"You will come and stay with us, won't you, Jan?" she asked earnestly, sounding as if she meant it.

"But of course," I answered, sounding as if I meant it too, then quickly moving away to allow others to express their felicitations.

Leila was standing next to Jean-Michel and his girlfriend from Marseilles. She left them and moved to my side. "What do you think of Gabrielle?" she whispered. "She frightens Lucien to death. She fancies herself as a *femme fatale.*"

Not another one, I thought bitterly.

That evening, when the family had returned from the hotel where the long, long celebration had taken place, and the newly married couple were preparing to depart for their honeymoon in Greece, I searched for Leila and discovered her sitting quietly in the privacy of her bedroom.

"I've come to say goodbye," I told her.

We wept on one another's shoulders, emotionally drained, acknowledging without words the gritty cinders of our shared dreams, crumbled castles in the spent coals.

My parents and Roddy were not leaving for another two days, but I had decided to spare myself the sight of Cassandra and Gérard leaving for their honeymoon and gave the excuse that my employers were in desperate need of me. Jean-Michel and Gabrielle, who were also making a speedy departure, drove me to the airport. Gabrielle seemed the kind of woman who sparkles in the presence of men and sinks into sulky apathy when left amongst her own sex. She talked incessantly to Jean-Michel, her long eyelashes, stiff with black mascara, flapping up and down in a manner that resembled a pair of tiny wings in a ritual courtship dance. Her pretty, cerise mouth was smiling and pouting in an all-out effort to be captivating. I sank into dejection behind them, not as fascinated as Jean-Michel was by the dazzling display and thankful not to have to contribute to the conversation. I had plenty to think about. While the car was waiting to pull out of the courtyard, away from the place I had learnt to love so well, I had overheard, through the open window of the family living-room, Leila speaking to her *belle-fille* in fluent, rapid Alsatian dialect and her elder son requesting her to speak in English because his wife was having difficulty understanding her.

13

"**I** THINK you should go, Jan," my mother says. "The children would love it. You used to love it yourself. How many years is it since you were last there?"

"That's easy. I haven't been back since Cassie's wedding. Eleven years."

It is a Sunday afternoon in late spring. We are sitting in the summer-house in my parents' garden. My mother is writing to Cassandra and I am reading a novel. On the grass a few yards from us, beneath the late-leafing ash trees, my two children are sitting on a fringed travelling rug from Otterburn, having a picnic. Alice is seven, Sebastian is five.

Mum regards me intently for a couple of minutes, then she advises quietly, "Think about it, Jan."

I think about it, my book open on my lap. Leila wants me to pick up where my parents left off and spend the summer holidays with my own family in Grutenheim. This is not the first time she has invited us, but this time her invitation is more insistent. She thinks our presence will be good for Cassandra who is two months pregnant, and that means, of course, good for Gerard also. Cassandra returns to Durham far too often, usually on her own, because Gerard is too busy to accompany her.

I think about Alsace. Although, once, I visited it in the spring, I only recall it in summer, a perpetual summer of deep enchantment which ended at the same time as my girlhood, when I fell in love. Love is reality. It brings pain. Thinking about Alsace is an indulgence, similar to allowing myself to dream an alluring and recurring dream, then forcing myself to wake before it reaches its climax. Occasionally, the ruse does not work and the dream changes without warning into familiar, miserable nightmare — but less often now. It is humiliating to want and be unwanted. The fierceness of a spurned love gradually dies down to a melancholy ache. Only my jealousy thrives undiminished, my sister's cruel legacy to me. I am a despicable green-eyed monster; not an agressive creature, but one which hides in corners, whimpering and ashamed. Out in the open, among family and friends, I appear the same as I have always been, lively and quick-tempered, too often acting on impulse, which can lead to regrets — but not always, thank heavens!

It was an impulsive action that brought me my present fulfilment. I close my book, place it on the rickety folding table next to Mum's leather writing case and get up to walk round onto the little verandah which overlooks the river. I lean on the rough wooden balustrade. The sparkling water with its bright reflections gradually fades into a uniform grey and all the small boats disappear, leaving it deserted.

I was looking down through a thick, soft drizzle from a dove-grey sky, which was mirrored in the flowing, darkly shining water, banked on either side with new green and daffodil yellow. The path directly beneath me was obscured by tree tops and bushes, but along the far path I could see three people walking towards the cathedral and the city centre; there was a couple, of indeterminate age, wearing hats and raincoats, with a dainty dog picking its way on a lead and, behind them, a tall young man, head bent, hands in pockets, loping along in a manner I found totally recognisable. Martin! I took an involuntary step towards him which brought me sharply against the rail, my mouth opened to call his name across the empty river, then I stepped back uttering a sigh of disappointment. He was no longer mine to summon. I watched him striding on. Where was he going? What was he thinking about? Suddenly, I could not bear to be isolated from all knowledge of him. Until that moment, I had not realised just how much I missed him. I did not stop to wonder whether or not he was missing me. I dashed from the summer-house, scrambling through the tall wet grasses down the muddy, overgrown path from the garden to the river. I ran along the tow path, my eyes on Martin's receding figure on the opposite bank. While I was running, I was thinking, Why do I want him? I did not know the answer. I only knew I could bear no longer to remain as nothing to him. What had become of the girl in

Philadelphia? I had not heard that he had married her. Please God, he had not married her!

Martin had reached the bridge and was climbing the steps in the narrow gap between the tall buildings, which would take him into the town. I raced up the steps on the other side and hurried back across the bridge, through the maze of sauntering afternoon shoppers, searching for him, inexplicably desperate for him, as if we had been torn asunder rather than drifted apart and this was a miraculous, now-or-never, chance encounter. There he was, halfway up the winding cobbled street, making towards the market square. I put on another breathless spurt of speed, darting through the aggravatingly obstructive shoppers until I was at his elbow. I touched his anorak. As I was summoning the courage to gasp his name, he turned. He smiled his attractive, slow smile and said, "Hello, Jan!" seeming not the least bit surprised. I could tell from the tone of his voice and the look in his eyes that he was not going to turn away from me.

"Where are you going?" I asked, as if I had the right to know, involuntarily catching hold of one of his arms with both my hands.

"To buy a light bulb, amongst other things. Coming?"

I went gladly. For the first five minutes we scarcely spoke. There was an awkwardness between us brought about by not knowing what had happened to the other during our long estrangement, but once we started talking, both together, we could not stop, except to sort out whose turn it was.

We talked over tea and sticky buns in a cafe, then I walked home with him, still talking.

Until that fateful day, had never properly visited Martin's home. I had called there with him once or twice, waiting for a short while before we set off again. I had called there occasionally on my own in order to pick him up in my car, but I had never remained long enough to feel anything other than a stranger.

Martin lived on a large, fairly modern estate. Originally, the houses had all looked remarkably alike, but over the years the owners had added bits to suit their growing needs and affluence. Many of the additions were at architectural variance with the overall cohesive look of the area. The Proudfoot family was one of the few which had added nothing to their home. All the extra money had gone into bringing up and educating the two sons.

That afternoon, to my consternation, I was given to understand by Mrs Proudfoot that Martin was very much her precious son and I was very much in her disfavour. She was sorry to see me turn up and even sorrier to realise that I would most probably be turning up again and again. She was too well-bred to chastise me for the hurt I had inflicted on her younger son, in fact I was not aware just how deeply I had hurt Martin until I saw the pained expression in the eyes of his mother as she politely welcomed me and expressed her cool pleasure at seeing me again.

I wanted to reassure her, to let her know that she was not the only person who appreciated what I had so casually discarded when I was reaching for the love of someone else. I resolved to court the esteem of Martin's mother. Mr Proudfoot accepted me more easily. Martin was happy to have me back and that was sufficient for his father.

During my first two or three visits, the atmosphere was strained and over-polite, almost wary. Martin knew how hard I was trying to fit into his family, which was so very different from my own. His mother was highly domesticated and proud of her role as wife and mother. She had devoted herself to the home from marriage and had never wished for independence in the form of individual development or earning power. She enjoyed a rigidly contained life-style which would not have suited my mother at all, but was similar to that of my maternal grandmother. Mrs Proudfoot cleaned the house vigorously and did a lot of baking. There was usually the smell of something delicious just out of the oven — biscuits, bread and cakes. Baking had never been one of Mum's favourite pastimes. She only cooked in order that we could eat, something quick and often expensive. Mrs Proudfoot made fragrant and filling stews, Mum put steak and mushrooms under the grill.

Martin's mother began to like me for his sake, not for my own. I was not the kind of girl she wanted for her son. They were a quiet, even-tempered family who never made rash decisions. I amused them with my impetuosity and sudden changes of mood, but they were suspicious of them, as they were of my father's affluence, which made life, so they considered, too easy for us all. Martin had been brought up to practise careful economy and expect value for money. Also, he had been taught true generosity, which means going without in order to give. They judged me as being thoughtless and extravagant and had considered Martin to be well rid of me — but here I was again!

Apart from when we were in his home, Martin and I were back on the old footing almost immediately. It was wonderful. I could hardly believe my good fortune. I kept thinking how dreadful it would have been if he had married the girl in America. She had probably deserved him more than I did. I would catch hold of his hand tightly, as if I would never let it go. Perhaps it is wrong to say we were back on the old footing, because I no longer took his devotion for granted, but felt the full privilege of it. My love for him was not passionate and delirious as my love for Gerard had been. It grew strong and steady, based on perfect trust and emotional dependence. It had always been easy to be fond of Martin and it had always been far too easy to hurt him. Having been hurt myself, I vowed I would be careful in the future to preserve him from that kind of pain. I tried to make his mother understand my commitment to this and, gradually, she did. We were friends by the time my first child was born.

Alice and Sebastian are fortunate to have two doting sets of grandparents. They see my parents at least once a month, usually on Sundays when we have lunch with them and their great-grandmother Harris. Her husband, my dear old grandfather, is dead. They never knew him. Nan and Grandad Proudfoot are visited more often. They are always at home, very willing to baby-sit and never too busy to give the children plenty of attention. There are always homemade cakes and biscuits to be had and if they make crumbs and sticky finger marks, Nan quickly and without complaint clears it all up, as if it is to be expected. One house is large and airy, containing many expensive objects which the children must not touch in case they damage them, and the other is small, tidy and shabbily cosy. The children do not make comparisons and have no thought of relative wealth. Their own home is small and, I like to think, cosy. It is a three-bedroomed, detached house on a new housing estate, the mortgage repayments commensurate with their father's modest salary.

"Mummy!"

The scene before me slips back into focus. The river shimmers in the bright sunshine. Summoned, I leave the verandah and walk round to the other side of the summerhouse.

"Seb has spilt orange juice all over the rug," Alice informs me officiously.

"It wobbled over," Sebastian explains.

The children are wearing thick sweaters knitted for them by Martin's mother. There is not a great deal of warmth in the sun, it is too early in the year to expect it. However, the long winter is well and truly behind us and the garden is inviting in its tender new greenery.

I sit down next to my mother again. The glass of the summer-house traps and enhances what warmth there is. Mum is about to seal her letter.

"Shall I tell her you'll go?" she asks.

"Could you really manage without me for a month?"

"Certainly," she says, pen poised.

Since Sebastian started school the previous September, I have been working for her on an erratic, part-time basis. She now has a chain of clothes shops throughout the North-East and is planning to open another in the prestigious, MetroCentre development in Gateshead.

"Martin will only be able to take two weeks in August. I suppose I could take the children on ahead. He's quite capable of looking after himself and I'm sure his mother would be only too delighted to keep an eye on him. She has always been critical of the way I iron his shirts."

"What's that about my mother?" my husband enquires with good humour. Here he is with my father, strolling across the lawn towards us. The children leap to their feet and run towards them. Alice makes for her grandfather who she knows adores her.

Sebastian is less sure of his worth and waits to be coaxed.

Dad is sixty-two. His hair is grey and as smooth and neat as ever. He remains brisk and self-assured. I am sure that he was never like Sebastian, in need of encouragement. I suspect that Dad no longer notices how much taller his son-in-law is compared with him. They get on well together considering how different they are in character. Dad likes to talk and direct, listening only when he must and with impatience. Martin prefers to listen rather than speak, proposes rather than directs and thinks prudently before he answers. One may be sure that he will give one the benefit of any doubt.

"I think perhaps we might go to Grutenheim after all," I tell him. "If I take the children over as soon as they break up, you could join us later and we could return together. What do you think?"

"Whatever you like," Martin says, settling down near me. Sebastian climbs onto his lap.

"I'll put that on the end of my letter," Mum says. "I'll tell Cassie that you will be letting Leila know the exact dates as soon as possible, so that she can tell the others."

The others are Leila's sister from Wallsend, her married niece and her family, and various friends. Now that the old couple, Marie-Louise and Mathias, are dead, Leila and Lucien have moved across the courtyard into the small house, Cassandra and Gérard have moved into the family house, and the flat above the bottling plant is let as a gite for all but the six weeks of the British school summer holiday, when Leila's family and friends are expected to use it. It is many years since my parents have been there during the summer, and when they do go they stay in the family house and never remain longer than a week. They are such busy people. My mother is as occupied with running her shops as my father has always been with his business affairs. I wonder sometimes what their marriage would be like if they had to spend more time together, especially now that Roddy is away at university, determined to do what is expected of him, be successful for his father's sake. Dad boasts about

Roddy's academic achievements, but he has no idea what efforts his son has to make to feed that fond pride. Roddy is not exceptionally clever. But what he lacks in genius he makes up for with dogged hard work. Mum often warns Dad that he expects too much from Roddy. Dad replies airily that she is talking nonsense.

"I think I'll pull this old place down and replace it," Dad says, surveying the summer-house critically. "I hadn't realised what a state it's got into." Which is not surprising. The bottom of the garden is a strange land to him, seldom visited.

"Don't pull it down, Dad," I entreat. I can imagine the kind of modern monstrosity he would put in its place — mostly glass and hardly any wood, the reverse of the present structure. "It only needs a few nails knocked in here and there. Just give it another coat of creosote."

Dad loses interest. "Well, if you're that fond of it," he says, wandering off to investigate the farthest corners of his property with the air of an intrepid explorer.

"The grass could do with a cut," Mum calls after him provocatively.

"I'll do that," Martin offers.

"No, you won't," Mum says. "Mr Garbey comes on Tuesday. I was only reminding Oliver that grass grows and weeds abound and that the tidy state of his garden is achieved by someone's hard work and not by miracles, now I haven't the time." She gets to her feet with the letter in her hand. "I'd better take a look at Mum. She's probably finished her after-lunch nap now. Would you like to walk to the post box with me, children? I think I have a stamp in my purse."

"I'll come," Alice calls, running over to her. "I don't want to go," Sebastian tells Martin quietly. "Seb's a bit tired," Martin says to Mum. "Seb's a bit lazy," I say, smiling at him.

Sebastian regards me gravely for a minute, then he asks, "Will I have to eat beefburgers at Paula's party?"

"Not if you don't want to. You're meant to have a lovely time, not be sick."

He wriggles off Martin's lap and scampers after Mum and Alice.

"I knew something was troubling him," I say to Martin, laughing. Sebastian and Alice have been invited to a Wimpy party.

My friend Mary's third child will be five on Wednesday.

Dad comes into sight from the corner where the compost heap is discreetly hidden behind ornamental vegetation. "By the way, you two, I saw a little house that would just suit you, about halfway between here and Chester-le-Street. Lovely big garden, almost as big as this one, ideal for the kids."

Martin and I exchange glances. Here we go again! Dad is always seeing 'little houses that would just suit us'. They are always at least twice the size of the one we are presently living in and nearer to Durham. He will not accept that we cannot afford a bigger mortgage and has even offered to put up the money himself. Martin will not hear of it. He does not want to be under a financial obligation to my father, it is against his principles and I do not want that obligation either, it would be too trying. Dad would never let us forget it and we would grow tired of having to be grateful.

"You'll have to move off that estate sooner or later," he says, standing before us on a patch of daisies in his position of intimidation — legs apart, thumbs in trouser pockets, rocking a little on his heels as if ready to spring into action the moment we acquiesce. His opinion of housing estates is as poor as his opinion of package holidays. Martin and I have been thankful to experience both.

"Why don't you have a look at it on your way home? You'd only have to make a small detour. I'll explain where it is."

We let him explain in minute detail and promise to take a look. It is the line of least resistance, a well-written leaf from my mother's book on the best way to handle Oliver Chandler. We know exactly where we shall be moving when Martin's salary takes the necessary leap, and it is not nearer to Durham. Kay and her husband Francis live in Northumberland and we would love to be close to them.

14

I HAVE received what I can only describe as a pathetic letter from Cassandra. In the manner of a little girl, thanking her elders for a present which she knows she does not deserve, she expresses her gratitude to me for consenting to spend a month with them in the summer. I am going to Grutenheim to please Leila, not to do my sister a favour. When has she ever put herself out for me, or indeed for anyone else?

The first time Cassandra came back to Durham after her marriage was to attend my grandfather's funeral. Gérard accompanied her and I contrived to see very little of them during their short stay. Then Cassandra started to return on her own quite frequently, twice, sometimes three times a year. Nobody knew why she came. She would suddenly inform Gérard that she intended to go home for a week and leave almost immediately. Leila said it was as if she took an urgent whim. A telephone call from Leila was sometimes the only warning Mum had that Cassandra was on her way. Was she miserable with her life in Alsace? This did not seem to be the case. She never complained or criticised it in fact she said very little about the Amberle family. she had left behind, but then she had never been one to talk freely about other people or herself, so that was not considered unusual. Leila remained convinced that all was well with her son's marriage. Although Gérard had occasionally expressed regret about not having children, Cassandra did not appear to mind one way or the other. There was no pressure put upon them to have a family: Leila and Lucien had two grandchildren already, produced by Jean-Michel and Gabrielle in Marseilles.

My mother always welcomed Cassandra warmly and asked no searching questions. Dad was cooler towards her. He was affronted by her coming alone and invariably greeted her by asking how long she intended to stay this time. He had no reservations about asking questions, awkward or otherwise, and most of them were about Gérard. How was he? How was the business? No sign of a family vet? Cassandra answered shortly, yet equably. The only sign that she might have minded was that she began to visit Durham when my father was away.

"I can't imagine what she does with herself all day," Mum said to me the last time Cassandra was over here. "She's not in the least interested in anything I do. If I take her to one of the shops, she drifts around it looking at the merchandise, but hasn't anything worthwhile to say about it — only whether it would or wouldn't suit her, as if we buy exclusively with someone like her in mind. She's become the perfect parasite, feeding off her husband's family and contributing nothing. When I visit them, I'm ashamed to see how little Cassandra does and how much Leila and everyone else does for her. Admittedly, Leila herself never took any interest in the business, but at least she has pulled her weight as a wife and mother — not to mention a dutiful daughter-in-law. Marie-Louise didn't make things as easy for her as she is doing for Cassandra."

When I tell Martin's mother about our

proposed trip to Alsace, she offers generously to keep the children until Martin comes across, so that I may have a fortnight on my own for what she terms a well-deserved rest.

"It'll do you good," she urges, "and you'll be able to have a lovely time, just you and your sister."

I protest quickly. "Oh no, I must have the children with me, overcome with a sense of panic at the thought of going alone. She looks offended, as if she believes I do not trust her to look after Alice and Sebastian. I am at a loss to explain my reasons for wanting them with me: they will be my safeguard, my anchor, my security against being hurt all over again; they will be the lure that will bring Martin over to me. I have not been far away from him since our fortuitous reunion, and the closer the holiday comes the less easy I am about going without him. I am frightened that my love for Gérard will once more rise to engulf me with its inexplicable power to put all other loves in the shade, and I am apprehensive that my sister, without apparently doing anything, will once more have a profound effect on my life.

"It's very kind of you to offer," I say to Mrs Proudfoot. "Perhaps we could leave them with you next year, while Martin and I take a short holiday together."

"Of course," she answers, disappointed.

Martin makes all the arrangements for our journey and takes us to the airport. The children are excited and happy to be going. I feel myself becoming excited too and pretend that it is at the thought of being in beautiful Alsace again, but nevertheless, I cling to Martin excessively when he kisses me goodbye. He does not realise that I am returning to a place where he has no dominion over me, a place he cannot even conjure up in his mind because he has never been there, only in my mind when he was by no means as important to me as he is now.

"See you in two weeks," he says as we leave him. He watches thoughtfully until we turn out of his sight, and waves from the air terminal roof while we board the plane. The children wave back frantically and call, "Goodbye, Daddy!" I lift my hand and quickly drop it. Go home, Martin.

Leila is there to meet us at the other end of our journey, looking middle-aged and careworn. She has lost weight everywhere except in her extraordinary bust and gives the impression of being top-heavy, almost grotesque: at her age it is not seemly to be so well endowed. She is still supported with sculpted craftsmanship, for comfort's sake, I suppose. She kisses and hugs the children and is obviously delighted to see us. I recall the other time when I arrived with Roddy, and am filled with affection and gratitude.

It becomes apparent on the long journey to Grutenheim that Leila has forgotten her Englishness. She has given up the drawn out and perverse struggle to preserve it. What was the point, after all? When she speaks to Alice and Sebastian her English sounds awkward, more like her second language than her first.

"Your children don't take after you, Jan," she observes.

It is true. Alice has a look of my father, Sebastian is a Proudfoot. Neither of them is very fair.

"I'm so glad you've come," she says. "Cassandra had an awful first three months. She was very sick, morning and evening. Now she's feeling better, but her spirits are low. When I was pregnant, I was cheerful and optimistic, weren't you? She was talking about visiting Durham again, but we didn't think she should make the journey on her own — that was why I asked you to come, but it wasn't the only reason: I wanted to see you here again." She smiled at me. "You and the children will cheer Cassandra up."

"Can't Gérard do that?" I ask with a trace of acidity.

"He's away. In California of all places, seeing how they do things over there."

The sun-drenched countryside becomes bleak. The roar of the traffic on the busy trunk road grows loud and intolerable.

"He'll be back next week," she says. "Lucien misses him."

Lucien, not Cassandra, I note.

"Seb's going to be sick," Alice informs us in a matter-of-fact voice, moving well away from him into the corner of the back seat. Hastily, I hand him a plastic carrier bag from a supply in my huge handbag. Immediately, he throws up into it and then sits holding the bag carefully, his face white, his eyes full of misery.

"All right now, darling?" I enquire.

He nods.

"It's too hot," Alice complains. "I might be sick in a minute."

I inspect her over my shoulder. She looks perfectly well. She is never sick in the car, she is just being awkward.

"We're nearly there," I inform them cheerfully.

"You always say that," Alice states, unconvinced. "When will we see some storks? Uncle Roddy said we would see some storks."

"We'll take them to the stork conservation park at Hunawihr," Leila says.

Cassandra is obviously and touchingly pleased to see us. She embraces me in the thorough French style and when she steps back there are tears in her eyes. I am embarrassed. It is not like her to be demonstrative and I put it down to the fact that she is five months pregnant. She kisses the children and they cling to her hands, just like Roddy used to do. She proceeds to ignore them, addressing herself to me while they gaze up at her in adoration. She asks after our parents and Grandma Harris, then she remembers to enquire if Martin is well.

"You look positively blooming," I tell her.

She grimaces. "I am now. The first three months were awful. I thought I was going to sick-up the baby."

Alice is appalled. "Can you do that?" she asks, wide-eyed.

This causes amusement and Alice is relieved to hear that Auntie Cassie was being ridiculous. Nevertheless, the remark has given Alice food for thought. She keeps glancing at Cassandra's rounded stomach and then up at her face, as if she is waiting for enlightenment.

"We'll leave the luggage for Lucien," Leila says. "Let's go and have a nice cup of tea." She has not lost all her Englishness, after all.

I start to walk across to the family house, then realise that I am going in the wrong direction — Leila is going to make tea in her own home. As we follow her over the courtyard I am overcome with the sadness of change. The last time I was here, Marie-Louise and Mathias were alive. Now I enter their kitchen to find it altered almost beyond recognition, with contemporary pine furniture and matching units.

Alice and Sebastian are given a refreshing cold drink and then sent out to explore, with strict instructions not to venture outside the courtyard into the tortuously narrow streets of the village, where lorries have to negotiate blind corners and cars and tractors have no room to squeeze past them. Cassandra, Leila and I take our tea into the living-room which overlooks sweeping green rows of vines. While we are talking, I notice a curious thing: every now and again one of them addresses a remark to me in English. I am made to feel like a foreign visitor — which I am, of course.

"Your French has improved dramatically," I remark to Cassandra, peeved.

She smiles enigmatically.

Leila says proudly, "Yes, she's really worked at it."

"I've got nothing else to do," Cassandra replies without a trace of shame.

I glance at Leila, ready to indicate sympathy for her on account of my sister's indolence. She is neither expecting nor wanting sympathy and our eyes do not communicate. I am made to feel even more of a stranger. Leila's expression as she regards her *belle-fille* is one of fond satisfaction.

I observe that Cassandra is as she has always been, softly radiant like the surface of a mill pond catching the glow of late evening sunlight; a very still pond with dark, unknown depths. One is drawn by her calm beauty, yet curiously repelled from intimacy. To disturb her watchful serenity would be destructive in the same way as the surface of the pond would shimmer and break up at the dropping of a pebble, before settling down once more upon its secret life. Her blue eyes, so like my own, return my critical appraisal.

"I'm glad you've come, Jan," she says slowly and seriously. "It'll be a relief not to have to look at everything for you."

"What on earth do you mean?"

She shrugs and smiles with a hint of apology. "You've always loved it here. I knew you would come back, eventually."

Lucien enters with Alice and Sebastian. He looks much the same as he has always done, apart from thinning hair and a thickening waistline. He is an older version of Gérard. My eyes light up appreciatively.

"How are you, Jan?" he asks. "It's

wonderful to have you back after so long."

"It's wonderful to be back," I say as we exchange kisses.

"I've taken the luggage up to the apartment," he says.

"I'll come and help you unpack, shall I?" Leila offers. "I can put the children's things away for you."

"I'll see you at dinner, Jan," my sister says. "I'm going to lie down for an hour. My blood pressure is rather high, which means I have to rest a lot. It's an awful bore." Sleek and languid, like a cosseted pet cat, she goes to seek her favourite god, indulgent Morpheus.

Martin telephones that evening when we are in the middle of dinner, to make sure that we have arrived safely. It is a short call because Martin is one of those people who detest the telephone and can never find anything to say to someone they cannot see, and I am not in the mood to help him out. The conversation peters out unsatisfactorily, and after assuring him once again that we have had a good journey and everything is well, there is nothing left to say but goodbye. I return to the table feeling unsettled and wondering what I should have said to him. I know that Martin will be experiencing exactly the same sense of dissatisfaction, but now that our voices have given up the attempt to bridge the distance, our minds are having no difficulty in communicating: he is already feeling lonely; he will find two weeks a long time. My mother telephones about an hour later, knowing that by that time only the dishwasher will be employed, and talks incessantly, first to me, then to Cassandra, and last and for the longest time, to Leila. We are not surprised to learn that Dad is away. Mum's telephone conversations are lengthiest during his absences. Just when we are considering the desirability of going to bed, the telephone rings yet again. Lucien gets up to answer it with a smile towards Cassandra. It is as he has conjectured, Gérard for his wife. While Cassandra is in the hall speaking to her husband, Leila and I continue our conversation about Alice and Sebastian. Cassandra returns and takes her place in the corner of the sofa, putting her feet up.

"He'll be home on Friday," she says to

no one in particular.

"Did you tell him that Jan and the children have arrived?" Leila asks.

"Of course.

There is a short silence, then Leila says to me, "He'll be looking forward to seeing you."

I wish he had said so himself. If he had, surely Cassandra would have passed on the message.

"I think I'll be going to bed," I say dully, making a move. "It's been a long day. Travelling with the children is always tiring. They are either overexcited or moaning about being fed up with the journey."

In the warm dusk, I cross the shadowed courtyard with its smell of freshly watered geraniums and slowly climb the stone steps to the balcony. Gérard is with me, his arm around me; we are moving as one, our minds centred on our love. I open the apartment door and I am alone again. The light is on in the passage so that the children will not be nervous if they wake. Like the small house once occupied by the old couple, the apartment is not the same as it used to be: it has been redecorated and much of the ghastly old furniture has been replaced by commonplace and inexpensive modernity. It has acquired an atmosphere of anonymity. Too many strangers make use of it during the course of each year. Groups of people come and go and all they leave behind are half-packets of soap powder, coffee, sugar, and if they are British, tea and sticky-topped bottles of tomato ketchup, plus black plastic sacks full of empty packets of convenience foods. All this is quickly disposed of within an hour of their departure, the place is thoroughly cleaned by a woman from the village and by late afternoon another group of people arrives, with sheets, towels, and, if they are British, wrong sized pillow cases, to begin a holiday in rural France and journey along the Route du Vin, sampling the produce.

I enter the bedroom which years ago Cassandra and I used to call our own. Alice and Sebastian are asleep in the twin beds. Nearer to the door, Alice, in pink pyjamas, is lying face down like a stranded star fish on top of the blankets, her arms and legs outflung, her long brown hair fanned out over the plump, square pillow. Only the very top of Sebastian's head can be seen. I gently turn back the covers to take a look at him. He is far too hot, his brow sweaty and his hair quite damp. I pull the blankets off and leave him with only the sheet for covering.

My double bed next door looks uninvitingly empty. When I eventually fall asleep, it is to dream confusingly of Gérard and Martin. I wake up expecting to find the latter beside me, only to be disappointed.

15

"THERE'S something I've got to tell you, Jan, before Gérard returns."

My children are playing contentedly at the edge of the lake. I take my eyes from them and turn towards Cassandra. Immediately, I am assailed by a strong sense of *déjà-vu*. She is sitting in the same place as she was sitting all those years ago, when I was watching the lake for a boat containing Mum, Roddy and Leila. She has a book open in her hand, as she had then, and is regarding me from beneath the brim of a protective straw hat; but she is not reclining on the ground. She is sitting on a light-weight, canvas and metal seat, the ubiquitous kind that folds flat and travels in the boots of cars, and her pretty plumpness is emphasised by her pregnancy.

She is going to tell me something important, something I do not want to hear. Drawn by a dreadful compulsion, I walk across the path towards her and sit very still on the grass beside the low seat, watching Alice and Sebastian.

"The baby isn't Gérard's," my sister says without emotion.

My head snaps round. I stare at her, aghast. She returns my stare. The moment seems endless, then she smiles, just slightly. Her sour amusement is for my expression of incredulity, not her predicament.

"Does Gérard know?"

The smile vanishes, the voluptuous mouth droops. "No! Absolutely no one knows, Jan. Only you."

"And the father? Who is the father?"

She gazes past me, out over the crowded water of the sparkling lake to the tree-clad hills encircling it. Tears fill her eyes. People are passing on the nearby path. They are happy and apparently carefree, intent only on having an enjoyable day. I envy them.

"I'll never tell you that, Jan. Never!"

The brightness of the day is spoilt. The holiday has become a prison sentence. I am sorry that I ever allowed Leila to persuade me to come. Since our arrival I have been anticipating meeting Gérard again with a mixture of pleasure and apprehension. The pain of losing him has long since dulled, and my passionate love has become a gentler emotion, a tender yearning for what might have been. I could have been contented just to be smiled upon by him with affection and trust. Now I do not want to see him. Cassandra has not lost the knack of ruining everything for me with a few words.

"You don't intend leaving Gérard for the baby's father, then?"

"There's no question of that," she states with flat finality.

"Is he married?"

She frowns with displeasure. "I'm not going to talk about him, Jan. Forget him! I only wish I could." She takes a delicately embroidered handkerchief from her skirt pocket and wipes the tears from her eyes in a fastidious gesture reminiscent of when she was a little girl.

"Why did you have to tell me?" I complain, aggrieved and suddenly suspicious, although I do not know why I should be.

She ceases to contemplate the far shore of the lake and looks into my eyes; a steady look, holding an expression I am unable to fathom. She is silently telling me something. I am mesmerised while I work out what it can be. All at once, I know. From now on, my love for Gérard will undergo another change: it will be tempered by pity. Inexorably, the first emotion will transmute into the second and already I sense the process starting. In a desperate and forlorn attempt to halt its progress, I scramble to my feet and join Alice and Sebastian at the waters edge.

"Can we go in a boat again?" Alice asks.

"May we," I correct her automatically. "No, we'll be going back soon. We'll come again when Daddy's here."

As before, Martin has slipped into the background of my consciousness. "What about Martin?" Cassandra had enquired in the past. Suddenly, I am afraid for him. I want to keep him away from this woman who sits and watches and waits for an unguarded moment in order to wreak destruction. I experience a poignant tenderness for my husband which is tinged with guilt. Sebastian is tipping water from his plastic bucket over his tiny sun-browned toes and smiling with pleasure.

Martin's son, Martin's smile.

Cassandra will never be able to look at her child and see her husband in him. She will see her lover, constantly. She took Gérard away from me only to cheat him. Angry and bitter, I turn my head to observe her. With the brim of her hat hiding most of her face, she appears to be engrossed in her book. The old emotions of jealousy and distrust well up in me. I utterly dislike her.

Alice throws down her spade and accidentally hits me on the instep.

"That hurt," I cry irritably and smack her thin arm, hard, as if I am exacting revenge on Cassandra's soft flesh.

"Ouch! I didn't mean to do it!" she yells, her eyes blazing at me in anger.

"Be more careful," I warn her. Cassandra has robbed my day of the sun, but must I tear it from the sky for everybody else? I am contrite. "Would you like an ice-cream?" I ask the children and we set off hand in hand along the perimeter of the lake towards the noisy crowds around the cafés and landing stages.

"What about Auntie Cassie?" Sebastian asks, looking up at me with an expression of concern for my forgetfulness.

What about her? I think ungraciously.

Alice calls back over her shoulder, "Would you like an ice-cream, Auntie Cassie?"

"It will melt by the time we walk back with it," I say, gripping her hand.

When one is chosen to share a disagreeable secret, it is not a favour. Any bond that exists between the chooser and the chosen becomes strained, perhaps to breaking point. Not only am I shocked to know that Cassandra has, or has had, a lover, I resent the knowledge. It is as if she has implicated me in her misdemeanour. I shall never be able to look innocently into the faces of those she has injured. Curiously, I share her guilt.

When we return later that afternoon, Leila's concern for Cassandra's health makes me wonder, uncomfortably, if she would be so solicitous if she were aware that she is not related to the unborn baby, regarded by everyone as so precious.

"You haven't walked too far, I hope, Cassie?"

"I haven't walked at all, Leila," Cassandra answers coolly. "I didn't even drive, Jan did. Now I'm going to have a refreshing shower."

"Jean-Michel telephoned," Leila says. "They are arriving on Saturday for two or three days. Do you mind having them in the family house? Or perhaps you'd prefer Jan and the children to move in with you and let them have the apartment?"

"I suppose I can put up with Gabrielle if it's only for a couple of days," Cassandra concedes without enthusiasm.

"Cassie and Gabrielle are so different," Leila explains to me apologetically, as if it is her fault.

I take the large plastic cool box from the boot of the car and go up to the apartment, leaving the children to play in the courtyard until their tea-time. While I am washing up the picnic things, I wonder about the identity of the baby's father. Who can he be? The fact that nobody seems to have the least suspicion that it is not Gérard brings me to the conclusion that the affair has not been a local one. Have I discovered the reason for Cassandra's frequent trips to Durham? My mother had wondered what she did with herself when she was left on her own all day. Counting back the months to her last visit, I am sure I know the answer. Cassandra had never brought her friends home, so it is possible that her lover is someone she has known for a long time, well before her marriage.

After dinner that night, when I am alone with her, I say firmly, "Cassie, I'm going to tell Martin about the baby." I expect her to object, instead she answers,

"I thought you might. Martin is to you as you are to me — the other dragon."

"The other dragon?"

"Yes. Individually they are perfect ornaments, but as book-ends one is useless without the other. I've always needed to know that you were available for support, Jan, just as you've always needed Martin. It's true, isn't it?"

"Yes, it's true," I admit. "That I need Martin, I mean. You've never seemed to need anyone, least of all me. Half the time we're more like strangers than sisters."

She is astonished. "No, we're not! How can you say that? I know you better than I know anyone else in the world." She sounds alarmed, as if I am taking away something upon which she has always depended, a certainty that I feel the same way about her.

The inexplicable urge to cosset and protect her overcomes my dislike. I have to reassure her.

"You can rely on me, Cassie, I promise. It would make things easier if you confided in people a bit more.

"If you mean, tell them the name of the baby's father, I won't!"

"No, I didn't mean that. What time are you expecting Gérard tomorrow?"

"About three o'clock."

"Don't you think you ought to confess to him?"

I receive another steady look from her wide, unblinking blue eyes. This time she appears to be asking herself why I have posed that particular question, then she says, "What would it achieve, apart from easing my conscience?"

It would ease mine, I think. I decide to be away all the next afternoon. I take the children into Colmar and we do not return until their bed-time. The first person I see when we get back is Gérard. He and Lucien are standing next to the pump at the entrance to the Amberlé *caves.* They are in animated discussion, judging by the dramatic dialogue of their hands.

As we leave the car, Gérard calls, "Hello, Jan! Hello, kids!" He says something to his father, then strides across to us and I am embraced in a brotherly fashion, warmly and briskly. He expresses his delight at seeing us and remarks how well I look and how much the children have grown since he last saw them in Durham. He is determinedly bright and cheerful, and I reply in a similar fashion.

"I'm happy to be here," I tell him. Two days ago that would have been true.

"When is Martin coming?"

"Not for another week."

"You'll have some friends to play with tomorrow," he informs Alice and Sebastian. "Candice and Armand will be here."

He turns back to continue his conversation with his father and I take the children up to the apartment. The crucial meeting is over. Gérard is the same as I remember him: lean and handsome, with the easy charm of a man who is aware that he is attractive to women. It is hateful to know something that would rob him of

267

that agreeable conceit. I send Alice across the courtyard with the various items of shopping that Cassandra requested from Colmar. Alice returns with a message for me.

"Auntie Cassie says you're to have dinner with her and Uncle Gérard."

I am surprised. I had taken it for granted that the whole family would be eating together. In Gérard's absence, Cassandra and I have been having dinner with Leila and Lucien in their home. All I had expected to change was the venue, simply because the family house has the larger dining-room and table.

"Auntie Cassie says she wouldn't mind some help."

"My goodness, that's a surprise!" The hint of sarcasm is lost on my eight-year-old. "I expect she's worn out with all the cooking."

"Yes. Uncle Gérard is kissing her happy again."

"Kissing her happy again?"

"That's what he said, when I asked him."

Desolately I imagine the scene. There is Cassandra who deserves to be miserable, and Gérard who does not deserve to be made miserable. She is unhappy about something and he, having not the least idea what it is, cannot bear to see it. He is coaxing and petting her until she smiles and graciously surrenders. Having been loved by him, I imagine the scene all too vividly; even the feel of his exploratory hands and the delicious sensation of relaxing and softening to his caresses. Cassandra, who confessed to a fear of being treated roughly, will have no fear of her husband's loving.

I send a note back with Alice, which says, "I would not dream of intruding on Gérard's first evening back. Enjoy your dinner *tête-à-tête*. Love, Jan."

Ten minutes later, Cassandra is standing beneath the balcony, imperiously calling my name. When I appear above her, leaning out over the wrought-iron rail and the long boxes of mauve geraniums, she says,

"You've got to come. The *traiteur* has already delivered the *dîner pour trois*." She does not give me a chance to reply, but turns and walks back to her house.

"Oh, hell!" I mutter. Why did she not ask Leila and Lucien as well and get the hard-working *traiteur* to conjure up a *dîner pour cinq?*

I give the children their supper and, while they are eating it, shower and dress for the evening. I am nervous and my stomach does not feel settled enough to do justice to the *traiteur's* culinary art. All I have to do is avoid mentioning the baby and pretend that Gérard and I have never been more to one another then fond in-laws. Will that be easy? I want Martin. I should never have come without him. Correction! I should never have come at all.

I go to see how the children are getting on. "Why haven't you eaten that?" I ask Sebastian, who has left half his first course in favour of his *tarte aux abricots.*

"It was yukky," he says, and they both giggle.

"There's nothing wrong with it. If I'd been here, I wouldn't have let you eat that tart."

He takes a big bite, in case I intend to make a snatch for it.

"Can I, I mean may I, have some more water?" Alice asks. "That one's empty."

I heave another two-litre plastic bottle

from the refrigerator and struggle to loosen the cap. It is tempting just to turn on the tap, but the water would be tepid and there is nothing so revolting as drinking tepid water. As I tip the gigantic bottle over the small glass, the water cascades over the sides. I wish they would make the holes in the bottles a bit smaller.

"You've made a mess," Alice points out smugly.

"It's only water," I remark irritably, going to fetch a cloth.

Here I am, where I least want to be! Pushing food round my plate between every difficult mouthful and pushing words round my brain between every difficult utterance. I am so anxious to behave in a normal manner — that is, the manner of a delighted guest who has nothing on her mind but enjoyment of the food and pleasure in the company — that I sound, to my own ears at any rate, slightly inebriated. I am laughing too much — a short, nervous laugh at every commonplace remark. I take a generous swig of wine, hoping it will ease my agitation, and pray that Martin will telephone as he usually does when we are in the middle of dinner. Martin does not. He has learnt to wait until later in the evening — much later!

Cassandra's health is under discussion.

"I hope you've been resting, like the doctor ordered, *chérie*," Gérard says fondly, regarding his wife with a look of tender concern; such a look as I have seen in my sister's eyes for nobody.

She answers that of course she has and I say exactly the same thing, inaudibly and with sarcastic emphasis. Quickly, Gérard turns to me, taking me by surprise so that instantly I have to recall what expression I am wearing and change it to one of thoughtful solicitude.

"Did you have high blood pressure when you were pregnant, Jan?"

"No, I was disgustingly healthy." I am amazed to hear a note of regret in my voice for something for which I had cause to be immensely grateful.

Cassandra asks me doubtfully if I am enjoying the fish. I assure her that it is very good and take a large mouthful to demonstrate that enjoyment. It refuses to go down my throat which has become alarmingly constricted, and I hold out my glass for more water. Obligingly, Gérard fills it. This is my first opportunity to observe Cassandra and Gérard alone in their own home — alone but for myself, of course — and I am keeping a low profile. He is warm and attentive towards her; she is cool and accepting. He is besotted and she is clever enough to keep him that way. Cassandra has always known which side her bread is buttered. The impression I am forming is that she quenches his desire with languid supplication, but never offers herself before he requests. He is another victim of the power of selfishness that lies active beneath her deceptively dormant nature.

Even as I wonder what Gérard's reaction would be if she told him about her lover, I know. His hurt and outrage would subside beneath a paramount urge to comfort and protect her. Some people may be forgiven anything. My sister is one of those people. I might have forgiven her myself had her marriage been an unqualified success, for it would have justified her poaching. To her initial betrayal of me. she has added the betrayal of her husband; the man I loved — still love. There was a time when he felt the same way about me, I am sure of it. I can still see that love in his eyes when he addresses me, but it is suppressed by an irresistible infatuation for Cassandra. Watching him gently take her hand to express how glad he is to be back with her, I yearn to be similarly favoured. She smiles at him, then looks past him at me, the smile lingering in her eyes, satisfied yet without triumph. Hastily, I glance down at my plate, experiencing a painful stab of jealousy.

"Gabrielle and Jean-Michel will be here by lunch-time," she tells Gérard. "And those dreadfully behaved children, of course. They are not a bit like Alice and Sebastian, Jan. They are allowed to do exactly as they please."

"We'll be firmer with ours," Gérard boasts in eager anticipation.

"Everybody says that," I remark drily.

Gérard chuckles, leaning back in his chair, relaxed and confident. "I intend to be the perfect father, strict but kind. With a perfect mother as well, think what the offspring will be like."

"Odiously ordinary, I shouldn't wonder," Cassandra says with ease. We do not look at one another. "Shall I take your plates? There's a delicious sweet to follow."

"Let me," I offer and I am on my feet, gathering up the plates and dashing from the room before anyone can gainsay me.

After loitering around the kitchen for a few minutes of reprieve, I return bearing the confection of fresh pineapple and ice-cream.

Gérard observes with amusement, "I'd forgotten what a live wire you are, Jan. It's no wonder you stay so slim." And when I sit down opposite him, he adds with what sounds like sincerity, "It's great to have you here. Cassie has missed you so much."

I glance at her in some surprise.

"Jan won't believe that," she says, and I am left wondering whether or not I should.

An hour later, when the coffee pot has been emptied and I am attempting to leave, against my sister's inclination to detain me despite her husband's politely concealed wish to the contrary, Martin telephones. I escape, gladly. The thought of Cassandra allowing her husband to make love to her later, as he clearly intends to do, when she is bearing another man's child, is utterly distasteful. That she will allow it, I have no doubt, yet she left the lover in London because she was disgusted by his apparent willingness to share her favours.

Before I lift the receiver, I shut the door firmly upon Cassandra and Gérard.

"Hello, Jan. How are you, darling? How's the kids?"

"Oh, Martin!"

"What's wrong? Are you crying?"

"No, not really. I miss you."

Martin breathes an audible sigh of relief. "Is that all? You had me worried, I thought there had been an accident. If it comes to that, I miss you. Only another week, Jan."

16

SOME people are so practical and unromantic that they bring order and sense to the charged emotions of others. Gabrielle turned out to be just such a person. I soon discover that I like her, despite the fact that behind a semblance of goodwill as becomes sisters-in-law, she and Cassandra are at polite daggers-drawn.

The only other time I have met Gabrielle was at Cassandra's wedding and I was not in a suitable state of mind to pay much attention to anyone there other than the principals, much less bother to assess anyone for nuances of character. All I remember of Gabrielle is that Leila had referred to her as a *femme fatale* and that she wore elaborate and excessive make-up, presumably to aid her efforts to be fascinating to every man who came within her orbit. That was eleven years ago. Now she is all too aware of what being fascinating to the opposite sex may achieve for a woman and has prudently given up practising the dangerous art, recovering a tardy affinity with her own sex.

Every day the courtyard is busy with the coming and going of cars containing people interested in Lucien's wine, either knowledgeable purchasers or itinerant samplers. For many years now, Lucien has employed a young woman from the village to help him and Gérard with the *dégustation* side of the business. Nobody else takes much notice of the constant traffic. However, when a car bearing relatives or friends pulls into the courtyard it is quickly surrounded by members of the family, who appear as if at a secret signal. When Jean-Michel, Gabrielle and the two children arrive, we all emerge into the bright sunlight, smiling towards the car as if it has magically borne them to us of its own free will. As the occupants pile out, I am amazed at the change in Gabrielle. There is no trace of *maquillage* on her pretty face to mask the faintly blemished brown skin. Her dark brown eyes are bright, her hair, which is black and glossy, is cut very short round her tiny ears, which stick out a little, but not unbecomingly. She is dressed like the rest of the family in a cotton, sleeveless top, faded cotton shorts and flat, scuffed sandals. I do not think she is wearing any underclothes. She appears to be an unadorned product of nature, well-scrubbed and healthy, and her once spare figure has thickened a little with her pregnancies. Jean-Michel, on whom the birth of two children has had no effect, is looking much the same as ever and I reflect how unfair life can be to women who only do what nature expects of them — prolong the human race — and in doing so are often transformed from siren to matron. Gabrielle does not merely allow herself to be hugged and kissed as Cassandra does, but accomplishes her own share of hugging and kissing, entering into the spirit of the occasion. Leila and Lucien are delighted to see them all, especially the children, who match the enthusiasm of the grandparents' welcome with excited chatter. The little boy, Armand, is seven, the little girl, Candice, is six. All of them are deeply tanned by the Mediterranean sun.

Alice and Sebastian, who have overheard their Aunt Cassandra complaining about the unruliness of these children, hang back at first, warily watching for signs of uncontrollable wildness, but as Candice and Armand are eager to make friends with them and are not shy or inhibited in any way, they are soon captivated and curious. Alice confesses to me later that she was embarrassed because her French is so poor compared with theirs, until she realised that her English is far better!

"It's a wonder Cassie isn't fatter, the way she sits around so much," Gabrielle says to me the next day, when we are in the loft above the apartment, hanging up our washing in the dusty heat. The sunlight is pouring through the apertures beneath the eaves in slanting funnels towards our feet.

"Cassie isn't fat," I protest loyally.

"She will be. Has she always had so little energy? She should go for long walks or swim. It would be good for her."

"Her blood pressure is too high. She has to rest," I explain.

"She likes to rest," Gabrielle amends with a smile. "When the baby is born, Leila will have all the work to do, you wait and see."

I fear she is right, but I do not say so.

The last thing I want to do is discuss the baby's birth. The voices of our children are heard clearly from the courtyard. They are making small difficulty of the language barrier. I recall how well Roddy had communicated with other children, whereas with adults who spoke no English he was inarticulate and stubbornly obtuse.

"You were going to marry Gérard, weren't you?"

I am taken by surprise. Has Leila told her that? I am annoyed. Before I can deny it, she says,

"I wish you had. I get on so much better with you than with your sister. I think she disapproves of me, but I don't know why. Perhaps it's because Jean-Michel and I aren't married."

"Cassie doesn't mind that."

Gabrielle shrugs. "It makes no difference." She bends down to take another article from the basket. "I prefer people who talk a lot and think little. They are often irritating, but harmless, don't you think?"

Does that mean she thinks I am talkative and empty-headed? I hope not. I am encouraged by her forthrightness to be the same. "Why haven't you and Jean-Michel married?"

"It hasn't seemed necessary. Perhaps we shall one day, who knows?"

We peg up a few more garments, mostly children's things. Gabrielle remarks on the numerous pants, vests and socks that I have washed.

"You must be a glutton for punishment. We don't bother with underwear in the summer." Then she adds, abruptly changing the subject, "It's strange, isn't it? Some women can keep men happy with little more than a smile, others have to work much harder. I'm not the complacent type, are you? I'm too frightened of losing Jean-Michel to another woman."

"Perhaps if you were to marry him, you would feel more secure," I suggest.

"It might make it more difficult for him to leave me, but it wouldn't stop him wanting to go, would it?"

We pick up the empty laundry baskets and leave the loft for the cooler, shuttered rooms of the apartment. I make coffee and we spend half-an-hour getting to know one another better and, in doing so, our mutual family and friends take on a further dimension, as perceived by the other. I am intrigued by this young Frenchwoman, once deplored by Leila as being the wrong type of girl for her fun-loving, irresponsible younger son and now providing their partnership with the stability of prudence and common sense, two qualities which Leila supposed she lacked. Gabrielle is the first person I have met who successfully resists the temptation to be kind to Cassandra, whether or not she deserves it. I am too close to my sister, close in consanguinity not empathy, to be objective about her. Gabrielle supplies that objectivity: she sees things as they are, not as she would like them to be. She is so alarmingly observant that I would not put it past her to guess Cassandra's secret. When she says,

"Your sister doesn't look happy. Perhaps she doesn't want the baby," I have difficulty in hiding my anxiety.

"Cassie doesn't become excited about anything," I explain. "She has an even temperament."

Gabrielle is regarding me with the unabashed stare of her countrymen which is so often interpreted as rudeness by foreigners. She shakes her head and purses her lips. "She boils beneath that smooth skin."

It is my turn to shake my head. "I've never seen her lose her temper."

Gabrielle smiles at my naîveté. "She boils with passion, not temper."

"Passion!"

Gabrielle is amused by my disbelief. "That's why she always gets her own way. Everyone is frightened of turning the pussy-cat into the tiger."

"Except you!" I suggest a little caustically.

She pouts and raises her eyebrows. "I am frightened also. Only a fool would not be."

I laugh, utterly rejecting her words and beginning to revise my opinion of her abilities of observation and objectivity. "Cassandra is placid. She always has been."

"Then I'm wrong," Gabrielle says easily, rising to her feet. "Let's go and see what the kids are doing. Trailing round after Lucien, I expect."

That is exactly what the kids are doing, and Lucien is loving every minute of their boisterous company and incessant, high-pitched questioning.

That evening there is a family meal, children included. We have it in the large house around the heavy, oval oak table where I have sat with my parents, sister and brother on numerous occasions in the past. Leila and Lucien are at either end of the table as they have always been, glowing with happy pride and generous hospitality, which means, in this country, sharing an appreciation of good food and wine. I relax in the cordial atmosphere, giving myself up to the pleasure of indulging a healthy appetite. The room is alive with voluble, excited conversation, punctuated by outbursts of merry laughter and spiced with the aroma of delicious dishes. How can one not take delight in participating in the reunion of a devoted family?

Suddenly, the smile on my face for Sebastian's latest 'Franglais' gem is wiped off by a question from Gabrielle to Gérard.

"Have you decided on any names for the baby yet?"

"Of course," he tells her with a smiling glance at his wife.

"We haven't discussed it," Cassandra contradicts him in a low voice.

"At least we'll agree on second names,"

Gérard says confidently. "Leila if it's a girl and Lucien if it's not."

Momentarily, my eyes meet those of my sister. She has the look of an animal that has no alternative but to turn and face the hunt.

Jean-Michel says, "Perhaps Cassie will want English names. Janine is very nice." And we all laugh at my very English name.

The awkward moment is over. The conversation changes course. Leila puts the cheeses on the table and Alice wrinkles her small nose at the smell of the Munster. Jean-Michel teases her and tries to get her to taste some of it, but without success. I take a piece of fruit and begin eating it with a knife and fork in the prescribed French manner, cutting it with the finicky precision of mindlessness.

Later, lying in bed going over what was said and what was left unsaid, I am unable to recall what kind of fruit I ate. All too soon, Jean-Michel and his family depart for Marseilles. I am left with my sister and her claustrophobic secret. I am counting the days until Martin comes. He will release me from the burden of silence. I spend as much time with Leila as I can and discreetly avoid being on my own with Cassandra, terrified that she will divulge another piece of startling information. Fortunately, now that Gérard is home, she is not so keen to accompany me and the children on our outings. I slip back into the familiar routine of doing the marketing with Leila in the mornings.

I have decided not to tell Martin the truth about Cassandra's baby until after the holiday.

We are sitting at a metal table outside a café in the centre square of a small town, which I am disappointed to find is as uninvitingly scruffy as it was on my last visit, twelve years ago. While Martin studies the map and the children draw in their new pads of squared paper, bought for them in the hope that it will assist them with their hand-writing as it does the local children, I analyse the reasons for my decision. Is it because I do not want to spoil his holiday? He is so thrilled to be here, participating in what for him has always been an unknown and enviable part of my life. He used to listen to me talking about France with the expression of someone listening to fairy stories. Now he is here, sharing the experience with me. Everything is new to him — the people, the scenery, the language, even the food and the different timetable of daily routine. My affection for Alsace is rekindled as I take him round my favourite haunts which invoke for me the insouciant days of bright, youthful summers. Martin and I have stepped into the shoes of my parents. I have a peculiar sensation of role reversal as we follow our own children along the paths I once ran along with my sister and small brother, revelling in the simple enjoyment of fresh, pine-scented air and the freedom to raise voices and kick up heels; scrambling on the crumbly slopes between the closely growing trees and slithering back down again. Perhaps the sandals of Alice and Sebastian are kicking against the same stones and tree roots that my sandals kicked against all those years ago. Why not? Tree roots do not move, neither do stones of their own volition. Walkers, who are infrequent here, melting snow and torrential rain do not shift the larger stones which are partially embedded in the ochre dust and dried pine needles of the winding tracks. These stones stub the toes of the unwary and trip the young children in their headlong exploration, painfully grazing brown knees beneath washed-out shorts.

We are going for many walks in the hills. It is a deliberate policy on my part. It means that Cassandra does not wish to accompany us. Picnics after long car journeys are her favourite things. When we went to Lake Gérardmer two days ago, Cassandra came with us and I made sure that we did not sit in our customary spot which she has spoilt for me. Uncomplaining and unburdened, she followed the rest of us and the picnic paraphernalia to a less secluded place which was nearer the hub of lakeside activity.

Martin folds the map and the children dutifully hand their pads and pencils to him. He puts them into the shoulder bag with his camera. As we are moving away from the café, we are approached by two young Algerian boys who are about the same age as Alice but with an advanced street cunning that makes them seem much older. They are thin and grubby, wearing khaki shirts and shorts which are far too big for them and they are each holding a pile of old-fashioned prints, prim and wishy-washy, carefully torn from an old book. They offer these for a franc each, sidling up to us and urging us to buy with rapid insistence. Martin, who cannot resist children no matter how unattractively opportunistic, gives them two francs and has one of the pictures thrust at him. The pair scamper off, highly delighted, to search for more easy game.

"They were begging," I remark disapprovingly.

"They look as if they need the money," Martin excuses himself, crumpling the dog-earned picture and pushing it in his trouser pocket.

We wander across the square of smooth stone setts to an ornamental fountain which has a low wall surrounding it and a stone column in the centre, topped by a statue with a froth of flowers around its feet. In the murky water swim plump fish of assorted sizes, their colours muted by the deep shade into a sludgy neutral. One fish, much larger and darker than the rest, circles sluggishly and disdainfully. We watch it with fascination. I feel certain that if Alice were to drop her brightly coloured ball into the water, the fish would solemnly return it to her.

"Do you suppose this is the fountain which runs with wine during the wine festival?" Martin wonders. "It looks as if it's still suffering from last year's hangover."

"Shouldn't it be in the sea?" Sebastian asks. "It's too big for that little pond. Who feeds it?"

"I remember that fish," I say incredulously. "I'm sure it's the same one that Uncle Roddy fed with bits of bread when he was a little lad."

"Shall I throw it some of my crisps?" Sebastian asks hopefully.

"No, you'll pollute the water," Martin tells him.

We walk back to find the car down the steep gradient of one of the narrow roads which lead off the main thoroughfare and which are hemmed in from the sunlight by tall houses with flaking stone and meagre paint. There is not a flower-box in sight.

The pavements are stained and dirtied by the passage of many dogs. The bold-eyed urchins appear from a scruffy alleyway and approach us again, waving the pictures and encouraging us to buy them in shrill tones which are more demanding now that there is no one else about. I wave them away, telling them to stop making nuisances of themselves. Belatedly, they recognise us and hurry off, running back into the alley, no doubt fearful that Martin will ask for his money back.

I am glad to get away from the place. I am sorry that I have taken Martin to visit it, but I discover that his impression is not the same as mine and I realise that my disenchantment stems from within me, generating from a vague, disagreeable memory of having been soundly smacked on a previous visit by my father for a crime I had not committed and subsequently hating the world, especially that little town, for the humiliation and awful injustice.

From the moment Martin arrived in Grutenheim, triumphant behind the wheel of our old car, having made the journey by overnight ferry from Hull to Zeebrugge, as we always used to do with my parents, I am able to relax. His tall, physical presence once more close by my side, and his quiet strength of character, give me a wonderful sense of returning to normality after a period of aberration. My husband does not go in for unpleasant surprises, thank goodness.

During his first evening here, at dinner with Cassandra and Gérard, I felt so very normal and secure that I actually set out to be noticed, boldly looking Gérard in the eyes for the first time that summer and laughing in a manner which suggested that I was no longer perturbed by our past intimacy. Gérard marked the change in me and was uneasy. By the end of the evening, I was satisfied that he had once loved me, and by the morning, conversely, Martin was reminded how much I still love him. If I could physically bind Martin to me, I would do so, I am so thankful to have him. That first night, the mood was set for the remainder of the holiday.

I am relieved that I made the decision not to divulge Cassandra's secret to Martin. Whenever the baby is mentioned, he is able to enter into the discussion with unassumed innocence, whereas when I am forced to take part in the conversation I do so with deception and feel ashamed. The happy anticipation of Leila, Lucien and Gérard is painful for me to witness. However, my sister remains amiably undisturbed and I have no idea what she is suffering inside, or indeed if she is suffering at all.

Nobody is a mystery to Martin. He does not delve beneath what people say in order to discover what they really mean. He listens to them with interest, giving them the benefit of judgement by his own standards. Martin only says what he intends to say, sometimes going to great lengths to make himself clearly understood, and he supposes that everybody else does the same. Subtlety to Martin means subtlety in expressing oneself, not in disguising one's true meaning. It follows that he finds Cassandra beautiful and uncomplicated; her calm temperament, allied to a slow grace of movement, is no doubt soothing in comparison with my sudden flashes of irritability and anger, and my buoyant energy which is a reproach to those who have to make way for me.

People must move their feet sharply when I approach with a vacuum cleaner. Usually they get up and go; only Cassandra can be cleaned around without losing her guiltless equanimity. I would rather walk than wait for a bus; Cassandra would not bother to make the journey. I am convinced that Martin, who admires organisation and drive — two qualities he does not possess — would be irritated by Cassandra if he had to live with her. I think I am amused by his evident admiration for her. I think I am!

Most days, Martin, the children and myself are away from morning until evening. I have so many places to take them that two weeks are not nearly enough.

"We can come again next year," he comforts me. "I'll see it all in time."

I cannot share his optimism.

In the mornings before we set off, and in the early evenings before dinner, while I am busy with the children, Martin takes a keen interest in the running of the vineyards. He would be content to potter about with Gérard and Lucien all day, observing and lending a hand, 'getting the feel of the place' as he calls it, but I will not let him tarry. By the time Leila is ready to drive off to a local street market or an out-of-town hypermarket, and Cassandra is making a fresh pot of coffee for the men's return from the vines, I am standing next to the car with the children, ready and waiting to be off on another expedition of escapism.

"Won't you have coffee before you go, Jan?" Cassandra asks me, one morning towards the end of our stay, as the three men make an appearance in the courtyard, amicably talking. My husband is easily distinguishable as an alien: he is able to talk with his hands in his pockets.

"No, I want to reach Munster before lunch-time," I tell her. "I'm going to buy something to take back for Martin's parents." The two-hour lunch break, which would be insupportable back home, is merely a slight inconvenience when regarded as a quaint foreign custom.

"I have a doctor's appointment this afternoon, otherwise I would come with you."

"Never mind," I say with hypocritical regret. "Another time, perhaps."

"Yes, tomorrow would be fine," my

sister says, before turning towards the approaching men. "Leila's gone into Colmar, Lucien. Will you have coffee with us?"

I open the car door and wait until my husband gets the message. He says a cheerful *au revoir* to his companions and joins us.

"We're going swimming," Alice informs him. "Mummy's got your trunks. Seb's going to play miniature golf. He takes ages. People have to overtake him." She rolls her eyes and sighs dramatically at his incompetence.

Sebastian grins and climbs into the car, happy at the thought.

We pull into a makeshift lay-by to consult the map on a quiet road a couple of miles out of Munster. The semicircular patch of rough ground is edged with bushes and small trees. Parked at the other end of it is a large, sedate car with a GB plate, and sitting beside it on brightly patterned nylon-covered seats around a small, collapsible plastic-topped table, are two middle-aged couples enjoying a snack. Martin and I smile an apologetic 'hello' in their direction and then do our best to pretend they are not there, in true insular style, but Alice, less sympathetic to their desire to be invisible to their fellow countrymen, takes in every detail of the group with her sharp eyes.

"They're eating Mr Kipling apple pies," she remarks with amazement, or perhaps it is envy.

It seems a long way to travel to indulge in something one may eat at any time at home.

When we return that evening after a day of unalloyed enjoyment, despite Sebastian's frustratingly painstaking attempts to place the balls in the holes, it is almost seven o'clock. The metal gates are shut, indicating that business for the day is over. I open them to let Martin drive through. As I am fastening them once more, I hear through the open window of her living-room, Cassandra speaking softly and indistinguishably to Gérard. It reminds me that she intends to accompany us tomorrow. When I join Martin and the children at the bottom of the stone steps to the apartment, I say, "Try and persuade Gérard to come with us tomorrow, will you, Martin?"

He gives me an enquiring look, but I have no logical reason to offer for my request. It has been made instinctively.

"He'll probably say he's too busy to take a whole day off."

"Please try!" I insist, following the children onto the balcony. Her husband's presence will protect me from Cassandra. It is very strange that I should think it is me and not my husband who is in need of protection from my sister.

After dinner we discuss where we shall go tomorrow. It transpires that Martin has no need to request Gérard's company, for he has every intention of coming.

"It'll be my last opportunity," he says. "Martin's two weeks have slipped past so quickly, and I haven't been able to spend much time with you."

I am greatly relieved and sleep that night without giving the next day another thought. It will be just another day of pleasure-seeking leisure, with Cassandra's secret tamped down into the back of my mind like an incipient headache that I am determined to ignore.

17

OUR destination is the Ballon d'Alsace. We travel in Gérard's car which is larger than ours, but without Gérard who had to cry off at the last moment. Martin drives, with Cassandra beside him where she will be most comfortable and safe from the children's feet.

At mid-morning we stop to wander round a street market. Martin buys a huge pot of local honey to take home. I buy tomatoes, cheese and a couple of *baguettes* for lunch. Cassandra buys green beans and peaches for dinner that evening. We sit outside a small hotel and order coffee and cool drinks for the children, while we watch the busy life of the streets going on around us. Across the stall-filled square is the village church, a bizarre building made up of fat cubes with a tiled roof, geometrically patterned in red, green and orange. It looks attractive here, squatting beneath the deep blue sky in a blaze of warm sunshine and surrounded by other buildings, amongst them the *Hôtel de Ville* and the *Marie,* all flaunting window-boxes of brightly coloured geraniums. At home it would look absurdly garish. Before the wide steps leading up to its massive, intricately carved door are two young girls in regional costume, consciously posing for photographs. They are dressed in lamp-black head-dresses which flow down their backs and stick out in large wings over their foreheads. They have white blouses, adorned with lavish red embroidery and three-quarter length, full black skirts. They look charming. Alice is quite envious and would move to Alsace tomorrow just to be able to wear these clothes and be photographed by admiring tourists.

We journey on to St Maurice sur Moselle, then start snaking upwards between the thickly forested slopes of the squat hills, until we reach the fragrant meadows above the treeline. After rounding each individual summit, the road falls steeply away to wind down again into the tree-filled valleys where isolated villages nestle, each a cluster of sharply-angled red roofs dominated by a church tower, often red-roofed also.

It is too warm in the car despite the wide-open windows. Our movement is on a constant curve, either to left or right, and is accompanied by the frenzied chirping of crickets in the thick, flower-scented scrub. We reach the dome of the Ballon d'Alsace by lunch-time and, after parking in a secluded spot away from the main parking area, walk across a field to take photographs of each other beneath the sculpture of a skier who is toppling landwards from halfway up an immense pair of vertical stone skis. Then we cross the road to climb up towards the summit on which is an equestrian statue of Joan of Arc, rearing up triumphantly towards heaven, pennant flying. Here again we take photographs, but not of Cassandra, who has elected to remain sitting near the souvenir shop and café.

We return to the car to collect the picnic things and carry them towards the trees to find an ideal spot. We do not have to go far before we are in comfortable isolation in a grassy clearing strewn with large boulders. While I am cutting bread and *saucisson*, Martin is opening a bottle of wine. Cassandra spreads a cloth and places cutlery and plastic plates upon it. We shall drink the wine from the familiar empty mustard glasses, and these are produced from the bottom of the picnic box and set ready. The children are content with paper cups for their fruit juice. They take no interest in the preparations but wander round watching the grasshoppers leap about their sandalled feet, trapping them in their cupped hands and squealing to one another to come and see.

We are munching away contentedly when Cassandra says to me, "I wish you weren't going on Saturday, Jan." There is an expression upon her face which reminds me to remember. Instantly, I am wary. My enjoyment of the present moment ceases.

"I'll be coming to Durham as soon as the baby is old enough to travel on a plane," she says. "Tell Mum and Dad, won't you?"

"Will Gérard be coming with you?" I enquire, hiding my anxiety.

"I don't know. We haven't discussed it."

There are a lot of things they have not discussed. I wonder if they ever will. Does she never have nightmares about having a child who may strongly resemble her lover

303

and be nothing like the Amberlé family? I have had that nightmare, even though I cannot give the baby a face, for I have no idea what the father looks like. Leila peers down into the crib which is festooned with white organdie frills and asks in a puzzled voice, "Who does the baby take after, Jan?" I stand transfixed, terrified to approach the pretty crib. The tiny face remains formless in my imagination.

"Have another glass of wine, Jan," Martin offers. "I'm limited to one as I've been lumbered with the driving."

"I'll drive back. Anyway, we won't be moving off for at least another hour, surely? The children won't want to get back in the car too soon and I want to finish my book."

"Fair enough," he concedes, contentedly refilling his glass. He takes three paperbacks from his camera bag and tosses one to me and another to Cassandra. We swop them wordlessly. Cassandra and I do not have a similar taste in books, but I would not expect my husband to be aware of that.

"I'm just getting to the exciting bit," I inform them happily, easing my back more comfortably against a mossy boulder and swiping at a couple of unidentifiable flying insects in which rural France abounds. Alice and Sebastian come to collect their own books and lie on their stomachs in the shade to read them, head to head.

A murmuring stillness of insect noises settles around us. It is as if we are miles from civilisation. Soon I am engrossed in the world of fiction and will remain there until recalled. I suppose ten minutes pass before Sebastian says he needs the loo.

"So do I," Alice says immediately, jumping to her feet.

"Go together," I tell them on a note of irritability, quickly returning to my book.

"I'll go with them," Cassandra offers, pulling my attention back again. "I'm dying to go myself. Being pregnant has a dire effect on the bladder. Come on, kids, we'll find a convenient bush."

I begin reading again, going back over the last paragraph which has not made sense. Martin shuts his book and leans back against the rock for a siesta.

"Where's Auntie Cassie?" Alice asks me.

I look up and glance around abstractedly. Alice is standing in front of me, Sebastian is kicking a ball a few yards away and Martin is fast asleep.

"I don't know. Wasn't she with you?"

"No, we went behind different bushes," Alice states, disgusted that I should think otherwise. "I came back with Seb. We couldn't see Auntie Cassie."

"She'll be here in a minute," I declare with confidence, starting to read again.

"But that was ages ago, Mum," Alice asserts indignantly.

I look up again, startled. "Ages ago?"

"Yes. Seb's nearly ready for another wee."

The only measure of elapsed time I have is the amount I have read. She is right. Cassandra has been gone for almost two chapters.

"Show me the bush," I command, following her and Sebastian into the sparse woodland which forms the upper reaches of the thick forest.

"I went there," Alice points. "Seb went there and Auntie Cassie went over there, where we couldn't see her."

"Cassie!" I call.

"Auntie Cassie!" the children yell in unison. "Martin!" I shriek.

Coming towards us through the trees, shuffling like an old woman with her hair and clothes in disarray and no shoes upon her feet, is my sister, distraught and wild-eyed, breathing with dry, difficult sobs.

"Get Daddy!" I shout to the children, rushing to her assistance. My God, what have I let happen to her? From the pleasant world of fantasy where horror is only make-believe, I am hurled into the harsh physical world where disaster is only too real. I put my arms around Cassandra, wishing I could pull a shutter upon the day as easily as I closed the covers of my book only minutes earlier.

While Martin waits impatiently at the wheel of the car, drumming his fingers, with Cassandra beside him, white and mute, biting her already bleeding lips, and the children shrink in the back, subdued by what they cannot understand, I race across to the shop to ask for directions to the nearest hospital.

We are halfway to it, locked in the welter of our imaginations, when Cassandra starts to moan dismally, clasping her arms around her body. The children tremble in sympathy. I am tortured by feelings of guilt. Martin could not have been expected to wander off into the trees with her — I should have gone. What has happened to her? I will not let myself explore the possibilities, they are too alarming, too disconsonant with the beauty of the day. While I had gently led her back to the car, Martin searched for her shoes and her attacker. He had found neither.

Driving as fast as the dangerous bends permit, almost too fast at times, impelled by alarm and urgency, Martin asks more than once, with desperation in his voice, "What happened, Cassie?"

Cassandra does not answer him. I do not think she hears. She is submerged in a private world of pain and shock. It is with profound relief that we hand her into the care of the friendly medical staff in the small town hospital. The journey there took twenty-five minutes, but it seemed endless.

Even while Martin and I are discussing in hushed tones who will telephone the dreadful news to Gérard and what we shall tell him, we are informed by a doctor with sympathetic reluctance that Cassandra has miscarried as a result of a brutal assault. Martin makes the difficult telephone call, sees the waiting *gendarme* and then drives the children back to Grutenheim. I sit by my sister's bed, watching her, but not holding her limp hand. She will not let me touch her, just stares at the ceiling, tranquillised into numb misery.

When Gérard arrives, goodness knows how much later, I cannot leave the room and my sister's suffering fast enough, neither can I look her husband in the face. I am sick with culpability and pity for his distress. He thinks he has lost his baby, when in fact he has lost his wife. All the petals have fallen from the crushed flower.

18

THINGS have changed. Less then two years have passed — fifteen months to be exact — and many things have changed.

We did not go to France this summer. Instead we went to the West Coast of Scotland with Kay, Francis and their ten-year-old twin sons. We stayed in a house near the Kyle of Lochalsh, belonging to a cousin of Kay who is working in Milan. We had a most enjoyable time. Kay and I are fortunate in that our husbands like one another and do not resent our closeness. One thing I discovered while we were there was that I have become neurotic about people wandering off in isolated places. A couple of times I was actually reduced to tears when my frantic shouts across a wild expanse of heather did not immediately bring the children into view. Fond friends make generous allowances for irritating behaviour, especially when they are aware of its cause, and even I was able to see the funny side of my strongly awakened herd instinct when the times came, as they inevitably did despite stoic endurance, to pick one's way amongst the heather searching for privacy.

"We'll shout to each other, Jan," Francis said reassuringly on one occasion, as we were fanning out from the car. "Keep in touch by voice, don't you know."

We had not been invited to Grutenheim, which was just as well, because I had no intention of going. I cannot conceive a circumstance that would entice me back. Cassandra has taken to writing to me. She unburdens herself to me in letters as she has never done in speech. Her correspondence is erratic and brief. She writes only when she is suffering from deep despondency. I answer her quickly with long, light-hearted letters meant to cheer her up and which she may read to Gérard and his parents. Cassandra's letters I can show to no one. I never did tell Martin that the baby was not Gérard's. I intended to do so on the ferry as we were returning from Alsace, but I did not. I could not bear to diminish regret for that lost life. It is enough that I should know the

311

problems that the traumatic stillbirth has solved. Cassandra's grief is intense: she has lost an irreplaceable and precious love-gift. Her letters reveal how much she still yearns for the giver of that unique gift, but his identity remains a mystery to me.

Mum and I have long discussions about Cassandra, when Mum does most of the conjecturing and I do most of the listening.

"Cassie appears to be more contented in Grutenheim now," she observes optimistically. "The miscarriage seems to have brought her and Gérard closer together. When she's completely recovered from that dreadful attack, I'm sure she'll want another baby. She's still young, there's plenty of time. Leila says she doesn't talk continually about coming home any more. When you consider how often she used to come! The last time I phoned, I asked her if she had any plans for a holiday, thinking a change would do her good, but she said she doesn't feel like making plans. It's understandable. When I think of all the plans they had for that baby, it's very sad."

Cassandra has never talked about the attack, nor discussed it in her letters to me, referring to it only obliquely. She has been encouraged to talk about it as a way of putting it into perspective when set against the many positive aspects of her life — as others see it, that is: a happy marriage, two supportive families, good health and considerable beauty. All anyone knows is that the assailants were two youngish men wearing shorts and T-shirts and that they spoke monosyllabically in French with foreign accents which Cassandra was unable to place. The medical evidence was that they had both abused her, taking it in turns to stifle her cries. Rape is a word that not one of us has used!

Unfortunately, my mother is wrong: Cassandra is not reconciled to life in Grutenheim, neither has the tragedy brought her and Gérard closer together. "I don't want his baby," she tells me in a letter. "He is patient and tender and his parents continue to spoil me with kindness. They hope that a time will come when I shall forget. I don't struggle against Gérard's loving, nevertheless, I am as frightened and subdued by his gentleness as I was by the brutality of those beasts. I lie, holding myself very still as I did then, screaming inside. I can't go on much longer, Jan. I am sick of living in pretence. What shall I do? I can't come to Durham. Mum and Dad are the same as Leila and Lucien, sympathising with me for all the wrong reasons and confident that everything will turn out fine in the end. If only they knew!"

I am concerned and worried about her, yet despite everything that has happened to her, deep down I am still jealous of all the attention she is receiving, the constant solicitude that surrounds her and, above all her possession of Gérard's love.

I was impatient with her in my last letter, telling her that she must pull herself together, forget her lover who has probably forgotten her, stop being utterly selfish and make amends to Gérard by concentrating on making him happy.

That was four months ago. I have not heard from her since.

My father,who is never ill, has become ill; not dramatically and acutely, but incipiently and irksomely. He is resentfully bad-tempered and must apportion blame, so he has turned upon the healthy and seems positively to dislike us all for our good fortune in not being sick. "If only he would learn to live with it," Mum laments. She is talking about his heart, that organ which has had the temerity to let him down and now dictates what he can and cannot do! "If he is sensible, the doctor says he has years and years to go yet. He stalks around the house and garden like a tiger in an unfamiliar landscape and keeps ringing up his office, demanding to know what's going on. It makes life very difficult for them there — after all, he is supposed to have retired. He thinks I should retire as well and stay at home to quarrel with him. Perhaps he'll be able to adapt better when Roddy goes into the business." Roddy will be leaving university in the summer.

What a reversal in the lives of my parents! I can remember when it was Dad who was always out and about, making exciting decisions, coming home only long enough to boast about his achievements and rush off again. Now he has to listen to his wife discussing her business affairs and watch her dash out each morning about her busy day, not knowing what time she will be returning.

"Why don't you try and interest him

in the shops?" I suggest. "Surely you can find something he can organise without too much exertion."

"I could try," she says dubiously.

Mum and I are having a lunch-time sandwich in Corbridge. We have half-an-hour together before returning to the clothes shop she has recently opened here — my shop! She has dropped by today to see how I am getting on and give me advice, but we have spoken more about my father than selling fashion.

Martin has been promoted and the upsurge in our combined fortunes has enabled us to buy a cottage in Northumberland near the grander country home of our friends, Kay and Francis. The children go to school in Hexham with their twin boys and do not come home for lunch, which leaves me more time free to work for Mum. I work school hours, more or less, except in the holidays when life becomes difficult to organise and Martin's parents are put upon more often than I like. If one of the children is poorly, then Mum has to manage without me as best she can, a sacrifice she is only too willing to make for her adored grandchildren.

"How's Roddy?" I ask her in order to divert the conversation from my father.

Mum sighs and frowns. "I don't care for his current girl friend."

I laugh, instantly picturing Uncle Daniel's 'currant woman'. Mum raises her eyebrows at me, affronted by my amusement. I recall Martin being similarly offended.

"Sorry, I just had a funny thought, that's all. What's wrong with Roddy's girl?"

"She's from Birmingham," Mum says.

"Well?"

"She sounds as if she's from Birmingham and what's more she's too clever by half. She runs rings round Roddy. It's not nice for a mother to watch another woman successfully manipulating her son."

"You've always managed to get your own way with Dad," I remind her, smiling.

"Only with craft and cunning. This young lady employs more direct methods. Head-on confrontation is more her style. It suits her politics better, I suppose. She is one of that elite band, the intellectual far left. I find her quite intimidating. Grandma Chandler died never knowing the influence I had and supposing that her son was the omnipotent demi-god he still thinks he is.

That time when I stayed on in Hong Kong I had the opportunity to reduce Oliver to the status of a mere man. The process had started by the time I returned and I realised that was not what I desired. I quickly halted it by taking most of the blame for the difficulties in our marriage, but first, of course, I had to explain to him what those difficulties were. He was shaken enough to readily accept that I needed more than domesticity to fulfil me. He was so relieved, poor soul! He had actually been wondering if it could, conceivably, be something he had done. It took me quite a while to persuade him back to Olympus, but once there he soon forgot that he had ever left it. Now he is gradually descending again and it makes me sad, because it's no longer in my power to do anything about it. I can only hope that he'll participate in the business again through Roddy. He's longing for the day when Roddy becomes his righthand man. Things should work out quite satisfactorily: Bill Trudge will be retiring next year, which means Roddy can be fitted in without too much upheaval. Heavens, look at the time! Have you finished? Hurry up, then, we have to get back."

That afternoon, when I pick the children up from school at four o'clock, reflections on my own day at work are promptly dispelled by their hassles at school, which appear far more dire to them than any crisis in the retail trade. While they clamber into the back of the car, full of doom and gloom, I exchange a few words with Kay who is collecting the twins, Angus and Fergus-two aptly named boys who resemble sturdy little bullocks, with large brown eyes, pugnacious chins and long, gangling legs ending in thin ankles and hefty school shoes. While their mother and I are talking, they are good-naturedly thumping one another with their school bags.

"Into the car, brats," Kay orders, after saying goodbye to me. Obediently they join the two excited, filthy dogs in the rear of the mud-spattered estate car.

I do not ask my children if they have had a nice day, the portents are too ominous; instead I ask Sebastian cheerfully if he enjoyed his packed lunch. He will not eat school lunches, yet Alice finds little fault with them.

"I didn't eat the sandwiches," he informs me. I detect a hint of defiance.

"Oh dear, I thought you liked ham."

"I told you last time that I don't like it any more," he says with exasperation.

"What do you like?" I enquire patiently.

Alice declares, "He doesn't like anything. He's a pain!"

"I am not."

"Yes, you are."

I interrupt to ask about casting for the nativity play which I know to be imminent. Too late, I realise that I have hit on a sore point.

"Tell her what you are," Alice encourages Sebastian with nasty glee.

"A silly ass," he says morosely.

"A what?"

"He means he's part of a donkey."

"Oh, only half a silly ass," I comment, trying not to laugh. I think I know which half.

"We're not doing a play," Alice informs me. She is in the junior school now and has gone on to more exalted things. "You can come and hear me play my recorder.

We're having a carol morning."

More time I shall have to wangle off work. I wonder how people manage who do not have the good fortune to be employed by their mothers. They are not able to attend many school functions, I suppose.

It takes us about ten minutes to reach home. The cottage is of grey stone with a slate roof. It looks austerely primitive and uninviting, especially on this dismal November afternoon with the light rapidly diminishing into a drizzly evening, but it has been thoroughly and sympathetically modernised by the previous owners and the space and comfort of the interior come as a pleasant surprise to the first-time visitor. We have a huge garden. The small patch at the front is cultivated, the remainder is field-like and blends into the surrounding countryside without distinction, so that the dour building appears to have been dropped haphazardly into position, and the fact that there is a very minor road running past the front hedge seems to be more luck than judgement. We owe our good fortune in acquiring the cottage to Francis, whose small family estate is only a couple of miles away.

My father grumbles about our house being situated in the back of beyond and rarely visits us. We have thwarted him in his desire to have us live nearer Durham and he does not intend to forgive us. We have Sunday lunch and tea with him and Mum about once a month, to placate him and give him some time with his grandchildren. He is far more tolerant with them than he ever was with his own small children, and actually sits and listens to them when they 'tell him the tale', as he puts it. He thinks they are exceptionally bright and boasts about them at every opportunity, whereas he was always urging us to do better. We never felt that we could achieve enough to satisfy him. Even my graduation ceremony was marred for him and, consequently, for me as well, by the fact that my room-mate at university had gained a first class degree while I had only managed a second. Cassandra opted out of education at sixteen, despairing of his unattainable hopes for her. Roddy is struggling on, clever enough to make success possible with much application. I do not think he is happy. I found learning a pleasurable challenge, but for Roddy it is a dreary chore which he will be glad to put behind him. I managed to work and play, once I had established a good balance between the two. Roddy only manages to work and that is undesirable for a young man. His first girl friend became bored with his dedication to his studies and found herself a more agreeable companion. Perhaps this new girl — I do not know her name — will stick it out for the six months or so before Roddy is released from ploughing long, concentrated furrows in the fields of academe in order to ramble with more freedom over the wider landscape of big business. Unfortunately, it will not be enough for Roddy to attain a first (an unlikely result): he will have to prove himself a worthy successor to his father in the company. Poor Roddy! I cannot see him as a dynamic leader in industry.

Martin usually returns home just before six o'clock. It is now five-twenty, and I am preparing the dinner. The children are in the living-room, watching the television. The door bell rings. Alice rushes to answer it and shouts from the porch that grandma has come. Having seen my mother at lunch-time, I wonder what could have brought her at such an unlikely hour. In the hall I stand still, too astonished to speak. Cassandra is here.

"It's Grandma's car," Alice says, explaining her mistake.

"Hello, Jan," my sister says in her controlled, quiet way. "Surprised?"

Instead of delight, I am experiencing a churning sickness in my stomach, the kind one has before opening the door at the dentist's.

"What on earth are you doing here? Come into the kitchen, I'm in the middle of cooking."

Alice gives up waiting to be noticed and returns to the absorbing rubbish on the television. Cassandra sits at the table and looks round critically. "What a lovely kitchen," she says, but it is an observation made without warmth.

"Yes, isn't it?" I open the oven door and shut it again, taking no notice of the state of the pork chops. I turn to her, bracing myself against the agreeable heat of the oven, and wait with my hands clenched in the oven gloves. Cassandra is pale and beautiful. Her fair hair, longer than she usually wears it, is curling softly on the velvet collar of her royal blue coat.

"I've left Alsace," she explains, undoing the large button at her throat.

"In other words, you've left Gérard," I say bitterly.

"I had to, Jan."

First she takes him from me, now she discards him. "I never loved him as much as you did. I know that."

"Then why did you marry him?"

"To escape. I wanted stability, security. I wanted to be surrounded by love like you are, Jan."

"I wasn't then," I remark coldly.

She ignores this, remembering only her own unhappiness. "I never told you the complete truth about Paris."

"When have you ever told anyone the complete truth about anything?" I cry. I wait, supposing I am going to hear it now. Not at all. Paris is to remain a mystery.

"May I stay with you for a while?" she pleads.

I am assailed by unreasoning alarm. "We've only got three bedrooms. Why can't you say with Mum? You could have your old room back."

"You know Grandma's in it."

Grandma Harris has been living with my parents for the last six months, since she became too frail to cope on her own. "She could move into mine," I suggest.

"I wouldn't ask her. She's cosy where she is. Anyway, Mum doesn't understand. She thinks I'll be going back to Alsace."

"Maybe you will," I say hopefully.

"No, I have other plans."

"What are they?"

She raises her eyebrows and shrugs; a gesture which tells me maddeningly that I am not to know.

I retaliate by saying cruelly, "You can't stay here, Cassie."

She begins to weep in her inimical heart-rending manner, her wide-open blue eyes on my face, the tears running down her cheeks, the way a small child cries before it has the words to explain its troubles. She does not sniff or wipe the tears away. They fall upon her blue-clad arms which are resting on the table.

I am ready to capitulate and comfort her, when Sebastian enters the kitchen with the intention of saying hello to his aunt. He is side-tracked by the intriguing sight of her tears.

"Why is she crying?" he asks me in awe.

"She's unhappy. She'll feel better when she's had something to eat." Sebastian understands the efficacy of food as consolation. "Go back into the living-room with Alice. I'll call you when dinner's ready."

Where is Martin? Surely he is not going to be late this evening of all evenings. I turn away from my sister to return to the mundane task of cooking the dinner. Perhaps she will disappear! I place four large, unpeeled and pricked potatoes into the microwave oven then, acknowledging the futility of my hope, I wash another one, stab it viciously, and put it in with the others, setting the timer with an uncalculated guess. I boil water to add to the sprouts and, opening the oven door again, notice that the chops are well and truly cooked. I turn off the heat. Everything is mistimed, and Cassandra's sudden arrival has given me such a jolt that I am having difficulty picking up a rhythm again; it is as if the earth has tilted and I am wobbling about trying to regain my balance, while my mind is seething. What has Cassandra told my mother? The truth? Unlikely. How are Leila and Lucien taking her departure? How sudden was it? Did she and Gérard quarrel or did she just take off?

"Did you quarrel with Gérard, Cassie?"

Cassandra, who has ceased crying, comes out of a motionless reverie with a slight jump. She regards me blankly for an instant, then hears what I have said.

"Yes, when I told him I was coming here. He tried to prevent me driving off. I almost backed into him. I could have killed him! I was capable of anything, I was so desperate to get away. I drove to the airport as if the whole world was conspiring to stop me."

I am about to ask her all the other questions which I have asked myself when the telephone on the wall beside me starts to ring. I answer it. "Yes, she's here." I turn to my sister: "Lucien wants to speak to you, Cassie."

She shakes her head vigorously, pushing herself back against the chair in repudiation. I let the receiver dangle against the wall

328

while I urge her towards it, then I thrust it into her reluctant hand.

"Lucien?" she whispers.

I hear Martin's key in the lock and hurry into the hall to intercept him, closing the door behind me, shutting Cassandra away.

"Daddy, Auntie Cassie's here," Alice calls from the living-room.

Martin's face is a study in surprise.

"She's left Gérard," I explain.

"For good?"

"So she says."

"Good God!"

"She wants to stay with us for a while."

"The kids will have to move in together," he says. Obviously, he has no objections. "What's gone wrong?"

"I'll tell you later." First I have to find out for myself.

Cassandra opens the door into the hall. "Hello," she says, barely looking at him, then addressing me, she says, "Lucien was trying to persuade me to return."

"What did you say?"

"I'm a coward. I didn't want to hurt him. I said I needed time to think to about it. He said he understood — as if he could!"

She is looking ill. I place an arm around her waist and propel her into the living-room. It is like taking liberties with a stranger, we have so little rapport. "Sit down, Cassie. When did you last eat?"

"I don't know." She perches on the edge of the sofa, tense and miserable. "I couldn't eat. I could drink some tea, though."

"Take off your coat," I encourage her. She undoes two more buttons.

The evening news is on the television. At a signal from Martin, Sebastian turns it off, then returns to loll on the carpet beside Alice. They regard Cassandra thoughtfully, with solemn eyes. Inexplicable and frightening things happen to this lovely aunt of theirs, things that are far removed from the tenor of life as they live it-attending school, playing with their friends, watching television, going to bed; all very humdrum, safe occupations.

Martin is hovering beside the sofa hoping for some enlightenment. Cassandra has left Gérard and he would like to know the reason why. Cassandra is unaware of him or anyone else, for that matter. Her eyes are fixed on the familiar oriental golden dragons on the book cabinet. They stare back at her, proud heads held high, with no pity for her plight. Unlike Martin, they appear to know everything without being told. Their large eyes, bold jewels of jade and lapis lazuli, glitter coldly in the electric light.

"They seem out of place in rural Northumberland," Cassandra comments listlessly.

I know what she means. I feel the same about the griffin heads in the grounds of Wallington Hall, every time I pass them in the car. Exotic pieces of stone which were brought back to this country as sailing ship ballast and are now embedded in an English lawn.

Martin, who has no idea what she is talking about, throws me a glance of exasperation.

"I'm not going back," Cassandra states as if she is addressing the ornaments.

"What are you going to do?" Martin enquires, frowning at me behind her back.

She turns her head and regards him expressionlessly for a moment, as if she is considering his question. She decides not to answer. Perhaps she has no idea. "Are you going to make some tea, Jan?"

"Of course."

Martin follows me into the kitchen. "I wonder how Gérard is taking this? What's wrong between them, do you know?"

"She has never got over that dreadful attack and miscarriage," I remind him, instantly taking umbrage against a male who can imagine that something so traumatic can be soon forgotten.

"Running away won't solve anything. Surely the one person who can help her get over it is her husband."

The time has come. "There's something you should know, Martin. The baby was not Gérard's."

"What!"

"It was her lover's."

"And who the hell is he?"

"I have no idea." I thrust a cup and saucer into his hand and ask him to take them to Cassandra.

When he returns he has thought of another question. "Has she been planning this or did she leave on impulse?"

"It's no use asking me," I snap, although I suspect the former. I am the one who acts on impulse. I serve the meal haphazardly on the kitchen table and shout to the children that it is ready. Martin and the children are hungry. I am too churned up inside to eat very much. I am making custard to pour over apple pie when my parents arrive. They have received a telephone call from Lucien, and Cassandra's arrival that afternoon, which they had considered an unexpected pleasure in the manner of similar visits in the past, is now seen, in the light of its intended permanence, to be an unmitigated disaster. I let them in with a surge of relief. From being a sister with a problem, Cassandra has become a daughter with a problem. I leave my husband and children to finish their meal and join the lively scene in the living-room, where Cassandra is blanching before my father's indignation.

"I want an explanation from you, young lady," he is demanding.

"Now, Oliver, remember you're not to get excited," Mum warns him.

He ignores her. "Well!" he says to Cassandra.

"I've left Gérard. That's all there is to it," she mutters sulkily.

"Of course that's not all there is to it," he shouts. "What are your reasons? You must have some bloody reasons."

"They're none of your business," she says defiantly.

"I'm making them my business. Lucien is my friend. I'm not harbouring you here when you should be at home with his son, doing your duty."

"What duty?" she flares. "If you mean having a family, forget it! That should be a pleasure, not a duty. And I'm not asking you to harbour me. I'm going to stay with Jan and Martin."

This is news to my mother. "Will you manage?" she asks me.

"For a while," I say, resigned to it.

"You'll be looking for a job, I hope," Dad says pointedly. "You won't be expecting Gérard and his family to go on supporting you." He thinks that the mention of a job may frighten her into changing her mind.

"I want nothing from Gérard or his family," she answers tearfully.

Mum sits on the sofa beside her and hugs her. "I'd no idea you were so unhappy, Cassie," she admits. "You need help, darling. You must see a doctor."

"A doctor? There's nothing wrong with

me. It's my marriage that's coming to an end, not my life."

"I think there's something wrong with you. You need to see someone who will help you sort out your problems."

"You mean sort out my mind, I suppose."

"Yes, I do."

She shrugs away from Mum with aggravation. "Just leave me alone for a week or so and then we'll talk about it again. All I want now is peace. Please, Mum."

Dad is still standing by the fireplace rocking on his heels, anxious to sort her out on the spot and pack her off back where she belongs. He does not believe in leaving problems to solve themselves with time. That is not the way he ran his business affairs. Positive action, taken on swift decisions, that is the way.

"Go back to Grutenheim and discuss it," he orders Cassandra. "That's how your mother and I sorted out our difficulties, by discussing them."

"Oh, Oliver." Mum sighs for want of words to express her incredulity.

"Well, we did," he states, challenging her to contradict him.

"Rather like we are discussing this," Mum says sarcastically.

My parents, Gérard and his parents, will never understand Cassandra's rejection of her marriage unless she tells them the truth about the baby, and that she will never do. They will have to go on believing that the mental anguish she is suffering is a result of the rapes and miscarriage and that if only she would return and become a wife again it could be assuaged by another pregnancy.

Mum helps Cassandra off with her coat and hands it to me to put away. As I am leaving the room with it, Dad says,

"Just you let me know when you're ready to go back, Cassie, and I'll take you. I don't believe in encouraging people to shirk their responsibilities."

That, no doubt, is a reference to Uncle Daniel's sympathetic connivance with his sister when she refused to return with her husband from Hong Kong. I hang the coat in the hall cupboard and go into the kitchen. The time has come to let the children loose upon the adults in the other room, in the hope that they will relieve the tension.

"Finished?" I ask them. "Then you

can go and say hello to Grandma and Grandpa."

When they have gone, I say quietly to Martin, "Only you and I know that Cassandra had a lover."

"Gérard deserves a better deal," he says heavily.

19

FOR the first three or four days of her stay with us, Cassandra is subdued and unresponsive, living inside her head. When I take the children to school in the mornings she is still in bed, when I return with them in the afternoons she is sitting in the living-room, surrounded by magazines, as if she has been there all day. It cannot be good for her to be left alone to brood for so many hours. It worries me.

At weekends the routine of the house changes. Martin looks after the children on Saturdays while I go to work. Usually, he takes them shopping in the mornings and to the swimming baths. They have a light lunch in town and in the afternoons visit his parents.

The Friday evening after her arrival, Martin invites Cassandra to accompany them. Surprisingly, she says she will. She brightens perceptibly as the evening wears on. I become uneasy. She has been with us for less than a week, yet already Martin is finding excuses for her.

The question whether or not she planned her departure from Grutenheim has been answered by the amount of luggage she has brought with her. She has enough clothes to see her through our North-Eastern winter and a few select items which will take her nicely into spring.

"Will you ask Leila to send on some more of my things the next time you speak to her?" she asked Mum on the telephone the other evening. Mum told me the next day at work what her reply had been.

"I said I certainly would not. If she wants anything from Gérard, she must ask him herself. Anyway, Leila has nothing to say to me. Why should she? Cassandra is driving a wedge between us. If Gérard had left Cassie with as little excuse, no doubt I would feel uncharitable towards his parents. It may not be fair, but it's inevitable. We expected the marriage to bring us all closer together. When you were little, it never entered my head that a time would come when I should find one of you incomprehensible. At least you and Roddy are easily analysed. When I

339

think how much I looked forward to your independence during the tiring years of wiping noses and bottoms! When children are lazy you tell them they are being lazy, and if they have a nasty habit you say, that's a nasty habit, stop it! Then they become adults and you are afraid to criticise them. Not because you may drive them away, oh no! Because you are terrified that they will retaliate by criticising you. The truth about oneself is too cruel, coming from one's children. Make the most of Alice and Sebastian while they are young and you are everything in the world to them, Jan. I toss and turn in bed at night worrying about Cassandra. It makes my blood boil to think that she has to live the remainder of her life suffering in her mind, while those who are the cause of that suffering are wandering about scot-free, perhaps preying on other women."

When I return home on Saturday, worn out after a busy day in the shop, I walk in upon a lambent and cosy scene. Martin, the children — who are lying on their stomachs on the carpet — and Cassandra are watching television in the warm, comfortable womb of my living-room. The curtains are drawn in heavy folds against the cold, damp night. In the manner of a new passenger on the London to Edinburgh train, or any long-distance train for that matter, my arrival on a reviving gust of chill air is disruptive of their easeful torpor.

"Had a nice day?" I enquire, loading the question with every ounce of false goodwill.

They inform me with assorted nods and grunts that they have, hardly taking their eyes from the bright animation on the screen.

"Did you go swimming?" I persist.

"Huh huh!" from the children

"I borrowed your costume, Jan. Hope you don't mind?" Cassandra says.

"You swam!" I am amazed. Cassandra dislikes getting wet, especially about the head. As a child she had to be cajoled into cool water. "Did it fit you?"

"It fitted her very nicely," Martin smiles.

I am about to remark churlishly that no doubt it will have stretched and be too big for me now, but realise I will only be drawing attention to my own lean body which will in no way detract from the allure of Cassandra's full curves. I leave them to the enjoyment of the noisy television programme and go to take off my coat, before grubbing around in the refrigerator for something to eat. Martin calls after me that they have all had tea at his mother's.

"Oh, good," I mutter. "I am glad."

While I am making myself a sandwich, I reflect that so far Gérard has made no attempt to contact his wife. He is right. Why should he beg her to return? Her absence is not caused by anything he might or might not have done. No doubt he is confident that when she feels able to cope with her inner misery, she will be able to live with him again. He believes that her misery is solely the result of the wrong perpetrated upon her. He knows of no wrong perpetrated upon himself, except that of inexplicable desertion by the woman he adores.

In bed that night I feel constrained to remind Martin that Cassandra deceived Gérard about the baby. "I know, but I can't help being sorry for her," he says. "She blames herself for marrying Gérard when she was in love with someone else. She had no idea that the other man would come back into her life. When he did, she couldn't resist him."

"She kept coming over here on purpose to meet him," I point out. "She should have left Gérard then, not waited until now. If the baby had been born, she would still be there, allowing him to think it was his."

"She was going to confess to Gérard as soon as he had grown fond enough of the baby to accept it."

"That's dreadful — if you can believe her. Don't you think that's dreadful?" I ask indignantly, moving away from him on the pillow the better to search his face for my answer.

"It was sensible. She has been through a terrible ordeal, Jan. Some people might think that was punishment enough."

I am perturbed that Cassandra has been confiding in Martin. Why Martin? Perhaps because she knows instinctively that he will believe whatever she tells him. People like my husband are alarmingly easy to dupe — for a while. He is not gullible, merely trusting.

343

"Why does everyone make excuses for Cassandra?"

Martin denies that he is excusing her, only trying to understand her.

"Yes, you are excusing her," I complain. "When she first turned up most of your sympathy was for Gérard."

The next day is the Sunday we are due to have lunch and tea at my parents' home.

Cassandra is not keen to go. She puts in an appearance in the kitchen soon after ten o'clock, wearing a peach-coloured satin dressing-gown, and says she has a headache. "I'll stay here. Is there any coffee in the pot, Jan, and an aspirin, please?"

"Stay here if you like," I say off-handedly, pouring her some coffee.

The children entreat her to accompany us. Martin says he is not keen to go either, but observes that, unlike Cassandra, he has no choice.

I am furious with him. He has never objected before.

"I had no idea you minded," I remark stiffly.

Cassandra decides, diplomatically, that she will come after all and join my husband in his day of martyrdom.

When we arrive, just before noon, it is
o find Roddy there.

I am delighted, until I see the expression on
Mum's face. "Another unexpected pleasure,"
she says drily.

Roddy smiles the apologetic greeting
of the messenger who brings ill-tidings.
Immediately, my protective instinct towards
him is roused. I kiss and hug him warmly,
trying to give him reassurance.

He and Cassandra embrace in the mutual
sympathy of those out of favour in the
hierarchy.

"Where's Dad?" Cassandra asks him
quietly.

"Trying to ward off a heart attack,"
Roddy tells her. "I'm afraid I've dropped
a bit of a bombshell."

Mum is unbuttoning Sebastian's coat,
quite unnecessarily, I might add. He is
perfectly capable of doing it himself, but
resembles his Aunt Cassie in that he won't
lift a finger if someone else will do it for
him. Mum looks up to frown at Roddy,
extremely displeased by his flippancy.

Roddy defends himself. "Well, he
shouldn't get so annoyed."

"What do you expect?" Mum asks him,

thoroughly annoyed herself.

"What's wrong?" I appeal.

Mum straightens up and says flatly, "Roddy has no intention of going into the company."

"Oh!" What else is there to say? We troop into the drawing-room like lambs to the slaughter, all except Mum who rushes off towards the kitchen, muttering about the vegetables. Obviously, she has endured enough argument for one morning.

The room is occupied by Dad and Grandma Harris.

Grandma is sitting where she always sits, in the upright, deeply buttoned blue velvet chair which she brought from her own home. Whenever she has to leave the room, I expect the chair to rise up with her. She struggles from its embrace as if the chair has similar expectations. We, the latest arrivals, kiss her soft cheeks with fond pecks. She smells of lily-of-the-valley, as she usually does. She is looking bright-eyed and alert, thriving on this latest domestic crisis which is alleviating her housebound dullness.

Dad is standing by the window, gazing out onto the quiet of the Sunday street.

He watched us arrive, but is ignoring our entrance.

"It's beef, Grandpa," Sebastian states triumphantly, unaware of the tense atmosphere in the room. It is a game they play. Sebastian has to guess the choice of joint by the smell in the hall on arrival.

"So it is, Seb." Dad turns and bends down to receive the children's kisses.

Martin, Cassandra and myself find ourselves seats as unobtrusively as possible.

"Sherry?" Roddy asks us.

We nod. Dad ignores him.

"Sweet or dry?"

We state our preferences.

Grandma says, "Still here, then, Cassie? That husband of yours must be missing you." She will not accept that Cassandra has no intention of going back.

Cassandra glances nervously towards Dad's stiff back. His attention remains fixed on the street. How upset he must be by Roddy's astounding, late decision. It is not often that my father is hurt so deeply that he cannot be vociferously angry. The only other time I recall him crumbling into a comparable silence of devastation

347

and perplexity was when Mum refused to return from Hong Kong. She set about restoring his confidence in himself again. Will Roddy be similarly affected by Dad's demise? No. A husband as a spent force is one thing, a father as a spent force is quite another. Mum had to go on living with Dad, Roddy can keep out of the way.

"Sherry, Dad?" Roddy asks, handing Grandma hers.

Dad glowers at him and marches from the room.

Roddy shrugs. "I only asked," he says as if he does not care.

"You've upset your father, Roddy," Grandma reprimands him. "Couldn't you change your mind? What are you going to do instead?"

"Social work, Gran."

"Social work?" I gasp. It is the last thing I would have expected from someone who has been reading electronic engineering and business studies with the intention of going into industry. "What kind of social work?"

"I haven't decided yet. Of course, I shall have to get the necessary qualifications first."

"What about the company?" I ask.

"Dad can always sell it."

"But he built it up from nothing into an international concern. No mean achievement."

"I'm sure it will go on being a success without either of us. He's made a lot of money out of it, which presumably is what he intended to do. Some of us have different aims in life, that's all."

"How long have you been interested in social work?" Cassandra asks him, appalled at the idea of someone wanting to take an active interest in the personal, even intimate affairs of others.

"For about a year. Rachel and I are going into it together. She'd like to become a probation officer."

"Rachel?" Cassandra enquires, looking interested.

"Yes, you must meet her sometime. What's this I hear about you walking out on Gérard?"

Cassandra's expression changes to one of guarded annoyance.

"I'll see if Mum needs a hand," I say. I find her in the kitchen leaning against a work surface drinking strong coffee.

"Anything I can do?"

"Yes, set the table. Grandma said she was going to do it, but she must have forgotten. Everything is under control here. I wish I could say the same for the rest of the house."

"When did Roddy arrive?"

"Last night." There is a pause, then she says, putting down her cup, "It's your turn now, Jan."

"My turn? To do what?"

"Tell your father and me something we'd rather not hear."

I blush with embarrassment, thinking of Cassandra's lover. Mum is regarding me in consternation.

"Oh no, you're not going to, are you?"

I laugh at her alarm and shake my head. "Don't worry," I reassure her, "I'm neither going to leave Martin nor chuck my job."

"How is Cassandra? Do you think she is missing Grutenheim?"

"I don't know, Mum. I hope she isn't planning to stay with us forever. I couldn't stand it. It's such an effort to be constantly trying to raise her spirits. She appears to be happiest when she's with Alice and Seb, but goodness knows what she's like when she's on her own all day. She'll have to find something to do, she can't just sit at home and read magazines or watch television."

"She can, you know," Mum says grimly. "I would offer her a job in one of the shops, but that would seem like encouraging the separation. I'm still hoping that she'll go back. The Amberlés couldn't have been kinder or more considerate towards her since she lost the baby. I don't know what more they could have done to help her over the ordeal." She takes the Yorkshire pudding from the oven. "This is ready. Get that table set, Jan. Where's Oliver? I could strangle Roddy, letting him down without any warning. He's allowing himself to be influenced by that Rachel woman."

When I enter the dining-room, I see my father through the glass doors, pacing backwards and forwards the length of the garden room. Alice and Sebastian are there as well, playing on the bagatelle board.

I set the table quickly, yet with care. Dad is fanatical about a neatly arranged table and I do not want to aggravate him any further. We shall be eating lunch in an atmosphere of enough acrimony. While

I am straightening the knives and forks and making sure the cruet is absolutely centred I recall the misery of past family meals when one of us has been in Dad's bad books. This time I shall find it difficult to defend Roddy. He should have brought the formidable Rachel with him. No doubt she could explain satisfactorily to Dad the superior merits of the underprivileged when set against his selfish capitalistic ideals.

20

OH, the misery of this meal! Why do we inflict such rituals upon ourselves? Despite the fact that all we want to do is rant and rave at each other, demanding explanations and arguing over excuses, we sit around the table making polite conversation as if our only interest is the cold rain and wind slamming against the windows and the hot food smelling deliciously upon our plates.

However, in spite of our endeavours to preserve a semblance of harmony, a few caustic remarks slip out and are countered by equally nasty rejoinders.

"I apologise for the excellence of the wine," Dad says to Roddy, while he is refilling his glass, "but no doubt you will soon lose such extravagant, bourgeois tastes." And five minutes later he remarks, "When are you going to copy your brother and sister and turn your back on affluence, Jan?"

Martin laughs. "She did that when she married me."

"You're not doing so badly," Dad says.

"Good for him," Roddy says approvingly. "At least he's doing it on his own."

"What do you think I did?" Dad demands.

"Exactly! That's why you should allow me to do my own thing."

"As long as you're not expecting me to pay for yet more years of study."

"Don't worry. I'll manage."

"And your mother won't help you either. Who do you think financed her business?"

"I shall do what I like with my own money, Oliver," Mum says quietly, but she is careful to make no promises.

"I don't want anything from either of you," Roddy says, reaching for his wine glass and then thinking better of it.

While my parents and Roddy are exchanging verbal punches, Grandma keeps asking Cassandra aggravating questions, such as, "Has Leila got rid of that bust of hers?" and, "How old are Jean-Michel's children now? Has he married his wife yet?" Consequently, Cassandra is becoming quieter and more exasperated as the meal progresses.

Martin and I are doing our best to keep out of the controversy. We shall have our say later in the privacy of our own home. Martin is fifteen years older than Roddy and has had very little to do with him. He knows how much I dote on my brother and this tends to make him critical.

Grandma and the children are the only ones who chatter without restraint and eat their food with positive relish.

"Will you be coming home for Christmas?" Mum asks Roddy, after Alice has been telling Cassandra some of the things she hopes Santa Claus will be bringing her. "You could bring Rachel, of course." She avoids looking at her husband.

"Sorry, Mum. We'll be going to her people in Birmingham. By the way, I'm moving out of my digs. We've found a decent bed-sit a couple of streets away. I'll give you the address before I go back."

Mum smiles at him sadly. "You're not going to cut yourself off from us entirely, then?"

"Of course not," he says, smiling back at her.

"If you're going to live together, why don't you marry her?" Grandma asks him. "I can't see the sense of it."

Everybody ignores her. We have heard it all before.

"May we enquire into the young lady's background?" Dad asks icily.

"It depends what you mean by her background. If you're asking if her parents are well-off, then the answer is, not by your standards, not that I can see what difference that makes; if you are asking about Rachel herself, that's different. She is sensible and intelligent with a highly developed social conscience, and I'm afraid she would disapprove of all this." He surveys the beautifully furnished dining-room and then the table, where the lavish meal is enhanced by Mum's carefully chosen, highly-prized Royal Doulton porcelain.

"Oh, dear!" Mum sighs in dismay.

"I've been seen as the enemy of the proletariat many times before," Dad observes witheringly, "but it's the first time for your poor mother. Don't worry, she'll get used to it in time."

Grandma says, "What do you mean, Oliver? Roddy didn't say anything about you being the enemy, did he?"

"It's all right, Gran. Dad's just being

facetious," Roddy consoles her.

"Facetious!" Dad blazes and that is when Martin steps in as peace-maker.

When at last the meal is over, we push back our chairs with a profound sense of release. Grandma toddles off to her blue velvet chair for a nap, worn out with all the excitement. Cassandra and I help Mum clear away. Dad shuts himself in the library with the Sunday papers and Martin and Roddy take the children for a walk along the riverside. The rain has stopped and they have only to suffer the bitter wind.

Tea is a less formal meal, eaten in the sitting-room. The children are allowed to watch the television while they eat, which means that nobody has to make conversation. Roddy leaves soon after tea to return to university, driving the sports car his father bought for him a year ago out of his obscene profits. When he kisses her goodbye, Grandma slips something that looks remarkably like a folded cheque into his hand. This is a gesture so familiar to him, he accepts it without demur, murmuring his thanks into her ear.

Then the rest of us take our leave.

"You'll be coming for Christmas as usual, I hope, Jan," Dad says when I kiss him goodbye. He sets great store by his hospitality. He loves to astound people with his extravagant generosity and be the great man of the occasion. Now that I am older and more tolerant, it is easy to humour him and show gratitude. However, this year Martin and I are planning to invite our families to our own home for Christmas.

"We have to consider Mr and Mrs Proudfoot," I remind him. "They won't be going to Martin's brother this year."

"They can come as well," he says, delighted at the thought. It would not occur to him that they might not want to be so indulged, knowing that there is no way they could match his largesse. Would he be willing to spend a modest Christmas in their home? Martin and I must be the catalyst in the delicate experiment of bringing our parents together under one roof, so it will have to take place in the cottage on neutral ground.

Nearly three weeks have passed since Cassandra arrived. She is alarming me by making herself useful. She does the washing and ironing and, on the days when Mum can let her have the car and use Dad's, she does the shopping and prepares the evening meal.

"This is great!" Martin declares to me, having been released from many of his chores. "You'll miss Cassie when she goes."

The trouble is that she shows no sign of going. I have tried to discuss the future with her, but she looks vague and tells me not to worry. This morning she received a letter from Gérard. As far as I am aware it is the first communication she has had from him. She took it to her room and came down ten minutes later looking as if she had been crying.

This evening I am determined to talk to her. I follow her into her bedroom and shut the door behind me. She sinks onto the edge of the bed and waits for me to begin.

"Has Gérard asked you to go back to him?"

"Yes."

"Will you?"

"No. I've told him I want a divorce."

"Cassie, I've often wondered why you didn't leave Gérard for your lover when you first knew you were pregnant."

"My lover's name is Colin, Jan."

"Colin! Wasn't that the name of the man you were living with in London?"

"Yes. He was married. He still is, so you see I couldn't just walk back into his life."

"Where is Colin living now?"

"I don't know," she says evasively and I do not believe her.

"Have you seen him since you came back?"

She looks me in the eye this time and says, "No!" and I do believe her.

"Then he's not in the North-East?"

"He's from Alnwick, actually, but he moved away years ago. I met him that time I went to stay with Grandma Chandler for a month, while Mum and Dad were in Grutenheim."

"But you were only fifteen."

"Yes. I've known him a long time, haven't I? I love him Jan. I always will."

"But Cassie, you left him because he was unkind to you. Didn't you tell me that he was willing to pass you over to a friend?"

"He said that to shock me into leaving him. It was for my own good. Anyway, one doesn't love only those who deserve to be loved, otherwise I should love Gérard. I'm not sorry that I took Gérard away from you, Jan. You and Martin were meant for each other."

"I'll be the judge of that," I retort angrily, turning to leave the room in order to investigate a sudden outburst of crying from Sebastian.

"What became of that picture of the girl with green eyes, the one Gérard gave you? I've been meaning to ask you."

"She was damaged in the removal," I inform her over my shoulder.

My father is becoming increasingly unwell. My mother blames Roddy and Cassandra for causing him anxiety and stress, but mainly she blames Roddy for betrayal.

We are to meet the estimable Rachel. Roddy will bring her to visit us on New Year's Eve. I am not feeling charitable towards either of them and do not care whether they come or not. I have to blame our perfectly awful Christmas on someone, so I have chosen them for being well out of it in Birmingham.

Dad was like a fish out of water. Martin would not have minded him playing the host — his favourite role — but Martin's parents kept reminding him, by their reproachful presence in their son's home, that he was a usurper. There was an understated rivalry betwen Grandma and Grandpa, Nan and Grandad, which we had never had the opportunity of observing before. The children were smart enough to sense it and made the most of the extra attention it afforded them.

Cassandra and I hid away as much evidence of Dad's munificence towards us all as possible, without making it too obvious to Dad and offending him. When he directed Sebastian to show off his magnificent train set, I told him that there was not enough room to set it out and that it might get broken, which was nothing but the truth — we would have to move house in order to give it a room of its own!

Mum and Mrs Proudfoot got along valiantly together with a festive determination to like and be liked. Dad and Mr Proudfoot were not so bothered. A lot of the time between admiring the excited children was spent in waiting to laugh at Dad's next jocular pronouncement. Martin's father does not make jokes or tell stories, but he loves to be entertained.

Cassandra, no doubt comparing this Christmas with those spent in her husband's home, was sad and pensive. She could have been in Grutenheim this year with her own child on her lap, watching it receive adulation from its French grandparents and basking in the approbation of her duped husband.

Rachel turns out to be ordinary. I do not know of a worse thing one woman can say about another, but it is true. She is neither pretty nor plain; neither dark nor fair; neither short nor tall. She has a very marked Birmingham accent, as my mother had informed me, and a commonsense line in conversation that is quite daunting in its lack of humour. She explains to me patiently why my daughter is behaving so precociously and tells me why I must excuse the behaviour and not give the obnoxious child a swift smack, which had been my intention. She explains at great length why Roddy is drawn to social work and how my father must come to terms with it if he is to keep his son's esteem. In fact, she has an explanation for everything, except what Roddy sees in her. I become exhausted by listening to her sensible, tedious conversation and gradually realise with umbrage that I am being patronised.

Kay and Francis, with more friends, join us in the course of the evening to see in the New Year. After listening to Rachel for so long, Kay's ultra-cultured drawl sounds ludicrous even to my accustomed ears, and I can see that Rachel is distinctly unimpressed by it, even a little offended. She probably thinks Kay is putting it on for her benefit. She is not the first person to think that.

Thankfully, she and Roddy do not stay long after the boisterous influx and once they have departed Martin and I feel free to let our hair down. Cassandra is drinking too much, probably hoping to drown her sorrows, and the toast at midnight is the one that sets her back teeth afloat. We are effusively wishing each other a Happy New Year when Cassandra bursts into tears. We all have a maudlin time comforting her and reassuring each other that it's the drink that has done it. Martin assiduously and lingeringly kisses her better. I suddenly feel like bursting into tears myself. Instead, I creep upstairs into the room shared by the children and nuzzle their warm, delightful faces, whispering, "Happy New Year, my darlings," wondering how they are able to sleep so peacefully in the merry din from downstairs.

21

THE children have been back at school for three days when we return in the afternoon to find the cottage empty and a note addressed to me on the hall table. Folded inside the envelope is a £50 note.

"What does it say?" Alice wants to know, watching me read it.

"Auntie Cassie's gone away."

"Back to Uncle Gérard?"

"I'm afraid not."

"Where then?"

"I don't know, Alice."

The note simply reads,

"Dear Jan, I am going to live with Colin. Thanks for putting up with me. The money is towards the telephone bill. I'll be in touch soon. Love, Cassie."

For the telephone bill?

Sebastian calls to me from the dining-room: "Mum, your picture's been mended."

"My picture?" What on earth is he talking about. I go to find out.

"Look!" he says, pointing across the darkening room.

The print that Gérard gave me all those years ago has been retrieved from the back of the cupboard on the landing and the broken glass has been replaced. I switch on the light the better to see it and experience a creepy thrill of shock. The young girl in the white dress gazes past me with eyes of a vivid blue. Stuck in the corner of the frame is a scrap of paper. I cross the room and pluck it out. It says, in Cassandra's neat handwriting, "Now she really does look like you.

I struggle with an urge to break down into tears.

"Can I go back into my own bedroom, now that Auntie Cassie's gone," Alice asks, quite pleased at the prospect.

"Can I have my train set over my bedroom floor?" is Sebastian's request. "There will be room for it without Alice's bed."

"We'll see," I say with the classic answer of the besieged mother, my eyes still on the haunting figure in the picture, untouched by time. For a moment I am standing beside Gérard, watching Roddy going round and round on the carousel, the mangy monkey on a stick waving frenziedly above his curly head, his arms reaching up eagerly to snatch its tail. Gérard's hand is on my waist and I am light-hearted beneath the summer sun, elated with love for him.

"May I have some crisps?" Sebastian asks.

I am back in the dining-room of my Northumberland cottage, on a snowy January day. I am a working woman, a wife and a mother, a supplier of crisps and glasses of orange juice, who has a dinner to cook.

As soon as Martin comes in at six, I hand him the note and the money.

"I thought you said Colin was married," he says after reading it.

"That's what Cassie told me."

"Fifty pounds! She didn't have to do that, it's not as if she's been telephoning Alsace."

When we receive the telephone account ten days later, we realise that Cassandra has not been over-generous in the estimate of the cost of her calls. We assume that most of the time she was in the cottage on her own she spent speaking to Colin and that he lives at a very long distance indeed!

Then Mum receives a birthday card from Cassandra with a Southampton postmark.

"I wonder if she's happy," Mum sighs, showing it to me.

We are Sunday visiting again. Dad and Grandma are dozing in their favourite chairs and Martin is playing Monopoly with Alice and Sebastian. Mum and I are preparing the tea.

"You once told me that to be happy one has to be utterly selfish," I remind her. "Cassie has a great capacity for selfishness, so perhaps she is happy."

"I often think about the people in Grutenheim and the lovely times we had there when you were all little, don't you, Jan? How different things would have been if you had married Gérard." She puts her hand on mine and gives it a fond squeeze. "I'm glad you didn't. I would have been happy for you, of course, but when I look at you now, with Martin and the children, I am thankful I've got you here. You've always been a great help to me, Jan. Now that Oliver's health is deteriorating, I'm relying on you more than ever. There was a time when you were jealous of Cassandra. I could never think why, until she married Gérard."

There was a time! Has that time gone at last? How can I be jealous of someone who has forfeited Gérard's love? I pity my sister and hope she has found compensation in the arms of her lover for all she has spurned.

That was a month ago. Spring is struggling to manifest its presence. Martin and I have been discussing holiday plans with Kay and Francis. Austria this year, we think.

I am driving home from work on the first Saturday in April in a mood of heady optimism, singing at the top of my voice. The shop — my shop — is doing well and when I see Mum tomorrow I shall be able to tell her the good news. Perhaps we shall be able to afford a new car before the holiday. Martin would like that. His car is a bit of a wreck and mine is not much better, but furnishing the cottage has had to take priority. Home at last! We have a visitor. There is a blue car in the drive at the side of the cottage. It's Dad's.

I park my car behind it and breeze indoors. I am met by silence and a sea of solemn faces. Something has happened! I remain poised between the bliss of ignorance and the pain of knowledge — an uneasy moment in limbo.

Martin steps towards me and I place my hand in his, holding on tightly.

Mum says dully, "We've had some dreadful news, Jan. Cassie is dead."

"Dead?"

"She has killed herself."

"Killed herself?"

Mum starts to cry and hides her face in her hands.

Martin leads me to a chair and gently pushes me into it. I look around, dazed, as if I have arrived on a strange planet. Dad is here, ancient in grief, Roddy is here and so is Rachel. Where have they come from? It's Saturday, I remind myself, just an ordinary Saturday. Have the children been swimming with Martin?

"Where are the children?" I enquire anxiously, looking frantically round the room.

"Kay has them," my husband says.

"Don't worry, they can stay there tonight."

I listen to my mother's wretched crying, numb with shock.

"What did she do?" I whisper in dread.

"She poisoned herself."

"My God!"

On Monday I receive a letter from my sister, posted in Southampton on Friday, the day of her suicide. I could not have opened it with more trepidation if it had been written from the grave.

Dear Jan,

Colin does not want me. He has gone back to his wife and children. I could have lived caring for his baby. I cannot live without either of them. I envy you, Jan. You have everything. I have nothing. Forgive me. I love you,

Cassie

The jealousy, which had always marred my love for my sister, and which, perhaps, had prevented me from understanding and helping her, dissolves into guilt and shame. I forget her deviousness and my reasons for disliking her. I am overwhelmed with pity at what she has suffered. I long to see her and put everything right between us. Knowing that I never shall is the greatest bitterness of all. She had possessed beauty and an indefinable quality that made those closest to her admire and adore her, and it was that quality which I had most envied; but she had also possessed an inability to share her unhappiness and that had destroyed her — that and my jealousy.

I collapse in a frenzy of sobbing that tears at my aching throat.

Martin comes and holds me in his arms to soothe me, but I cannot calm down. I am grief-stricken, left with an unending legacy of remorse. I am also left with fear. I try to explain this to Martin, gazing desolately into his face through my tears.

"Cassie says she envies me, Martin. For years I envied her and look where it has brought us — to catastrophe! Don't you see, she's condemning me to a similar fate. I know I deserve it, but I fear it. Cassie was right, I have so much to lose."

I bury my face in his shoulder, repeating in a hoarse whisper, "I fear envy, Martin."

Other titles in the
Ulverscroft Large Print Series:

TO FIGHT THE WILD
Rod Ansell and Rachel Percy

Lost in uncharted Australian bush, Rod Ansell survived by hunting and trapping wild animals, improvising shelter and using all the bushman's skills he knew.

COROMANDEL
Pat Barr

India in the 1830s is a hot, uncomfortable place, where the East India Company still rules. Amelia and her new husband find themselves caught up in the animosities which seethe between the old order and the new.

THE SMALL PARTY
Lillian Beckwith

A frightening journey to safety begins for Ruth and her small party as their island is caught up in the dangers of armed insurrection.

THE WILDERNESS WALK
Sheila Bishop

Stifling unpleasant memories of a misbegotten romance in Cleave with Lord Francis Aubrey, Lavinia goes on holiday there with her sister. The two women are thrust into a romantic intrigue involving none other than Lord Francis.

THE RELUCTANT GUEST
Rosalind Brett

Ann Calvert went to spend a month on a South African farm with Theo Borland and his sister. They both proved to be different from her first idea of them, and there was Storr Peterson — the most disturbing man she had ever met.

ONE ENCHANTED SUMMER
Anne Tedlock Brooks

A tale of mystery and romance and a girl who found both during one enchanted summer.

CLOUD OVER MALVERTON
Nancy Buckingham

Dulcie soon realises that something is seriously wrong at Malverton, and when violence strikes she is horrified to find herself under suspicion of murder.

AFTER THOUGHTS
Max Bygraves

The Cockney entertainer tells stories of his East End childhood, of his RAF days, and his post-war showbusiness successes and friendships with fellow comedians.

MOONLIGHT AND MARCH ROSES
D. Y. Cameron

Lynn's search to trace a missing girl takes her to Spain, where she meets Clive Hendon. While untangling the situation, she untangles her emotions and decides on her own future.

NURSE ALICE IN LOVE
Theresa Charles

Accepting the post of nurse to little Fernie Sherrod, Alice Everton could not guess at the romance, suspense and danger which lay ahead at the Sherrod's isolated estate.

POIROT INVESTIGATES
Agatha Christie

Two things bind these eleven stories together — the brilliance and uncanny skill of the diminutive Belgian detective, and the stupidity of his Watson-like partner, Captain Hastings.

LET LOOSE THE TIGERS
Josephine Cox

Queenie promised to find the long-lost son of the frail, elderly murderess, Hannah Jason. But her enquiries threatened to unlock the cage where crucial secrets had long been held captive.

THE TWILIGHT MAN
Frank Gruber

Jim Rand lives alone in the California desert awaiting death. Into his hermit existence comes a teenage girl who blows both his past and his brief future wide open.

DOG IN THE DARK
Gerald Hammond

Jim Cunningham breeds and trains gun dogs, and his antagonism towards the devotees of show spaniels earns him many enemies. So when one of them is found murdered, the police are on his doorstep within hours.

THE RED KNIGHT
Geoffrey Moxon

When he finds himself a pawn on the chessboard of international espionage with his family in constant danger, Guy Trent becomes embroiled in moves and countermoves which may mean life or death for Western scientists.